Beat
The
Cross

Even with a lecturing brother and an extremely violent partner, Rico Adams attempts to advance from small-time creative criminal to national mastermind. Settling down with just one beautiful woman and spending more time with his only child would have to come later.

Dan Kapata, a professional criminal with no compassion for those who interfere with his business operations, has received an important fax with a name on it. The hunt for the black guy that robbed him begins, but Rico isn't done stealing from Dan yet.

There's only one thing that beats the cross...
and that's the double-cross

.

Beat
The
Cross

Leon Blue

Infraread Publishing
P.O. Box 233
Bronx, New York 10462
www.infraread.net

Infraread Publishing
www.infraread.net
© 2009 Presented by Leon Blue
Story by Cordless Sims
All rights reserved.
Printed in the United States of America
10 09 08 07 06 1 2 3 4 5 6 7

ISBN: 978-0-9746237-9-5
Paperback Elite Edition

Library of Congress Control Number: 2004118109
San number: 256-7474

Book edited by James B Sims
Book composition by Thomas Mulligan tom2776@yahoo.com

Series: The Cross/no. 1

Advance Endorsements

"BEAT THE CROSS is non-stop action from the first page to the last.. This book is a <u>must</u> read!"

..Teri Woods, publisher and author of
the Dutch and Deadly Reigns series

"In an overcrowded genre of "street lit the formula remains the same gangsters and their women. If you expect more from a thriller and are looking for complex and full developed story, BEAT THE CROSS is the book for you! Compelling characters, (Roc deserves his own book), and a plot that rivals a Walter Moseley novel. This is not your average tale from the hood."

..Beverly Smith, TV Personality

"Dangerous! Wicked! Forbidden! You Bet! Puts the pedal to the metal at the cross roads of reality, always on the cutting edge. His men, cool and laconic. His women, lush and volatile."

..George Jung, Johnny Depp played his
real life story in the movie, BLOW

Acknowlegements

I would like to thank all those who supported me during my struggles to obtain success: Doris Blue, Leon Blue Sr, Leniqua Blue, Lequan Blue, Jeffrey Blue, Joanna Lopez, Robert "EU" Williams, Scotty, Big Tex, Tinko, Delson Hollaway of Don Diva, Teri Woods, Cordless Sims, Scooter Rockwell, my nieces, nephews and godchildren. To my partner Kim Jackson and our group The Diva Model CoverGyrls (DMcG). To Mack and Don Media, thanks for all your support. To The Dream Team (Brian Luv, Jiton & Legendary Blue) your events are top of a line. To my Don Diva Rydazs. Last but not least, thanks to all my friends and family which are too numerous to name, you know who you are! If I forgot anyone, blame it on my brain and not my heart!!!

CHAPTER 1

Rico Adams was expecting a call that would either make him wealthy or get a lot of people killed. Maybe both. He was at the car wash vacuuming his brother's Lexus LS 400 when he heard a vehicle pick up speed. The driver was coming for him. He caught a glimpse of the approaching car and wasted no time jumping up on the concrete base of the vacuum cleaner.

The driver slammed on brakes, threw the car in park and got out laughing. "Get your muthafuckin scared ass down."

"Why in the...fuck..." Rico stepped down from the cemented vacuum base and kicked the hose as hard as he could. "Trex, the stupid shit is funny to you? You gonna make me fuck your momma's son up." Their attention shifted to the police car that cruised by.

The cop glanced at the two black males but kept

going.

"How long you got the Lexus?" Trexler Orson looked inside the back window of the car.

"Fuck the Lexus. Don't your black ass get tired of playing?"

"Playing? I don't even play the muthafuckin radio. I was tryin to kill you for real."

Rico's pager sounded off. He checked the display then walked to the driver's door of the Lexus, leaned inside, and dialed the number using the car phone.

"Computer 411, Dave speaking."

"What's up, Dave? Why didn't you put in your code? I almost didn't call your ass back."

"How fast can you get here?"

"Ten minutes."

"Did you find a good thief with balls?"

"Yep."

"Bring him if you can, but remember the game plan. And not a word about the casino."

"I'm on my way." Rico terminated the call. He pulled himself out of the doorway of the car and smiled at Trexler. "Drive to my house and park. Dave at the computer shop is waiting for us."

"The white guy? And I thought you was lying about having that connection." Trex rubbed the tips of his fingers with both thumbs. The marred, gritty feel was fresh. "You got your fingerprints straight?"

"They're coming back now. I'll clip them again when I get to the house."

"Wait a minute." Trex rushed to his Camry and retrieved the fingernail clippers from the console. He pitched them to Rico. "I stole them from your house last night."

"I don't know why; you didn't have a job to pull off."

"It's a business world...stay out of mine." Trex got in the Camry and drove away.

Rico was driving down Heckle Boulevard when the car phone rang. He answered it by pressing the button on the steering wheel. "Tank is at work, and can I take a message?"

"Dad, I ain't looking for Tank; I'm looking for you."

Rico lowered the volume on the intercom. "Roc, why do you talk so damn loud?"

"Shit, I don't know. My momma say I take after you."

"What's up? I'll be there in a few minutes."

"Two of your girlfriends called here at the same time."

"Same time? You sound like they was together."

"No, I clicked over and Sequerria was on the other line."

"You didn't mix the damn names up, did you?"

"Hell no. You know I got your back, dad."

Rico laughed. He thought about how fast his son was growing up. The boy was already passing to the ninth grade. "Did your momma call you today?"

"Yeah. She asked me if I was ready to come home."

"What did you tell her?"

"I told her that school only been out a week. She knew I was staying the whole summer."

"You told her I was gone?"

"No, because she think I'm too young to be here by myself. She wanted to speak to you, but I told her you was outside arguing with one of your girlfriends. She started laughing."

"Boy, you're the smartest little fucka on the planet."

"Then stop by the store and get me some Doritos."

"You got that." Rico terminated the call and smiled.

Dave closed the blinds and displayed the *Closed* sign in the all-glass front door. He heard someone knocking at the back door of his shop. On the way to the back, he stepped inside his office and pressed the button on the smoke detector. The chirp was sharp, and he knew the recording would be just as clear.

More knocking.

Dave made it to the back door and saw Rico through the peephole. He unlocked the door and invited him in.

Rico was closely followed by Trex.

"Wait a second. Who's your company?" Dave attempted to keep Trex at bay with an open-hand gesture.

Trex stared at the hand and walked around it.

"That's my business partner. I have no business without my partner."

"But I asked you to come alone. This is—"

"You're just wasting good time. I trust my man here more than I trust you."

"Well, I have a business partner, too, but I didn't want you to feel uncomfortable with his presence."

"If it's any consolation, I make my own comfort by bringing along my own partner."

Trex walked closer to Dave. "Call your partner; we'll wait for him. Otherwise let's shorten the language arts and get to the purpose of this visit."

Dave turned away, avoiding the menacing stare. "Let's go to my office."

Rico and Trex sat on the leather sofa and watched Dave on the other side of the desk.

Dave looked at Rico. "Are you familiar with Novelty Bread?"

"Everybody in Rock Hill is familiar with Novelty." Trex leaned forward.

"The question wasn't directed at you." Dave feigned a smile.

Trex leaned back and stared at the painting above the file cabinet.

"Yeah, what about the bread store?" Rico made eye contact with Dave.

"There's two van-like trucks parked in the back of the store; I want you to steal them between 5:10 and 5:20 on Monday morning."

"You want me to steal some silly-ass trucks—"

"Don't concern your—"

Rico got up from the sofa and Trex followed suit. "I don't steal cars and trucks. Ain't enough money in that shit."

Dave opened his desk drawer, but before he could remove the contents, Trex had drawn a .45 caliber handgun.

"Take your hand out of the drawer, slowly, or I'll lower your muthafuckin blood pressure."

Dave eased his hand out, gripping a band of hundred-dollar bills.

Rico calmly pushed Trex's extended arm away then took a seat again.

Trex remained standing, anxious.

Dave dropped the money on the desk. "Five grand. Just for stealing two trucks. Half the money is up front right now. The other half when you get the trucks to the desired location and—"

The telephone rang.

"You mind?" Dave looked at Rico.

"Answer it; it's your phone."

"Computer 411, Dave speaking."

"I'm on my way to the shop. Did the Rico guy show up? I have the ID ready."

"Yeah, Mark. You just interrupted our meeting. I'll see

you when you get here." Dave replaced the receiver.

"Five grand for some bread trucks." Trex tucked the gun away. "Sounds like there's some risky shit you ain't telling us about."

"Could you shut your partner's mouth before he blows this deal for you?" Dave frowned at Rico.

Trex inhaled deeply and released.

Rico looked down at the floor, scratching his head. *What the fuck was my next line?* He flinched at the sound of the .45 and looked up, surprised.

Trex jumped up on the desk and squatted, looking at Dave's bleeding shoulder. "Blow the deal? We takin the twenty-five hundred and everything else you got in this muthafucka."

Rico shook his head in disbelief. He heard the sound of the .45 again.

CHAPTER 2

Mark Aldridge parked in the rear of the computer shop. The front lot was empty but he had expected to find Dave's car in the rear. Nothing. Mark left the engine running, got out, and hurried to the back door. He turned the knob and the door opened. He was confused. He stepped inside. "Dave?"

No answer.

He headed for the office, looking around for anything out of order. Mark stopped at the doorway of the office. No sign of Dave, and the shop's main computer was missing. Mark stood silent, listening for any sounds in the building. He walked around the desk and saw his business partner on the floor. The blood still looked fresh. Mark looked up at the smoke detector; the LED indicator was on. He hurried over and removed the face from the smoke detector. He pulled the audio and video chips from the circuit board, stuffed them in his pocket, and finally dialed 911.

Sequerria Truesdale was reclined in the tub, lost in the hot water, the steam, the old Anita Baker song—*I Apologize*. The first ring from her cordless phone seemed to invade her privacy. "Hello."

"May I speak with Sequerria?"

"She's not in. May I take a message and ask who's calling?"

"Would you let her know that Les Hansen called?"

"Hansen? The Cop?"

"That's a good guess."

"What the hell do you want now?"

He smiled, but she would never know it. "I was hoping you were in the mood for some conversation."

"With a damn detective?"

"This call isn't job related or—"

"What's wrong with your phone? Sounds like you're frying chicken."

"I'm on a cellular. I'll pull over and talk when I reach a clear area."

"So what's this conversation about?" She stepped out of the tub and reached for a towel.

"I was just riding and thinking: If I called her and said all the right things, maybe she would give me the opportunity to take her out to dinner or something."

"That's a nice line—if you was trying to get with a white woman in a church parking lot." She laughed, still drying off. "Tell me, why would I wanna date a cop?"

"Honestly, I have no idea. But when I'm off duty, I don't consider myself a cop. I'm just your everyday black man looking for a good woman."

"Whatever caresses your emotions."

Silence.

"If you saw me robbing a bank while you was off duty, you telling me that wouldn't concern you?"

He pondered to respond with a good answer. "That depends on whether we were going to split the money."

"Ain't it something unethical about what your doing?"

"What am I doing?"

"Just before dark I'm in a restaurant that gets robbed; you find the robber dead in the parking lot and then get my unlisted number from your damn interview notes."

He laughed. "I asked for your number; I don't recall saying it was for my investigation."

"Yeah, right. Listen, I have things to do. Sorry, but I don't have an interest in fuckin with cops." She ended the call and dropped the towel. She placed the cordless on the sink and stood before the mirror, holding both breasts in her hands. *Damn cop don't know what to do with this.*

Rico and Trex sat on the trunk of the Lexus. The 40-watt porch light wasn't worth a damn beyond the doorsteps. The car had been backed in Rico's driveway, windows down, CD player trying to fill in the blanks of silence. "What did you shoot the white guy for, Trex?"

"His mouth was too fly."

"So you killin everybody with a fly mouth?"

"That ain't all to it, and you know it."

Rico hesitated. "Trex, I had something big set up with Dave."

"Stealing some bread trucks?"

"The trucks was just...something small to help with a million-dollar casino scheme."

"Honey buns and poker chips. That shit don't add up."

"Dave had access to the Kapata bank account. It's off-shore and in some black guy's name—Robert Mayes. Me and Dave was working on getting the money out through a Vegas casino."

"Why am I the last one to know your plans?"

"I still haven't told my bother. But as for you, I knew you couldn't handle big-time shit in a professional way. You let your gun—"

"So you're talkin about taxing a muthafuckin casino and leaving me out?"

"You damn right. I need you and Tank's help with the bread trucks; that's enough to help me with the casino scheme. The split is three ways, but you need to stop fuckin up with that madman attitude."

Trex got off the trunk and sat on Rico's doorsteps. "Why was you fakin like you didn't know about the bread trucks when we was in Dave's office?"

"I was suppose to find a thief who's crazy enough to steal from Dan and Arnold Kapata. Dave heard that they used to be in the Mafia or mob or whatever. He wanted me to play that role around whoever I found to steal the trucks."

"So I jacked off the million-dollar scheme?"

Rico leaned back against the car window. "Looks that way for now. And I don't even know what's in the bread trucks, but me and Dave figured it must be something valu-able."

"How did Dave find out about the trucks? How does it help the casino scheme?"

"Dave repaired and planted some kind of spy shit inside of his customer's computers. That's what..." Rico shook his head and leaned up from the window. "I still don't understand why you shot him."

"When he asked you to shut me up, I thought you was thinking about saying something to me."

Rico shrugged. "What does that have to do with—"

"I think if you woulda said something to me, making him think his money could buy some control over me, that woulda complicated things between you and me." Trex paused. "So I shot him before you could make your mind up."

Rico leaned forward. "Trex, I been fuckin with you since I was eleven. In twenty-four years, you can't name one goddamn time I crossed you."

"I never crossed you, either."

"That's beside the point, Trex! I'm saying, why would I go against you just to get a damn hustle?"

More silence.

Rico looked at him. "Ran out of answers?"

"You misunderstanding things. I don't think you'll go against me, but you can easily say something wrong in the spur of the moment. Anybody could."

"Learn to trust my judgment as a muthafuckin friend. Who else—"

The front door opened. "Dad, Tremaine is on the phone."

"Tell her I'm...Just tell her to come over here and spend the night."

Roc dipped back inside, leaving the door partly open.

Trex watched the headlights on the approaching vehicle. "I think you just fucked up. Here comes your girl with the big ass, big mouth, and big fake-ass weave."

"Damn. I'm getting rid of her ass."

The car pulled in and stopped in front of the Lexus.

Rico met her at the driver's door before she could get out. "What's up? You look beautiful and...most elegant."

"I'm not trying to hear that shit." Sequerria opened the door. "I been calling you all day. Why don't you ever stay at home? You don't have no damn job. Got that little boy answering calls and here by hisself."

"You know what..." Rico closed her door.

"Move, let me get out. I'm staying over here."

"No, stay in the car. I don't feel like fuckin with you tonight. I don't play that shit—telling me how to handle my son."

"I'm not telling you how—"

Trex walked up to their argument. "What's up, Sequerria?"

"Trex, please stop speaking to me. You know I don't fuck with you."

"Yes, ma'am. But would you please back this raggedy-ass Escort out of the way. Your man was about to take me home."

She glanced at Trex's Camry, which had been parked across the lawn. "Drive your own damn car. Your broke ass must be out of gas."

"Call me sometime tomorrow." Rico tapped twice on the roof. "I don't like your attitude tonight."

Roc came to the front door again. "Dad, she said she's on her way."

Trex turned to Rico again. "I'll get your sister to take me home when she gets here." He smiled at Rico. "I think I rather ride with Yvonne anyway." Trex headed inside the house.

"Yvonne don't have time for that fool." She looked up at Rico. "I wasn't telling you how to handle your son. I miss you, and I just wanted to be with you. Don't treat me like this."

His eyes cut toward the street. Her soft words were beating him down. "Sequerria, not tonight. I'm in a bad mood, and I just want to spend some time with my son."

"Come here." She pulled on his T-shirt. He leaned inside and she kissed him. Her wet lips and slow-moving tongue went inside his mouth then back out, and erotically lapped at the side of his face. She pulled his head down and sucked on his ear lobe.

He pulled back. "Fuck this shit. Get out of the car and go inside."

She couldn't resist smiling. "And I gotta tell you what happened to me at Gadden's Restaurant earlier today. I was there when it got robbed, but somebody killed the robber in the parking lot with a knife and took the money from him."

"Leave the keys inside. Trex is driving it home and Roc is spending the night with him."

She got out of the car. "I don't really want Trex driving my car after he talked shit about it."

"This is plan B; you want to go back to plan A?"

"Nope." She laughed and headed for the front door.

"Go to my room and strip down, no covers. Just wait for me." Rico watched her go inside. He leaned against the door of her car, wondering how this would turn out.

Trex came out and started laughing. "You fuckin up real good now."

"Drive Sequerria's car to your place. Take my son with you; I'll get him in the morning."

"When Tremaine rings that doorbell, you'll be my hero if you let her in."

"I'm tired of this sneak shit. Tremaine is coming in, too."

"Stop fakin. You talk that lesbian shit, but you can't work it out. Not between those two women anyway."

Rico walked by Trex and headed inside the house. "Come on; I'll get Roc's clothes ready."

"Okay, but I'm not pulling out of the driveway until Tremaine pulls up, and I'm not pulling off until me and Roc actually see her come inside and close the door."

"I don't give a damn what you do. I told you, I'm tired of this sneaking-around shit."

Tremaine entered the house and closed the door. Prince's album could be heard from one of the rooms. She looked at Rico on the sofa and heard the Escort leaving. "I know that isn't Sequerria's car that Trex is driving."

"Of course it is, but who gives a damn? Have a seat; I need to talk to you."

Tremaine sat on the arm of a matching chair. "You're still messing with her? What did you call me over here for?"

"Because I'm still messing with you."

She was silent.

"Listen, sit right here and watch some television while I get in the shower. When I get out, I got a surprise for you."

She slid herself off the arm of the chair and relaxed on its cushion. "Yeah, I bet you do."

"It's not...Believe me, this is a real surprise. Don't leave out of the front room until I get out of the shower."

"Roc, you know what? Your crazy-ass daddy is my hero."

"Why you say that, Trex?"

14

"Right now, you too young to understand, but the muthafuc...My man got *two* women up in that muthafucka."

"Why you didn't say muthafucka the first time?"

"Hey, hey! Your dad lets you curse, but you know he don't let you say *muthafucka*."

"That's only if he around. Where we going? This ain't the way to your house."

"Me and you going to break in somebody's house. You scared?"

"I ain't scared of shit. Whose house we breaking in?"

"Sequerria's. But you can't tell *nobody*, not even your damn dad. It ain't really breaking in; I got the key." He rattled the keys that hang from the ignition.

"You going in to steal something?"

"Hell no. Girl ain't got shit worth stealing. I'm just testing your creeping skills."

Rico walked into the living room wearing only silk boxer shorts and a damp towel around his neck. He stood before Tremaine. "Strip down."

She got up, kicked her shoes off, and began unbuttoning her shorts.

He moved in closer and gently sucked on her neck. "Leave the G-cut undies on." He pulled back and helped her out of the T-shirt. His erection bulged at his boxers with the look of deformity. He moved behind her and unfastened her bra. He kissed the back of her neck. The shoulders. The spine. The top of her voluptuous ass cheeks. He sat back in the chair and shook his head at the provocative sight before him. He jiggled her ass cheeks from the bottom with the tips of his fingers.

She turned around and grabbed one of his hands.

"Why are your fingers so rough?" She looked closer. "What did you do to the tips?"

He stood. "Just trying to stay out of trouble." He pulled her closer, with an arm around her waist, and fitted his mouth around her lips.

Tremaine closed her eyes and moved her tongue around, trying to meet his. She pressed her body against the erection and grabbed his ass with both hands.

The bedroom door opened. The music poured out, much louder now. Tremaine released Rico and covered her breasts with her forearms. She stared at Sequerria who was now standing naked in the hallway.

"What the fuck is going on?" Sequerria walked toward them with regard for neither their half nakedness nor hers in full.

Tremaine looked Rico in his eyes. "You're an ignorant-ass man, you know that?" Without warning, she began swinging and clawing at his face.

He managed to grab her wrists, but the knee to his thigh compelled him to protect his groin. He put a leg behind hers and fell to the floor on top of her.

Sequerria entered the fight, stomping Tremaine's free leg.

Tremaine let out a loud cry and bit Rico's chest.

Sequerria went for Tremaine's long hair. She had heard that it was real; now she would find out for herself. She gripped Tremaine's hair with both hands and yanked at it.

Rico released Tremaine and lunged at Sequerria, grabbing her neck. "Girl, what the fuck you think you doing?" He squeezed with both hands.

Sequerria freed Tremaine's hair and struggled against Rico's grip. She needed air.

Tremaine crawled over, feeling pain in her knee, and

slammed an elbow into Sequerria's ribs.

Rico loosened his grip on Sequerria's neck and was slapped square in the mouth by Tremaine.

Tremaine got up from her knees and limped over to her clothes. She picked up her T-shirt and shorts and took the keys out of her pocket. She headed for the door, wearing only underwear. She didn't care about leaving her shoes. She stopped at the door and looked back at Rico. He was no longer holding Sequerria's neck. "Don't think that I was fighting over your sorry ass; I was fighting *because* of your sorry ass." Her eyes cut to Sequerria. "He's all yours now, bitch!"

Hansen had driven from his weekly poker game. He was under the influence of alcohol, but he was nearly home now. He thought about Sequerria and her shape and wondered what she was doing at 1:36 in the morning. He smiled to himself, remembering the lies he had told his poker buddies. About he and she.

He slowed the Camaro and parked in his driveway. He got out, staggering once. He heard the gun shots but didn't have time to react. Sharp, splitting pains attacked his upper body. Within seconds he was on the ground. He could no longer hear anything. His eyes stared into another world, retrieving an unfamiliar view. Officer Les Hansen finally blacked out. Forever.

CHAPTER 3

After watching the Saturday morning news, John Caston discovered that he'd killed an off-duty policeman. He tried Arnold's pager number.

The number you are trying to call is no longer in service...

He tried the number again and received the same message. He didn't understand. He had reached Arnold with that number as recently as yesterday. He was sure that no paging company would disconnect services on a Saturday. He dialed the number to the bread store then sat up in bed. He decided to make the necessary calls while his wife and daughter were out.

The old lady behind the counter at Novelty Bread was extremely nice to everyone she came in contact with, even with the rude, hostile man on the other end of the phone. "I'm sorry but both owners are out at this time. If you'd like, you can leave your number—"

"You sound like a real goddamn answering machine. You just tell old Danny Boy and that fat-ass Arnold to get in touch with John real soon."

"I sure will."

"Tell them that goddamn set up will cost an extra fifty grand." He slammed the receiver, ending the call. He wanted to dial Arnold's pager number again, but he knew it was useless. He leaned to the floor and checked the pockets of his pants for Kayla's number.

Gone.

Shit! He imagined his wife rambling and finding the strip of paper. He'd have to hear her bitch at him for a week now.

Dan and Arnold Kapata were on Interstate 77 in Dan's Jaguar.

Arnold ended the call with the bread store attendant. He lowered the power window a few inches and threw his head back against the headrest. "Caston called the store and made a demand for an extra fifty."

Dan kept his eyes on the highway and did not respond.

"I told you that fucking nut was gonna be a problem. We probably need to suspend the store operations until we get rid of him."

"What makes him think we have fifty grand?"

"Maybe it's because we never tried to negotiate the contract fee. We gave him what he asked for."

Dan veered off at the first Rock Hill exit. "I'm not so sure about that. I think he knows about the other side of our business."

"Nah. How could he?"

"I don't...I'm just thinking out loud." Dan slowed the car at the end of the ramp and blended with the light traffic on Celanese Road. "John was too concerned about whether Hansen was a prominent or public figure. I shouldn't have taken that risk with Caston."

"You gonna beat yourself up over it, or are we gonna handle the matter and get on with our normal life?"

Silence.

"Did you hear me?"

"Yeah." Dan dialed Caston's number on the car phone. He heard the voice of a young girl after the second ring.

"Hello."

"Yes, is John in?"

"No, he's not. May I take a message?"

"Well, I'm with his former employer, Liverpool Construction. When do you expect him in?"

"In about another hour; he's out looking for my mom's birthday present."

"I'm sure he'll find her something nice. In the meantime, would I be able to stop by and leave some photos and sketches with someone? He'd have to be familiar with the work by Monday."

"Of course. Me and my mom will be here."

Dan smiled at Arnold and ended the call.

"We should have killed the cop ourselves."

"Come on, Arnold, that Mafia shit ended in Philadelphia thirty years ago. We're professional businessmen now."

Kayla Seegars opened her front door.

"Ms. Seegars?"

"Yes."

"I'm Detective Harold Greenburg. Does anyone else live at this residence?"

"My boyfriend, but he's at work."

"We'd like for you to come to the station and answer a few questions concerning the murder of Officer Les Hansen."

"A murder?" She had heard about the cop from the news. Her heart was beating faster now. "I don't know anything about a murder."

"Well that's fine, but maybe you can help us understand why your telephone number was left at the suspected ambush area."

She thought about John Caston. Before yesterday, she hadn't given her number out all year.

Dan pressed the doorbell. He smiled when the teenaged girl opened the door. "Matthew Johnson of Liverpool Construction." He held up a manila envelope and stepped aside.

She pushed the storm door open. "Where's your car? I hope you didn't walk in this heat." Her innocent smile was genuine.

Dan shoved her face with the palm of his hand, sending her to the floor. He entered the house and closed the door.

"Stacy, what's going on in there?" Caston's wife turned off the hair dryer.

Dan had a handgun aimed at the young girl. He held a finger to his lips with the other hand. He and the girl could hear the woman approaching.

"Stacy?"

Tears ran down the young girl's temples and into her hair as she lay on her back. Her eyes moved from the gunman to the ceiling fan.

Caston's wife stepped into plain view.

Dan let two rounds fly. He watched the woman fall backward against the wall.

The young girl let out an unbearable scream.

Dan turned the gun on the girl and pulled the trigger again.

He remained still, listening to the sounds of a TV coming from a different room. He followed the sound to a bedroom and turned the television off. He returned to the living room and heard the sound of vehicles arriving. He peeked through the window and saw four police cars. *How?* The shooting had only been a minute ago. He scrambled through the house, looking for the back door. A natural choice led him to the kitchen. He used his shirt to handle the lock and doorknob. He jumped from the house, skipping the doorsteps, and ran for the woods.

Two policemen saw the figure before it disappeared into the woods. "Police! Freeze!" One officer fired warning shots, but the runner had a much better chance now.

Trex parked the Escort in front of the Lexus. He and Roc got out and sat on the doorsteps. "Well, Roc...Tremaine's car is gone; shit more than likely went bad for my hero."

"What does that mean?"

"That means your nothin-ass dad probably ain't my hero no more."

"Why you won't ring the doorbell?"

"It's your damn daddy's house; *you* ring it."

"I ain't ringing shit; I can sit out here all day."

"Your little smart mouth is about to make me kick a new hole in your ass."

"And you better unkick before I find out about it."

Trex laughed. "You steal all your dad's lines. Make your own shit up."

"Why you so scared to ring the—"

Rico opened the front door. "Why the hell you two sitting on my steps with that big-brother-little-brother shit?"

Roc stood. "Trex is scared to ring the doorbell because he knows you don't get out the bed before eleven."

"You got me fucked up. I don't care about waking your—"

"Come on in here and stop arguing with Roc."

Trex sat on the sofa and finally noticed Rico's face. "Your lip's swollen, your face is scratched the hell up...I told you to call me if somebody ever jumps you."

"Roc, go in your room and let me talk to Trex. And knock on my room door, and tell Sequerria to put her damn skates on." He waited for Roc to leave the living room. Rico sat on the coffee table in front of Trex. "Listen, I was thinking about the bread trucks. We have to be ready Monday morning. Some rumor had Dave scared of the bread store owners. I don't see that bullshit."

"That's a good point. Let's steal them shits tonight."

"No. The owners load the trucks shortly after five on Monday morning."

"Wait a minute. Novelty Bread sells nothing but bakery products—bread, cakes, donuts and shit."

"That shit is irrelevant—"

Sequerria opened the bedroom door and approached

the living room.

Trex smiled at her. "My man got his ass whipped last night; why didn't you help him?"

"Where's my keys, Trex? I don't have time for your mouth."

"The keys is in the car."

She headed out the door.

"Oh, I put two dollars worth of gas in—"

She slammed the door.

"And that's the thanks I get for getting your shit off E!"

"Open your mind, Trex. There's something more valuable than snacks in them bread trucks. We can sell the stolen goods; I need something to gamble with as a front when I hit Vegas."

Trex got up and walked to the kitchen. "What happened with Tremaine?"

"She wouldn't go for it; she went off. Sequerria ain't even down for the lesbian shit. It was a cat fight up in here."

"At least you kept one."

"Yeah, but that's the wrong one." He hesitated. "I got to get Tremaine back."

Dan fired two shots from the woods. He knew that that would make the cops think twice about running in after him, at least until they could gather enough men. He kept running, batting and swatting the weeds and thin branches. His wind was short, and his time was running out. It was only a matter of minutes before the cops could get the area closed off. Dan made a turn through the woods; he didn't want to reach the next street over by running in a straight line.

Less than a minute later, he stopped at the end of the

woods and scanned the street. The Jaguar was nowhere in sight. He looked at the line of houses and saw everyday life: children playing, a man washing a car, a dog rolling around on a lawn. Then he watched a police car turn onto the street.

The car cruised at a walker's pace.

Dan took his dress shirt off and waited for the cop to drive by. He pulled the back of his T-shirt up and over his head, creating an impromptu disguise. He wrapped the dress shirt around his neck for feature distraction—an old Mafia trick that he could never forget.

The cop cruised by, looking at a house, then turned his attention toward the woods again.

Dan's aim was excellent from the ten yards. The bullet traveled through the driver's window and hit the cop under the left eye. Dan rushed from the woods toward the police car, which was moving even slower now.

Someone screamed. Children ran. Dogs barked.

Dan opened the driver's door and steered the vehicle back on course while hustling alongside it. He pulled the policeman out of the seat and watched him fall to the street. A rear wheel ran over the dead man's hand and wrist, but Dan paid that no mind. He jumped inside the police car and sped off.

When the call came in over the radio, the search of Arnold and the Jaguar was called off. The four policemen had left Arnold sitting on a curb. They were no longer concerned with stopping and checking vehicles in the area. Their shooter was somewhere in a city police car.

Arnold closed the trunk of the Jaguar and got back in the car. He thought his brother had only a slim chance—a chance that was better than reaching the Jaguar as planned. But just in case Dan could get away, Arnold knew exactly where his brother would be waiting.

Roc rang the doorbell and waited. He looked back at his dad who was waiting in the Lexus.

Tremaine opened the door. "Hey, Roc, with your handsome self. Whatever your daddy is up to, tell him it'll never work."

"Can I come in?"

She laughed. "Yeah, but your daddy can't. Not ever."

Roc turned and waved his dad away.

Rico drove off.

Roc sat in her recliner without invitation.

Tremaine smiled and sat on the love seat. "That's terrible the way your dad uses you to fix his problems."

"I can't fix the shit he gets in."

"Roc, you know I don't want you to curse around me. You haven't forgotten what I told you about cursing."

Roc looked at the fish in her aquarium. "I'm sorry. I ain't gonna curse no more."

"Yes, you will; just don't curse around me."

"I won't."

"Now, why did your dad send you here?"

"He didn't send me here."

She cocked her head and shifted her eyes with disbelief. "Then why are you here?"

"This morning I asked him why you was over there last night with Sequerria."

"And what did he say?"

"He said he wanted you and Sequerria to live there together because he was tired of cheating and sneaking around."

"Well, his ass don't have to worry about cheating on me no damn more."

"Watch your language; you know I'm just a kid."

Tremaine laughed and clapped twice. "Boy, you are just like your daddy."

"Anyway, he told me that y'all was fighting and you busted his lip and scratched his face."

"If I was strong enough, Roc, I would have thrown your trifling daddy out the window."

"I asked him if you was still his girlfriend, and he said you was too mad; you probably won't never come over there again."

"He was right, Roc."

"But I don't even like Sequerria. I told him you was his best girlfriend."

She smiled. "Come here, Roc."

Roc got up and stepped to her.

She leaned forward and hugged him.

"So I told him to bring me over here. I don't want you to break up with my daddy. He ain't gonna do it no more."

Tremaine held Roc in her arms. The tears were on the way.

Roc heard her sniffle. He smiled. His dad would have to pay up that thousand-dollar bet.

CHAPTER 4

Arnold drove down the dirt road, eyes on the parked police car forty yards ahead. Fifteen yards later, a figure rose from the front end of the police car. His brother had evaded the police.

Dan got in the passenger side of the Jaguar and Arnold made a three-point turn. "What happened to you?" Dan tossed his dress shirt to the back seat.

"I saw all the cop cars coming, so I decided to circle the block. They ended up pulling me over and searching the car."

"Then it's a good thing I didn't make it back to the Jaguar."

"How'd you get away? I mean, how'd you get the police car? I heard it over their radio."

"I shot him while he was cruising. I'll tell you all about it later."

"Did anybody see you?"

"No. Not well enough for a line-up." He rubbed his forehead. "I don't understand it; the cops arrived maybe thirty seconds after I erased the wife and daughter."

"They might have been onto Caston about Hansen. They must have been." Arnold stopped at the sign at the end of the dirt road. He pulled out, falling in behind a car with protruding fishing equipment.

"If only I could have waited for Caston at his house. Hell, I didn't even get a chance to check the place for the ten grand we paid to the cocksucker."

"Did you leave any prints in the house or in the police car?"

"No. I wiped the door handle of the car, inside and out, the steering wheel case, and the gear knob. I was careful not to touch nothing else."

"What about inside the house?"

"Didn't touch a thing."

They rode in silence for a few seconds. "What happened to the manila envelope? Your prints were all over that."

No answer. Dan was thinking. Picturing. Worrying. He'd certainly fucked up. Because the cop wasn't wearing a seatbelt when he'd pulled him, Dan thought luck had been up for grabs. Truth is, a seat belt would have only given him a problem for a few seconds; the damn envelope could give him a lifetime of problems.

"You left the goddamn thing in the house?"

Still no answer.

"That would put the both of us up shit creek."

Rico's pager sounded off. He checked the display and

saw code 88 behind a North Carolina number. The code meant that the caller was using a fairly safe phone line; returning the call should come under the same conditions. He pulled the Lexus over at a convenience store and used a pay phone to dial the number collect. The operator connected the call and a female voice was on the other end.

"Hello, Rico?"

"Who am I speaking with?" He could think of no one who would call him outside of South Carolina.

"This is Lynn. How are you?"

"I don't know any muthafuckin Lynn."

"Calm down, Rico. I'm Lynn Gardner; Trex and I used to—"

"Oh shit! Trex's girl."

"Trex's ex-girl. It's been two years now."

"Yo, Trex will be with me later on; I can give you—"

"I don't want to talk to him; I want to talk to you."

"Slow the fuck down, Lynn, and make your case. You know I don't get caught in the cross."

"I don't mean it like that. Listen, the police came to talk to me about a gun less than an hour ago. The same gun that Trex took from me in our last fight."

"What's so special about it?"

"They said it was used in a robbery or something."

Rico turned and stared at the poster in the store window. "And you told them Trex got the gun from you?"

"Of course not. A week after I moved up here, someone broke into my car and stole my CD's and tapes. I had reported the gun stolen, too, just to get my insurance to pay for it all."

"I tried to tell Trex he lost a good woman. You fucked him up when you left him; he said he would never put his hands on a woman—"

"Rico, I believe Trex is in trouble over that gun."

His pager sounded off again; he ignored it. "How? you said you didn't tell them Trex got—"

"They asked me about Trex."

"How the hell they know you used to mess with him?"

"You remember taking us to apply for a marriage license? Somehow they know about that, even though we never went through with it."

"What was the gun used to rob?"

"Well, the gun was used to rob Gadden's Restaurant, but the robber was stabbed and killed in the parking lot."

"Damn, that was yesterday. Sequerria told me about that shit; she was there. She was interviewed by some cop named Hansen. How the cops get that information and trace the gun to you that fast?"

"The police use online retrieval for information, too. They even kept a damn record of a two-year-old marriage license application. The government have their own files and internet system. I don't know how it works, though."

"Is this a number I can reach you at?"

"No. I'll give you my home number, but don't give it to Trex."

"I don't have nothing to write with. Just call my pager again and put it in without the code."

"I'll do it as soon as we hang up. How is Trex doing, anyway?"

"Write this number down."

"Go ahead." She listened and wrote the number.

"That's Trex's new number. Call and ask him how he's doing." Rico hung the phone up. He stared at the poster again. *In Rare Form*. It was a thriller and novel-writing manual by Cordless Sims. *Probably some more bullshit about the dope game. I like the cover, though.* He got in the Lexus and drove off.

Mark Aldridge was restless. He stared out the window, waiting for his brother to come inside. Mark had driven from South Carolina to his brother's trailer in Wytheville, Virginia. He had a key to the place but hadn't used it in over seven months. He backed away from the window and sat on an ottoman when his brother reached the doorsteps.

Norman unlocked the door and entered the house. He paused at the site of his brother. "What's wrong?"

"Does something have to be wrong for little brother to come see you?"

Norman laughed. "That's usually the occasion. How's mom?"

"Fine, last time I checked."

Norman closed the door and cleared some old newspapers from the couch. "So how long have you been here?"

"A little over an hour." Mark slowly rubbed his hands together.

"Tell me about it." Norman took a seat on the worn cushion.

Mark hesitated. He was considering the opening line to his story. "Dave is dead."

"The guy you worked for?"

"I didn't work for him, Norman. We were partners."

"He was always fixing and repairing, and you were always delivering and picking up computers and parts and shit."

"You'd never understand how a business is run."

"Maybe not, but I sure as hell understand how an employee like yourself is ran."

"I didn't come here to argue with you."

"Yeah. Hey, I'm sorry to hear about your boss...er, your partner."

Mark made eye contact with his brother.

"How did he die, an accident or something?"

"He was shot twice at the computer shop."

"Big shit! A robbery?"

"No...Well...I guess so. But the only thing taken was the main computer."

"Where were you, out picking up something?"

Mark ignored the question. "Dave hired a guy named Rico to steal some bread trucks. At least he was *supposed* to hire the guy."

"Bread trucks. Why would—"

"He was paying the guy twenty-five hundred up front and the same on delivery."

"Why didn't you have him call me? I would've gotten him some Wells Fargo trucks for that."

"It's not really about the trucks."

"Why bread trucks?"

"The owners of the bread store are hauling something inside the trucks, and we were willing to pay to find out what it is."

"How do you know?"

Mark took a deep breath and exhaled. "Whenever Dave would fix the computer of a business, he would plant a Share-Link program inside."

"Break that down for me; don't forget that NASA turned down my application."

"A Share-Link allows you to view the contents of another computer as long as it's online. It's like snooping around in a file cabinet."

"So what was he looking for, good porn sites or children's chat rooms?"

"Try company bank accounts, passwords, and codes."

Norman sat up, interested.

"We searched the files of an automotive custom shop and saw before-and-after images of Novelty's bread trucks."

"Why would a bread store want something customed for its trucks?"

"I don't know, but the trucks have hidden compartments in the floor."

Norman nodded with approval. "And who's the guy that Dave hired?"

"Rico. I know he's the one who shot Dave. I talked to the cops and told them how I found Dave in the shop's office. I didn't tell them anything about the Rico guy, though."

"Why not?"

"Because Rico has the main computer. We need to get that back; we don't want the cops to seize the computer with the Share-Link."

"What's so important about the Share-Links?"

"We'd have access to the bank account of the Novelty Bread owners. All we'd have to do is figure out how to withdraw the money."

"And how much money is that?"

"At last count, six and a half million."

Silence fell over the room.

"I have the audio and video chips that Dave made for the main computer. Dave initiated a recording in the office but I can't see or hear what went on until I link the chips up with that main computer."

"Why can't you use the chips with a different computer?"

"Because the chip doesn't have any memory in them; they're not for storage. They serve as a trigger when connected with the main computer."

"Does that mean Ruso can't access the audio-video without the chips?"

"You mean Rico. And the answer is no, he can't."

Norman stood and stretched. He walked to the kitchen and grabbed two beers from the refrigerator. He returned to the living room and sat one of the beers on the coffee table.

"No, thanks. You know I don't drink."

"Then you're in luck, because that's not for you." He popped the top on the beer. "So what do we take first, the trucks or the computer?"

"I think Rico may be interested in the trucks. We'll wait and watch. If he shows up for the trucks, we get the computer from his house while he's out."

"When is all of this supposed to take place?"

"Let's just hope that Dave told him about the owners loading the trucks on the first Monday of every month. They're usually done with the loading around five in the morning."

"How do you know all this?"

"After learning about the hidden compartments, we watched the store for five months."

"That's big shit."

"Get your things; you're going to Rock Hill for a few days."

Rico tapped the horn and waited for Trex to come out of the apartment. The door opened and out came a woman that Rico had never seen before. She entered a Toyota and drove off.

The door opened again and Trex walked out. He

approached the passenger door. "Tank must have gave you this car. I ain't saw him all week." Trex got in and closed the door. "You look upset. What the fuck's wrong with you? The little trick with Roc and Tremaine didn't work?"

He backed the car out of the parking space, opened the moonroof, and cruised slowly. "You robbed Gadden's Restaurant, didn't you?"

"Gadden's? What the hell I look like robbing a restaurant? Where did you get that shit from?"

"Don't worry about it. If you say you didn't rob the joint, that's the end of that."

"But I still wanna know who got my name fucked up in some shit like that."

"The cops. They investigated Lynn, your ex, because the dead robber in the parking lot had the gun you took from her."

"So she told them I took the gun from her?"

"No. The gun was reported stolen two years ago, but—"

"You planning on staying at this stop sign forever?"

Rico turned onto Mt. Gallant Road. "For some reason they're investigating you because, we figure, the marriage license application. They know you used to be her man."

"Makes sense when you think about my two prior weapons possession charges."

Silence.

"Wait a minute. When did you talk to Lynn?"

"Less than an hour ago."

"She's in Rock Hill?"

"No. She paged me from...Charlotte, I guess."

"So Lynn looked out." Trex smiled. "I need to get her back on the team."

"That girl ain't about to fuck with you."

"This is a new dance; get out of my video."

"You caught the news this morning?"

"About the computer shop? No. What did they say?"

"They don't know shit."

"The girl that just left my apartment was telling me about some white guy that killed a cop at one-something this morning."

"I heard about that. The muthafucka killed two more people in a house and shot another cop and took his car while it was still rolling. That white dude is straight up hard."

"Yeah, he's hard. But if he ever cross the Trexter's path..."

"You'll just get your nothin-ass shot up." Rico laughed.

"I don't play when it's time to stop the violence; I don't play the muthafuckin radio."

"Whatever, you tough-ass villain."

"You got a plan for the bread trucks yet?"

"No question. You're bound to love this one."

CHAPTER 5

Detective Harold Greenburg studied Sequerria's graduation picture. "So you never dated Officer Hansen?"

"Hell no. I already told you that. He was probably dating something your color."

"You said no to having sex with him?"

"The first time I ever saw him was when he interviewed me at Gadden's two days ago. I never saw him again."

He looked at a framed picture of a white Jesus. "He was coming from a poker game the morning of his murder. He told every man in that house that he had just had sex with you at your place."

"Then the lying fucker need to be dead. He even said he was a detective when we was at Gadden's. That was a lie."

"He told them he talked with you on the phone before you asked him to come catch you before you got out of the tub. Is that true?"

"I always knew cops lied, but *goddamn!*"

"So you didn't talk to him over the phone?"

Sequerria shook her head. "No. He took my number down for the investigation at the restaurant, but he never called me. I ain't got no rap for no police."

"Do you recall where you were on Friday night, early Saturday morning?"

"I was with my boyfriend, Rico Adams. I even had a fight over there with him and another woman."

"Sounds interesting." He jotted a few notes down. "Did you win?"

"I don't know; you woulda had to be there to judge for yourself."

He smiled. "Thank you for your time, Ms. Truesdale. I'll be in touch if I need you for anything else."

Roc sat on his bicycle, leaning against the fence, watching the men play basketball in the park.

Rico and Trex walked around inside the park; they were waiting for Tank to show up. "What makes you think your brother wanna get down with the bread truck lick?"

Rico glanced over at Roc on the other side of the park. "Because we can't pull it off like I want without a third person."

"Tank work too hard for a living to get caught up in our type of shit."

"Me and Tank did shit together plenty times when we was in our teens."

"Man, that was ninety damn years ago."

"From now on, I'll tell you what to worry about. I know..." Rico and Trex saw the black Suburban pull up. They watched Roc ride the bicycle toward the truck.

"I bet you Tank will have something negative to say about the plan." Trex looked at Rico.

Rico watched another child on a bicycle attempt to intersect Roc's path. The child sped up but Roc could not stop or turn away in time.

Roc's front wheel scraped the boy's back tire, and they both fell.

Trex was about to dart over, but Rico grabbed his shirt. They watched Tank rush to the accident, and three guys from the basketball court trotted over. Rico knew the accident wasn't that big of a deal. They continued walking toward the scene at a normal pace.

Tank dusted Roc off and stood the bicycle up.

"What happened, Lil' Tim?" The muscular ballplayer helped the boy up.

Lil' Tim was dusting himself off. "I turned in front of him, but he speeded up to try to hit me."

Roc looked at Tank then turned to the interrogating ball player. "That muthafucka lying his ass off."

The ballplayer looked at Tank. "That your son?"

"Nope."

The ballplayer grabbed Lil' Tim by the arm and pulled him toward Roc. "Tell Lil' Tim that you're sorry, and squash the shit."

Roc took a step back and frowned. "You got me fucked up. Lil' Tim ain't got nothing coming."

Tank laughed. "Hey, I saw the whole thing. Shit was an accident."

Another ballplayer stepped forward. "I saw the shit, too. It happened the way Lil' Tim say it happened."

Tank smiled. "You and Lil' Tim both telling a mutha-fuckin lie."

The second ballplayer jumped at Tank but was held

back by the first.

The first ballplayer stared at Tank. "Well this is how it's going down: Lil' Tim gonna whip the little nigga's ass for callin him a liar, and you and my man can get your shit off next."

Tank gripped the handlebars and the back of the seat and held his position. "Oh, this is a beautiful day in the park."

Rico and Trex arrived and watched as spectators.

The first ballplayer pushed Lil' Tim.

Lil' Tim walked closer and pushed Roc.

Roc looked at Rico.

Rico looked away.

Lil' Tim took another step to push Roc again.

Roc hit his opponent with what his dad calls a two-piece facial.

Lil' Tim fell to the ground, and Roc rushed to sit on top of him.

The first ballplayer pushed Roc off to help Lil' Tim with an advantage.

Rico and Trex dashed forward but fell back when they saw the bicycle in the air.

The first ballplayer could not dodge the bicycle in time. He was knocked to the ground, unconscious.

Roc scurried out of the way.

Tank looked at the second ballplayer. "The main event belongs to us."

The tallest ballplayer moved in to help his partner against Tank. There was no such thing as a fair fight on the streets.

Rico whipped out a handgun and smashed it across the back of the tallest ballplayer's head.

The tall man staggered and weaved out of the scene.

He had no problem with running away.

The second ballplayer watched his partner run then showed respect for the man holding the handgun.

With a closed fist, Tank bashed the right ear of the second ballplayer, sending him to the ground.

He looked up at Tank, with a hand over his ear.

Rico aimed the handgun at the second ballplayer. "Now get your ass up, get the kid, and put your muthafuckin skates on before I shoot the shit out your momma's son."

Lil' Tim was kneeling by the first ballplayer, waiting for him to come to.

Trex walked up behind Lil' Tim. "Is that your daddy?"

The child's head turned, looking up at Trex. "Yeah."

"What's his name?"

"Anthony."

"Last name?"

"Patterson."

Trex kicked the child in the ass—just hard enough to knock him on top of Anthony. "Tell him I know his name. And tell him to stay off the streets; I got this."

Roc walked over and picked up the bicycle. The handlebars were crooked; the front tire was warped. "And you and your retarded-ass dad quit jumping in front of bicycles."

Roc and Rico sat in the back; Tank and Trex sat up front in the Suburban. Roc's bicycle was in the rear area of the truck. "What the hell is this, family day? Y'all up and decide to walk to the park on Sunday." Tank lowered the driver's side sun visor.

"Unc, you owe me another bicycle."

"I don't owe you shit, boy. Be glad I stopped Lil' Timmy from smashin that ass."

Roc laughed.

"What the hell you and Trex need to talk to me about?" Tank looked up at Rico, using the rearview mirror.

"Grown folk shit. Ain't made for Roc's ears."

"Bullshit. Roc curse more than anybody in this truck. Hell, you just pulled a gun out in front of him, now you concerned about what he hear?"

Trex flipped through a *Robb Report* magazine. "Tank, it's a big lick. Roc don't need to hear about it."

"What's a big lick to you?" Tank glanced at Trex. "A laundromat full of quarters? A warehouse full of clock radios? How long y'all think that petty shit will last? Either knock over a...global bank, or get a damn job." Tank continued driving and inserted a CD. Nobody else said another word on the way to Rico's house.

Rico, Trex, and Tank talked while Roc was in the bathtub. Tank and Rico sat on the doorsteps; Trex leaned against the Lexus. "Trex, why did you shoot the white dude?" Tank held a look of confusion.

"He was a threat to society."

Tank shook his head.

Rico watched an ant wander near his foot. "Tank, I need your help for this truck scheme."

"You don't even know what's in the trucks. Might not be nothing but biscuits in them damn trucks."

"Might be twenty keys of coke in each truck." Trex smiled. "Look at every angle."

"Angle your ass, Trex. Even if the trucks got a *thousand* keys, it's more snitches in the dope game than all the keys in the country."

Rico crushed the ant. "Tank, whatever is in the trucks must be worth a lot. Now, you talk about me and Trex going after petty shit all the time; this shit ain't petty. I been plottin this for a minute."

"What's in it for me?"

"We split three ways; you know what time it is."

"You and Trex just came off with twenty-five hundred. Get the calculator and figure out my third. That's about a grand—rounded off."

Trex laughed. "But you didn't do shit at the computer shop."

"I don't give a fuck. That's still the white guy paying me in advance for taking the trucks. He gave y'all an advance, but y'all want me to...put in work—on the house—and hope for a profitable surprise inside a stupid-ass biscuit truck. Cough that money up and quit playin with me."

Trex grinned. "I'll give you my share for the Lexus."

Rico got up from the steps. "You work three days a week, twelve hours a day. How long you think that shit will last? You keeping that up till you sixty-five?"

"Nope. One day I'll own my own company, and you two petty larcenists will have somewhere to work." Tank laughed.

John Caston drove past the bread store. He was driving Hundred Proof's car. Hundred Proof, a former drunk, was in the passenger seat enjoying the conversation. Caston had told him nearly everything that had happened. It was almost dark, and Caston had not spotted the Jaguar all day.

"I don't understand why the police would think that

you'd shoot your own wife and daughter."

"The goddamn cops don't believe that shit. That's just their way to stir my emotions; they think it might flush me out."

"You never told me why the Kapatas wanted the first cop dead."

"They never told me. Hell, I didn't even know the black guy was a cop."

"Would you have killed him if you knew?"

"As sure as hell, but it wouldn't have been for a lousy ten thousand."

Hundred Proof shifted in the seat of the Volkswagen Jetta. "What difference does it make?"

"Killing a cop gets you the death penalty. It's almost like an incentive to kill the regulars."

"Maybe you're looking at it all wrong."

"Maybe. But it's too late now."

Silence.

Caston pulled the car over. "I don't feel like driving no more. You take the wheel." He got out and walked to the other side.

Hundred Proof moved over to the driver's seat. He watched as Caston got in; he saw the water in his eyes. He knew that Caston was thinking about his family. "You think there's any truth about the rumor concerning the bread store?"

Caston closed the door but gave no answer.

"I knew a guy that used to work for the cable company. He said that the president of the cable company had some kind of private business going on with one of the owners of the bread store." Hundred Proof began driving.

Tears ran down Caston's face. He wasn't paying any attention to his friend.

"He said that the owner was doing business with a lot of owners and managers of different companies."

Caston reclined his seat and cried some more. He had been holding it back for nearly nine hours—the emotions were overdue.

Hundred Proof decided to shut up. He didn't know how to console Caston; he didn't want to upset him any worse.

A full bottle of Baccardi rum liquor was on Hundred Proof's kitchen table. Caston took a seat and began reading the label. "I thought you stopped drinking."

"You thought right. I've had that full bottle sitting there for two months now. That increases my will power."

"Say, listen, Hundred. I appreciate you helping me out. You know every cop in the city is looking for me."

"No sweat, John. And I'm sorry about your family."

"Yeah, thanks again."

"About that five thousand dollars...Look, you don't have to give me anything. You've helped me during some rough times before."

"Naw, the money is yours, and I wanna give it to you. Besides, after I kill the Kapatas, I'm turning myself in."

"But what about the death penalty you'd be facing?"

"I think they'd have to prove that I knew the guy was a cop. Otherwise it's just a homicide. I'd probably get a life sentence, though."

Hundred Proof took a seat at the table. He bit into an apple. "What's the next step?"

"The bread store opens at six in the morning. I'd like to be there when it opens. Monday is a good day for business."

"Who do you think opens the store?"

"The owners—Dan and Arnold. They don't have a manager. The old lady comes in at seven, but I should have the party going by then."

"If the store is open by six, that means the owners are probably there by five-thirty."

Caston grabbed the bottle of liquor and opened it. He got up and fetched two glasses and gave Hundred Proof one. "That also means that I should be there before the owners show up." He sat down again. "Have a drink, Hundred. This one's on me."

Hundred Proof hesitated. He pushed the glass away. "Help yourself. I told you, I don't drink no more."

Caston poured a shot and drank up, no chaser.

CHAPTER 6

At 3:15 a.m. Tank waited in the woods with two sheets of plywood, both four feet by eight feet and both a half-inch thick. From his position he could view the side and the rear of the bread store. There had been absolutely no signs of life inside the store since his arrival fifteen minutes ago. The bread store had no windows on the side, and the front windows were protected with bars. These factors made Tank appreciate his brother's plan.

Rico sat in the driver's seat of a stolen Oldsmobile; Trex was parked beside him in a stolen Ford pick-up truck. They were about a hundred yards away from the bread store, waiting behind a drug store on the other side of the street. Lights out. No talking. Rico had one of Roc's Radio Shack walkie-talkies; Tank had the other.

At 4:30 a.m. Mark and Norman drove past Rico's house and saw the Lexus in the driveway. "How did you and Dave meet Rico?"

"Dave had a wide-screen TV for sale in the newspaper. Rico called and said he'd buy it if Dave offered free delivery. I helped Dave deliver the thing, but I never really had any words with Rico."

"So him and Dave stayed in touch?"

"Something like that. When he learned that Dave runs a computer shop, he wanted to know what kind of hot products Dave would be interested in." Mark pulled over and finally stopped the car.

"And how are you so damn sure he lives alone?"

Mark gave Norman a cellular phone. "The moment I know they're moving in on the bread store I'll call you."

"That's not the answer to the question."

"He told Dave that he enjoyed living alone because of all the women he was fooling around with."

"And so you want me to break in his house, armed with your .38, based on some hearsay shit?"

"For the last thirty-six hours you were busy talking about the computer and the offshore accounts. Why didn't you ask these questions before now?"

"Because at the time, the computer was big shit. Now this is the big shit."

"You're wasting a lot of time. I think you should go and get set up."

Norman got out of the car. "You're gonna owe me for this." He slammed the door and ran off.

At 4:43 a.m. Tank watched a white van pull into the

bread store parking lot. The van stopped in the back of the store and a passenger got out. The passenger used a key to unlock the rear doors of both bread trucks. The doors were opened, and the driver of the van pulled closer and positioned the side sliding door of the van with the rear doors of the bread trucks. The passenger seemed to be watching out for anything out of the ordinary.

"I got a white van." Tank squeezed the button again. "Two guys—one on the lookout; the other probably loading something in the trucks."

"Let me know when you're ready." Rico increased the volume on his walkie-talkie.

A few minutes later, Tank saw the van back up and obstruct the view of the rear doors on the second bread truck.

Mark was parked in the parking lot of a convenience store. He had a nice view of the bread store as he watched through binoculars. He could only see the north side of the bread store, but he expected the action to occur on the south side. The side of the convenience store was the only feasible spot from which he could watch.

He saw some movement in the dark near the bread store. He prepared a mobile fax about Rico Adams for the bread store owners. *This one is for you, Dave*. Besides, he couldn't let Rico get away with whatever was in those damn trucks.

The truck doors were locked now and the two men were inside the bread store. Tank hurried across the paved lot with the heavy sheets of plywood. He stopped at the side of the building, near the rear, and propped a sheet of the plywood against the wall. He hurried toward the front and propped the other sheet against the same wall. He stood silent, listening.

Nothing.

He scanned the side of the building for the telephone line connection but found nothing. *Damn!* He knew it was probably on the other side or in the rear of the building. He squeezed the walkie-talkie. "Get set; I'm looking for the phone connection now." He hesitated at the rear corner of the building. He listened again.

Nothing.

He peeped around the corner but did not see any outside line connection. He crept closer to the back door and listened for inside movement or voices.

Faint noises.

Tank darted past the back door and didn't stop until he'd reached the other side of the building. He listened again.

Nothing.

He scanned the side of the building and saw the telephone line connection.

Rico turned on the headlights of the Oldsmobile, and Trex did the same with the truck. Trex pulled out of the drug store parking lot and Rico followed. They drove the speed limit for eighty yards then slowed for the turn to enter the lot of Novelty Bread. Lights out again.

Tank watched the truck rush toward the front door. He hurried with the plywood and propped it against the front door entrance. He ran to the back to do the same.

Dan and Arnold were receiving a fax when they heard the vehicles outside the building. They drew their weapons and walked to the front of the store. The inside light made it difficult for them to see outside, so Dan hit the light switch. They saw an image dash by the window. The all-glass front door seemed to turn black. The image dashed by again, and Arnold shot at it, breaking a hole in the thick glass. They heard something smack against the front door and could hear the vehicle engine. Dan fired three shots at the front door, breaking more glass. He didn't understand why the door was black now.

Another smack, this time at the back door.

Hundred Proof slowed the Volkswagen and stopped about thirty yards from the bread store.

Caston got out and bolted for the woods.

Mark had watched the pick-up truck roll up to the front door of the bread store. It was happening; there was no need to wait and see the outcome. He started the car and called Norman.

Norman answered on the first ring. "What is it?"

"He's here. Get in the house."

"Are you sure it's him?"

Mark ended the call. He didn't feel like getting into a discussion. He was headed back across town. He wanted to be there by the time Norman could get out of the house with the computer equipment.

John Caston watched from the wooded area. He was only ten feet down from where Tank had been waiting. He watched the two guys smash out the driver's window of both bread trucks. He thought he had heard gunshots but wasn't sure. He had no idea that the sounds had come from the inside of the building.

He saw the Oldsmobile's back end kissing the rear door of the building. He grinned in the dark. "Somebody's after some goddamn bread trucks." He heard the sounds of what he thought were two more gunshots and finally put it all together. He wondered if there was another car in the front blocking the other door. He raced through the woods, moving toward the front, until he saw the pick-up truck kissing the front door. He knew that his enemies were trapped inside.

Tank was waiting in the woods again, watching for any incoming traffic. He heard something or someone scramble through the woods not far from where he was positioned. The scrambling noise was moving toward the front. Tank squeezed the walkie-talkie. "Somebody is in the woods; hurry the fuck up."

Roc was awakened by the sound of broken glass. He sat up in bed and rubbed his eyes. He heard more noise coming from the kitchen. He stared past his room door, out into the hall. He eased out of bed and retrieved a black handgun from under his mattress. He could hear someone snatch open the rear storm door. He thought about hiding in the closet but was running out of time. He heard the back door open, and he crouched on the side of the dresser.

Norman entered the kitchen, gun visible from his waistband, and searched for the light switch. He flipped it on and looked around.

No computer.

He walked to the living room, and the light from the kitchen was enough to help him scan the area. He nodded at the wide screen TV then looked down the hall and saw light escaping on his right. The light led him to the bathroom. Norman opened the room door that was across the hall from the bathroom, flipped the light switch on, scanned the bedroom, then checked the closet.

No computer.

He turned the light off and walked out into the hall again. Two more rooms. The door to one of the rooms was open. He walked in, felt the wall for a light switch, and found it. He scanned the bedroom but saw no computer. He walked to the closet door and opened it.

No computer.

Roc sprang from his crouched position and turned the handgun on the man at the closet door.

Norman heard the noise and reacted with a jerking head turn.

"Now just sit your ass down and don't try no dumb shit."

Norman threw his hands up inches away from his chest. He feigned a smile. "Hey, kid, did I wake you up? Ruso...Rico sent me here."

"I thought I told you to sit your ass on the floor and—"

"Is that a real gun?"

Roc lowered the handgun and pulled the trigger, aiming near the side of the dresser.

Norman cringed at the sound of the loud gunshot.

Roc aimed the gun at Norman again. "Sit your muthafuckin ass down. My daddy ain't sent no white man up in here."

Heart racing now, Norman squatted.

"Indian-style, ass on the floor, and keep your hands on top of your head."

Norman complied with the child's orders.

"Use your pinky finger and pull that gun out of your pants. Drop it on the floor and kick it over here with your foot."

"Hey, I can leave and you won't even have to bother your daddy. You can—"

"Shut up and minus that gun."

Norman removed the gun and kicked it toward the child.

Roc kicked the gun under the bed then began dialing a number using a cordless handset.

"Hey, kid, I promise—"

"Shhh!" Roc entered *113*, his birthdate, instead of a phone number. He placed the handset on the base again. "My daddy say if somebody break in the house and try to leave, just keep shootin them in the back until he get here."

Trex had hot-wired the bread truck and was leaving the parking lot. Rico was close behind him in the other truck but stopped to wait for Tank to come out of the woods. He heard shots fired. Rico leaned over and unlocked the door. There was no passenger seat, just two steps and a space used for standing.

Tank emerged from the wooded area in a rush. He opened the door. "Go, go!" He jumped inside the truck and closed the door.

Rico stepped on the gas and heard his pager sound off.

Sequerria, take your ass to sleep.

Tank smashed the passenger window out with the butt of his handgun. He waited until they were near the front of the building then fired nine rounds into the wooded area, hoping he would hit whomever was in there.

Rico whipped the big truck out in front of an oncoming car.

The driver of the Pontiac Grand Am slammed on brakes, locked the steering wheel to the right, and still smacked the rear end of the bread truck.

Rico ignored the impact and the fact that it had sent Tank to the floor. He was more concerned with the gunfire and the few bullets that struck the truck.

Tank picked himself up and rushed to the back. He would begin his search.

Caston got up from the ground. He had no idea why the man in the bread truck had fired shots in his direction. He scrambled through the woods, towards the back, and came out headed for the side of the building. He saw the interior light glowing inside the Grand Am across the street. The rear end of the car was visible, but the damage could not be seen from his angle. Several cars stopped; others were driving around the Grand Am.

Caston rushed toward the front of the building and glanced around the corner. The engine of the pick-up truck was running, but he was sure that there was no one inside the truck. With the transmisson in drive, the vehicle kept the plywood pinned against the front door. He heard police sirens in the distance. He stepped around the corner and was now in front of the building, pressed against the brick wall, next to the window.

Dan had used every round in his gun to fire at both bread trucks. He'd hit both trucks with several shots but hadn't had the position and lighting he knew he needed. He walked away from the window and kicked over a gumball machine.

Arnold was in the back pressing his 290-pound frame against the back door. "Give me a hand with this goddamn door." He had seen the car backed against the door, engine still running, while looking through the bullet holes. He hoped against the odds that the car could be budged just enough for Dan to squeeze through the door.

Dan walked toward the light switch. "Relax, the cops are on the way."

Arnold could hear the sirens himself. He pushed away from the door and looked around when the light came on. He walked toward the front area and stopped when he heard the gunshot. He never heard the next three; the second shot had entered his head.

Dan Kapata hit the floor. He had reacted fast. He threw the empty gun at the light switch across the room, missing it completely. He heard the gun and his brother fall to the floor at the same time.

CHAPTER 7

The grocery store was out of business and was therefore the perfect spot. Trex was standing behind the place when the other bread truck arrived. He ran up to the door in front of the broken window. "You left Tank?"

Tank walked from the back of the truck. "Don't be so optimistic. Open the back of the Suburban; we got stacks of money."

"Good, because there ain't a damn thing inside the other truck."

"Has to be." Rico grinned. "Pull up the carpet in the back."

They began loading the money in the Suburban. "This is a lot of muthafuckin money." Trex flipped through a stack of hundred-dollar bills.

"Load the shit up, Trex. We ain't got time to cherish no damn moment." Rico's pager sounded off for the third time, now indicating an unchecked page. "Man, I gotta get rid of Sequerria's ass." He pressed the side button on the pager, and the illuminated display revealed 113. "I gotta go." He dropped the money from his hand and rushed from the bread truck, racing toward Trex's Camry.

Roc heard the cellular phone ringing. He was leaning against the dresser with his right arm resting on it, right hand holding a black gun. "I know damn well that ain't my daddy calling back on your cell phone."

Norman felt foolish; he was being held prisoner by a child. "Can I answer it? It might be important."

"If you answer it that means *you* ain't important, because I got something for your ass."

Outside, Mark drove past Rico's house again. *What the hell is he doing in there?* He thought about pulling in the driveway and tapping the horn. He still felt protected by the darkness; he had maybe twenty minutes before the sun could run him off, but he was thinking that Rico might arrive long before then. Mark waited at the stop sign and pondered. Again he called the cellular he'd given Norman. *Maybe he'll answer this time.* Mark allowed the phone to ring five times. After getting no answer, he was headed for Rico's driveway.

Rico made a left turn and stomped on the gas pedal. From the top of his street he saw a vehicle turning in to park in his driveway. But the vehicle's lights were out, and he thought it might have been headed to his neighbor's driveway instead. The closer he got the clearer it became. The

Acura Legend was parked inches from the Lexus. He whipped the Camry in behind the Acura and banged the bumper.

Roc heard the horn blow once. "That ain't my daddy's horn; that ain't my uncle's horn; and that ain't Trex's horn. Sound like Tremaine's Honda." Roc glanced at the alarm clock. "You know what that mean? You just might have fucked my thousand dollars up, and I worked hard for that. When I tell my daddy you made Tremaine leave, he gonna kick a new hole in your ass."

Norman wondered if all black parents raised vulgar, aggressive children. "Why don't your daddy have a house cat?"

"Why the fuck he need a cat?"

"That's what I use when I wanna get rid of mice and rats."

"We don't got no damn rats."

"There's one behind you, up against the wall."

"You must think I'm a kid or something. You want me to look?" Roc fired the handgun toward the closet, above Norman's head.

Norman flinched and turned away.

"They shootin...Ah, I made you look." Roc laughed.

Rico stepped out of the Camry, his handgun drawn, and approached the driver's door of the Acura. He tapped on the window with the barrel of the gun.

Mark lowered the power window. "Excuse me. I was trying to find the Archer residence."

"Oh, that's me. I'm Mr. Archer. Now arch your ass up out that car."

Mark opened the door and got out with pleading hands.

"If anything happened to my son, I'm waking the whole block up. I'm unloadin this clip in you, draggin you out the house, and running over your ass with every car in the driveway."

Rico backed up the steps and stuck his key in the door, unlocking it as he watched Mark. "Now lean against the trunk of the Lexus and spread your shit."

Mark followed Rico's orders. He was nervous and scared, and he thought his legs would buckle at any moment.

Rico stepped closer and frisked him thoroughly. "Let's go inside; you first."

"Please...I..."

Rico delivered an open hand slap to Mark's face, knocking him up against the trunk of the Lexus. "Put some close on your mouth, and get the fuck inside."

Mark entered the house, and Rico followed closely.

"Roc?"

"Dad, I'm in my room. A white man broke in the house and he's in here with me!"

"Mr. Muthafuckin Burgular, I got your friend from the Acura at point blank. Hurt my son and we gone tear this muthafuckin house down! Ain't no getting away."

"Dad, I'm the one with the gun. Come and get his ass so I can go back to sleep."

Tank parked the Suburban on the front lawn. He and Trex got out and walked over to the Acura and the Camry.

The Acura's engine was still running. Trex studied the fender-bender and wondered why Rico had parked in the driveway rather than on the lawn. Trex pulled his handgun from his waistband. "Some shit must be going on inside—something fucked up."

Tank entered the house first, aiming a handgun at the two white men who were sitting next to one another on Rico's sofa.

Trex entered from the back door. He noticed but did not study the damage to the doorjamb and window.

Rico had been standing by the front room window, watching and waiting for their arrival. "Put your guns up; they're just here to talk."

"Where's Roc?" Tank closed the door and leaned against the wide-screen TV.

"He's in his room. He hemmed a fake-ass burglar up with the blank gun you warned me not to buy him."

Trex smiled. "Sound like they knew your damn schedule."

"You know I was thinking the same shit?" Rico smiled at the white men.

Trex threw his hands in the air. "So what's the hold up? I could throw them in the Acura—"

"Don't even worry about it; I got a better idea." Rico walked over to Mark. "I know we met somewhere before. Where was it?"

Mark shrugged. "I don't think we've ever met."

"I can't remember, but you can bet I won't forget this meeting." Rico sat on the arm of the sofa, next to Mark. "Trex, you take the fake burglar in that first bedroom on the left." Rico pointed at Norman. "Tank, you go with him to make sure Trex don't beat the gentleman to death or shoot the fuckin room up. I'm staying here with Mr. Acura."

Trex stepped forward and kicked Norman in the chest. "You heard my man; get your ass up."

"On second thought, Trex, you stay in here with me. Tank, take the man in the first bedroom and just calmly ask him to tell you everything. Me and Trex will do the same out here."

Trex shook his head. "That ain't hard enough."

"Of course it is. They'll tell us everything they know about the bread trucks; why the fuck they was on my property; who else they might be fuckin with; how they know about the bread trucks; and anything else they can think of relating to any of this shit."

"And why you think they gonna talk if we don't shoot them muthafuckin knees up?"

"Trex, this is how the cops discover their snitches. They should have the same story. If one leaves out any detail that the other gave, that's the one who gets killed off the top."

Tank shook his head at Norman. "I just got a funny feeling that you're gonna leave out a bunch of shit."

"If both of them give full, consistent stories, then this one gets locked up for burglary and whatever charges the cops can think of." His eyes shifted to Mark. "And when I let you get in that muthafuckin Acura, you better stay missing forever."

Tank and Trex went along with the scheme. They knew that both men were as good as dead no matter how consistent the stories they were about to tell.

At 6:30 a.m. Tremaine parked on the side of the street and got out. She walked across the lawn with her mind on the Acura.

Rico opened the front door. He came out and met her on the lawn. "Tremaine, you look beautiful."

"What's going on inside; you got an orgy going?"

"No, just Tank, Trex, and one of their friends...a white guy."

She smirked. "Let's go inside and talk; you called me over here."

"When did I call you?"

"Your son left a message on my answering machine last night. I called him back and we talked while you were out, and he told me to come by on my way to work this morning, and said it was important."

"Oh, I didn't have nothing to do with that."

"Well, can I go inside and talk to Roc about it?"

He scratched his head. "Roc went to sleep not long ago."

Tremaine folded her arms below her breasts. "Rico, if you got some dizzy bitch in the house or if you're having some kind of freak show for your brother and your friend, please tell me so I can leave and never come back. Either tell me that or let's go inside and talk."

He smiled. "Let's go to your house and talk."

"No." She leaned against the front end of Tank's Suburban. "We're going to talk in that house, or else I'm getting out of your life forever."

He thought about it. He moved closer and wrapped his arms around her shoulders and held her. "Tremaine, I just want you to know that I love you more than any woman I ever fucked with before. I'll try never to disrespect you again. I'll move you in with me. I'll stop you from working. I'll throw three bad-ass kids up in you." He paused. "But I can't let you go in that house right now."

She pushed him away. "I love you, too, Rico. But

apparently that's not enough to keep us together." She walked toward her car. "Have fun."

"I'll call you on your job at 9:30."

"Please don't. And don't drop Roc off at my house anymore."

He watched her get in the Honda and drive away. He felt bad. He walked to the back of the Suburban and pressed his cupped hands and his face against the tinted window. He saw the blanket that covered the pile of money. He was hoping that it would help him to get over Tremaine and the depression she'd left.

Caston and Hundred Proof were watching the news. Caston was sitting on the floor, his back against the couch; Hundred Proof was kicked back in a Lazy-Boy chair. "So why'd you have to go and steal the bread trucks, John?"

Caston laughed. "Whoever did that shit had a damn good plan, but I sure as hell wouldn't have wasted it on some goddamn...oatmeal pies."

"Did you see the guys that took the trucks?"

"I was too far off, and it was dark, remember? But one of them was a black dude."

"Whoever thought of that plan was more'n likely a white guy."

Caston drank more liquor, this time chased with Coca-Cola.

"So Arnold's dead, and there's no telling when the store will open again. How are you gonna get Dan?"

"That's a hard one; I'll just have to find out where he lives."

"You think the cops know you were there?"

"Maybe not but Dan probably knows I was. That makes me feel a lot better."

"Shouldn't be hard to find out where he lives. You got the internet and...all kinds of ways to find out."

"I'd really rather let him live for now and go after his family. You know, make him feel what I'm going through."

"John, I'll help you as much as I can. But I never killed anyone before. So I don't think I can help you there."

"Hundred, I appreciate everything you've done."

"It's the least I could do for you. I wish I'd been able to pay you back for helping me with Marsha's funeral."

"I told you to forget about that. Your wife treated me like I was your brother."

Hundred Proof smiled. "Don't say that; she couldn't stand my brother."

"But you know what I mean."

"Yeah, she was a good woman. I told her I'd quit drinking one day. Too bad she's not around to see it."

"She's still around, Hundred. She's with you; you gotta believe it."

Hundred Proof did not respond.

"Later on today we'll drive to my stash area. From now on everything is on me."

"John, you don't have to do that. I get by with my unemployment check."

Caston drank more liquor and soda. "Listen, Hundred, I'm talking about having a good time. Pay a few bills, pay to find out a few things, and eat real good."

"Sounds like fun to me."

"I'm gonna give you five thousand to put in the bank for yourself. I think we can manage the rest."

Hundred Proof got up from the Lazy-Boy and headed for the kitchen. "First, let's figure out what kind of groceries we need in here."

"Get some of everything. If my money starts to get low before I find Dan or his family, there's a few nice spots I've always wanted to rob—quick in-and-out jobs."

"John, I envy your balls."

"I don't know if I like the way that came out." They laughed.

"Listen at us. It's like we forgot about the fact that you're wanted for killing two cops, not to mention your own family."

Caston looked at the television but wasn't listening to it at all. "I suppose it's silly to think there might be a way to clear my name."

"I could say you was with me at the time they claim you killed your family and the cop in the car, but I don't think my word weighs anything."

"I'm wondering how they found out I killed the first cop."

"Oh, that one's easy. One of the Kapatas told them or gave them a lead."

"Wouldn't make sense."

"Why not?"

"Because if I was arrested for it, they don't know for sure if I'd implicate them."

"Good point." Hundred Proof stood at the kitchen entrance, facing the living room window. "Maybe one of them told another friend; who knows?"

Caston gave it some thought. "No, I think it might have been something I done." He stared at his friend. "I feel like I'm missing something."

CHAPTER 8

Detective Jimmy Neely parked near the mailbox and studied the Lexus in the driveway. The fact that it had been backed in made him think that the owner had reason to hide the license plate. He got out and walked down the driveway, admiring the apparent wax job on the vehicle. He rang the doorbell and waited on the steps.

Rico parted the bedroom curtain and saw the Crown Victoria. *Looks like a damn police car.*

"Dad, want me to answer it?" Roc pushed away from the kitchen table.

"No. I got it." Rico shook his head. "Now that you done told them I'm here." He walked to the front door and looked through the peephole. He saw an older black man wearing a shoulder holster and a badge. He opened the door. "Yeah, can I help you?"

"I think so. Hi, I'm Detective Neely." He extended his

hand.

Rico did not shake hands with the detective. "What can I do for you."

"Uh, I'd like to ask Mr. Rico Adams a few questions about a murder and a robbery that took place at a repair shop called Computer 411."

"I'm Mr. Adams. Why do you think I can help you with that?"

Neely looked away. He stared at a motorcyclist who was speeding down the street. He looked at Rico again. "Mind if we talk inside?"

"Not at all." Rico stepped outside and closed the front door. "Let's go talk inside your car."

They walked up the driveway. "I can understand you not wanting a policeman in your house. Most people don't feel comfortable around the police."

"As long as you got the air conditioner on in that big ugly-ass car, I'm comfortable."

Neely laughed then got in on the driver's side and unlocked the front passenger door.

Rico got in and closed the door. "Plus the cops don't ever invite nobody in their house to sit and talk around their family and shit."

"Your point is well taken." He pulled a pad and pen from his hip pocket. "Did you know the owner of Computer 411, Dave Rutherford?"

Maybe they got some documents that shows I bought the TV from him. "Yeah, I know him, but I never hung out with him or nothing. I never even had a computer for him to fix."

"How did you come to know him?"

"Bought a TV he had in the newspaper. What the hell is this all about? Did he tell you I robbed and murdered him or something? Why you can't just get to the point? Cops like to fuck around and stall and fake break—"

"The last three calls made from Mr. Rutherford's office were to 9-1-1, his business partner, and a pager number that eventually led me to your address...not in that particular order, of course."

"I get it. Routine procedure, check the last numbers called."

"Did you talk to Mr. Rutherford last Friday?"

"No. I saw a number in my pager that I didn't recognize, so I didn't call back."

Neely jotted a few notes on his pad. "When was the last time you talked with the owner?"

Rico looked out the window and saw Roc standing on the steps. He lowered the window. "What's up, Roc?"

"Tremaine is on the phone. She wants you to hurry up."

Rico looked at the detective. "I gotta go; you ain't talkin about shit."

"So when was the last time you—"

"I told you, when I bought the TV from him—six, seven, maybe eight months ago." Rico opened the door then looked back at the detective. "You got a boring-ass detective job, investigating muthafuckin numbers." He got out of the car. "Nice air conditioner, though." He ran inside and heard the detective drive off. Rico picked up the phone. "Tremaine, what's up?"

"This ain't no damn Tremaine. Why in the fuck do you—"

Rico slammed the receiver down. He walked into the kitchen and sat at the table with Roc. He grabbed a spoon and ate some of Roc's cereal and sipped a little of the milk. "I thought you said Tremaine was on the phone."

"Tremaine? Sequerria was on the phone."

"But you told me Tremaine."

"I meant to say Sequerria—"

The telephone rang, but Rico ignored it. "Tremaine is mad at me again."

"Why?"

"Because you told her to come over here the other morning, and when she came I wouldn't let her come in."

Roc shot his dad a look of confusion. "But you still owe me a thousand dollars anyway."

"No question. You got that."

"Why you didn't let her come in?"

"Remember when I sent you back to bed and closed your door? Well, I had the burglar and his friend that I caught in the living room. You know I couldn't let Tremaine in here."

"You still didn't tell me what happened to the burglar."

"Maybe one day I'll tell you when you get older."

"I already know."

"No the hell you don't."

"You took him somewhere and shot him and threw him in a creek."

Rico laughed. "You watch too much TV, but in a few more years I'll tell you how close you was."

Roc tapped the spoon against the bowl of cereal. "How much do I get if I can get Tremaine back over here again?"

Rico smiled and shook his head. "Your little shit won't work this time. She don't even want your gnat-ass at her house again. She was—"

"But how much do I get if I do?"

"Okay, another extra thousand, with your tough ass."

"Give me my first thousand, and I'll put my work in again."

71

"No. You just tell me what you wanna buy, and I'll get it."

"What if I wanna buy something that cost a hundred dollars and keep the rest?"

"Then I'll have your momma open you a bank account."

"But I'm almost fourteen; why I can't keep my own money?"

"Because if somebody take it from you, you might be too little to whip their ass good. Damn that; just tell me how you plan to get Tremaine back on the team?"

"Tell me what you want with her, and why you like to make her mad?"

"Damn, you startin to sound like her now."

"Just break it down to me, so I'll know how to break it down to her."

"You must be planning on calling her; I told you she don't want to see your narrow-ass."

"You don't believe that shit, do you? You ever watch Oprah?"

"The hell *Oprah* got to do with it?"

"Women love little kids. Especially the ones who listen to whatever they say." Roc grinned.

"I never knew a...thirteen-year-old that watches Oprah."

"Me neither. I be hearing my momma and her girl-friends talk about that shit."

"May I speak to Lynn?"

"Who's calling, please?"

"Trexler Orson." He was sitting on the doorstep of his apartment. He hadn't opened the photo album yet.

She hesitated. "Hello, Trex. How are you doing?"

"Much better since Rico told me you called. I see you still got that same beautiful voice."

"Wait a minute...What did Rico tell you?"

"He said you called and told him about the police asking about me."

"What else did he tell you?"

"That you said you miss me, and you was wondering how I was doing."

"I can't believe Rico told that lie. I asked how you were doing, but I didn't tell him I missed you."

"I think he told me that because I always tell him I miss you."

"Yeah, right."

"Why is that so hard to believe?" Trex was flipping through his photo album.

"You know what happened between us, Trex. What are you saying? You miss putting your hands on me?"

"No. I'm saying I hate that ever happened."

"Maybe you—"

"Lynn, I treated you wrong; I was a no-good boyfriend, and I know I didn't deserve you. But I had two years to suffer for that. If you think I need twenty more years to suffer just let me know."

She sighed. "Well I am glad to hear from you, Trex. I see that you're still getting in trouble."

He closed the photo album. "I'm not in trouble. The police got to justify their paychecks by doing something and harassing anybody with a record."

"You might not have that problem if you had a job."

"So, are you happy with your job?"

"No, but I have to work, Trex."

"No, you just think you have to work. A woman like

you could have people working for her."

"You make it sound like I'm wasting my time by working for a living." She walked in her bedroom with the cordless phone and sat at the foot of her bed. "I can't afford to take the year off like you and your friend. I bet he still doesn't work, either."

"Would you, if you didn't have to?"

"No, I wouldn't. But just because..." She decided to change the subject. "So where's your girlfriend?"

"She left me about two years ago."

"Oh, I'm sorry to hear that. You must have treated her bad."

"Yeah, but I licked her good. I used to try to wet her whole body with my tongue, but I couldn't move fast enough; the air used to dry her up."

Lynn laughed. "Trex, I thought I would never leave you—once upon a time ago."

"I don't think you really left me; I pushed you away."

"Well, yeah, that's true."

"Your current man treating you like he should?"

"Hell no. I don't think there's a man out there willing to do that. But he's cool."

"No, he's not. Tell me the truth."

She laughed again. "How can you tell me? You don't even know him."

"But I still know you. If he was cool, you wouldn't be still on the phone with me."

"Okay, he's some shit, and I haven't seen him in five days. Whenever he comes around again, he'll just claim that he's been on a business trip or some other bullshit."

"I feel better knowing he's messing up. Maybe I can get the chance to show you the all-new Trex."

"What are you getting at?"

"I'm trying to see you again. I'm ready to settle down, divorce the streets, marry a woman like you, and plant two seeds."

"Trex, I'm already married with two children."

Silence.

"Trex?"

"I'm still here."

"Boy, I'm just kidding."

Trex smiled. "You fucked me up with that one."

"If you plan to divorce the streets, then you have a job lined up."

"I got a question for you."

"I'm listening."

"You used to stay on the computer all the time. You still use it a lot?"

"Whenever I need to. I had enrolled in a computer programming course, but I quit after nine months."

"You ever heard of a Share-Link program?"

"Yeah. That just helps computers to share information. Some people use it as remote access, some use it to spy and record every key entered on the keyboard."

"I need to come pick you up today."

"You must be crazy."

"I need you to do something for me with a computer."

"Whatever it is it can wait."

"Why not today? This is important."

"No, it's not. You'll get me down there and I'll catch hell trying to get you to bring me back to Charlotte."

"What's wrong with that? I might be able to talk you into lettin me lick you for three straight hours."

She clinched her teeth and sucked air through them. "Sounds real good, Trex, but I'm sorry; I have to go to work in the morning."

"Lynn, I need you right now. I can't trust nobody else with this. Do me this one favor and you won't never have to go back to work again."

"I like the idea of that, but for some reason that shit don't sound right."

"Tell me how to get to your place; I'll tell you all about it on the way back here."

Kayla Seegars walked out of the house and approached the Volkswagen Jetta. "I haven't seen you in months, Hundred Proof. How did you know I live here?"

"I didn't. I thought this was Darlene's place."

"Oh, she's been living in Chester for nearly a year now. My husband and I moved in here right after she moved out."

"You're lookin as good as ever."

"You're just saying that."

"Where's your husband now?"

"He's at work. He won't be home until 11:40 tonight." She looked at the empty backseat area. "I know you got something to drink in here."

"I stopped drinking going on eight months now."

"Well that's good to hear."

"Not really. Shit, I started messin with that damn cocaine."

"You're kidding me."

He opened the console and showed her three grams of the oil-based crack cocaine. "That's why I came by to see Darlene; I wanted her to get high with me."

"If that stuff is as good as they say it is, hell, I'll try some."

"Hell yeah. This is some good shit. I know the fella

that brought it back from Florida."

"Why don't you cut your car off and come on inside?"

"I have to get back to my place; I got dinner in the oven."

"Doesn't make much sense for me to stay here being bored. Want me to keep you company?"

"Yeah. I'd like that."

"Wait here until I slip on some shoes and lock up. Don't go anywhere; I'll be right out."

He watched her walk away. He knew Caston was right. She still has it. He and Caston had no intentions of using the drugs. The three grams were for Kayla.

Kayla locked the front door and hurried to the car.

Hundred Proof pulled up at his house and retrieved the drugs from the console. "Come on; let's get the fun started."

Once inside, Kayla stood in the living room while Hundred Proof headed for the kitchen. "Why don't you take everything off and get comfortable."

"Everything?"

"Yeah. Want something to drink?"

"Yeah. What do you have?" She was coming out of her shirt.

"Baccardi; you know my name."

"I thought you said you didn't drink anymore." She unbuttoned her shorts.

"I was almost telling you the truth. Yesterday I started drinking again." He glanced at her in the living room. She was standing in her panties and bra. "I thought you were taking everything off?"

"I wanna try some of that stuff first."

He brought her a small glass of liquor and some Coca-Cola and ice. "Try this first, and I'll fix you a few hits of the good rocks in a few shakes." He turned the television on and entered the kitchen again.

Kayla drank the liquor and watched *The Andy Griffith Show*.

Hundred Proof finally returned with a saucer that held small rocks, all resembling off-white soap shavings and crumbs. He placed the saucer on the coffee table along with a cigarette lighter and a pack of cheap menthol cigarettes.

Caston finally emerged from another room and saw Hundred Proof screwing Kayla from behind.

She was smoking a rock that she'd buried at the tip of a cigarette. She kept grazing the lighter flame against the tip, ignoring Hundred Proof's work, oblivious to Caston's presence.

Caston pulled his erect penis out and calmly walked around them.

Kayla paused and looked up at Caston. "What are you doing here?" She smiled.

He reached for the cigarette, and she gave it to him. He placed it in the saucer and moved it out of her reach. He stood in front of her—Hundred Proof still humping away—and waved his penis in her face. "I couldn't remember where I put your number, but I can never forget where you put your mouth."

She smiled, grabbed his penis with a gentle grip, and took it all into her mouth. She knew there would be no more smoking until both men were satisfied.

CHAPTER 9

Detective Greenburg stopped at Dan Kapata's jail cell. "I got some good news...for the city of Rock Hill. Might even be for the whole state of South Carolina."

Dan sat up against the wall in the cold holding cell. "How much longer do I have to stay in here over a fucking gun charge? You should be out looking for the dickheads that trapped me inside, killed my goddamned brother, and stole my trucks."

"I just got some preliminary results from ballistics."

Dan thought about the manila envelope. He had wanted to get a quick hearing and make bail before any tests on the envelope could be had.

"The gun we found in your store, on your brother, seems to give the same strike impression compared to the bullets found in John Caston's wife and daughter and the police officer that was killed on the next street behind the

Castons."

"Bullshit. My brother wouldn't be involved in—"

"That's what I say...bullshit. Your brother was stopped and searched near that incident when the call came in over the radio. So, you know what I think?"

No answer.

"I think you put that gun in your brother's hand before we arrived and rescued you."

"You're holding me because of what you think? I think you're full of shit; you couldn't get ballistics in less than three days—"

"Where have you been since the invention of computers, scanners, and laser technology?"

Dan stared at Greenburg, who was on the other side of the steel door, looking through the tray slot.

"But you don't have to worry about the preliminary results; they're only eighty-nine percent accurate."

"You still haven't placed me at the scene."

"Maybe not, but the shit is good enough to hold you for a while." Greenburg's face held a serious expression. "By the way, your bread trucks were found behind Nathan's Groceries. The investigators are trying to determine what you might have been hiding in those secret compartments."

Dan's head tilted back; he closed his eyes.

"I'll let you get some rest now. You probably don't want to be disturbed." Greenburg walked off, whistling.

At 6:55 p.m. Trex and Lynn were leaving from her apartment. She carried an overnight tote bag, and Trex walked beside her, smiling.

"Why are you so happy?"

"You still look like lick material. Wanna stop right here

and get licked on the sidewalk?"

She laughed and turned to face him, still walking backward. "Yeah, come on." She laughed again.

"You think I'm playin? Lynn, I still don't play the muthafuckin radio."

"Trex, right now you make me smile and laugh. I'm happy for a moment. But how long can you keep that up?"

He reached out and grabbed her belt, stopping her. "Lynn, just like all people, I know we'll have our ups and downs." He looked down at his crotch area. "But I'll try my best to keep that thing *up* all the time."

She pushed him away. "You're still crazy as hell."

He stepped to her again. "Lynn, I think the main problem you had was with me fighting you." He stared in her eyes. "Something big changed my life. We fought because you nagged; you nagged because I stayed in the streets, trying to get money. I can't see me fighting you again."

"So you're saying you're not the same violent Trexler Orson that I used to know?"

He threw his arm around her and they headed for the Camry. "I ain't no Christian or nothing, but you don't have to worry about me."

The Mustang GT made the turn and the driver picked up speed.

Lynn turned and waited for the car to arrive. "I don't believe this shit."

"Your boyfriend?"

"No, but he doesn't know that yet."

Trex silently took a deep breath and released.

The driver pulled up next to Lynn and her company, CD player banging, passenger bobbing with a ball cap lowered to the eyebrows. The driver turned the loud music off.

"What's up, baby? You eloping on me, or is that the cousin I never met?"

"I haven't seen you in almost a week. Haven't heard from you, not even a postcard."

"Business, baby, business."

"I know. You did that shit before, and I told you that was your last time."

"Yo, damn, that was quick. I guess you already had that soft-lookin nigga waiting on the side." He stared at Lynn's new friend.

Trex removed his arm from around Lynn's neck. He turned her face toward his and licked her lips. He stopped and looked at the driver. "And that's about the only thing soft about me."

The driver pulled the hand brake up and got out of the car, and the passenger joined him.

"Trex, go and get in the car." Lynn's hand was on his chest. "Thomas, get back in your car and leave."

"Trex?" Thomas stopped six feet from Lynn. "This must be the reunion. Go in the house, Lynn. Me and you need to talk."

"There's nothing to talk about. When I wanted to talk, you were gone. This time I'm gone."

"Lynn, take your muthafuckin ass in the house and stop bitchin about a grown man handling—"

Trex lifted his shirt and pulled out a handgun.

Thomas had seen Trex's movement without shifting his eyes.

Trex swung at his face with the gun, trying to connect with the nose or the mouth.

Thomas turned his head away and tried to shield the blow with his arm. The gun struck the side of his face and ear, scarring his jaw. Thomas fell to his knees.

Trex turned the gun on the ball-capped guy who was trying to back away.

"Trex, don't do that." Lynn eased closer to Trex. She looked around at the few neighbors that were watching.

Trex looked evil and anxious. He walked up to the guy with the ball cap and calmly reached for the cap. He removed it to get a good look at the guy. Trex looked inside the cap then tried it on, turned backward. He glanced at Thomas, who was getting up now. Trex slipped the gun back in his waistband and rushed toward Thomas, kicking him once in the ribs.

Thomas hit the concrete sidewalk.

Trex stood over him. "Disrespect Lynn again and you die. I'll turn myself in and still take that shit to trial." He removed the ball cap, tossed it toward Thomas, then backed away with Lynn.

Lynn was driving the Camry down Interstate 77. "I thought you said you didn't fight no more."

"You misunderstood me. I said I wouldn't fight *you* no more. I'm still the world's favorite street villain."

"I'm glad you didn't shoot anybody back there."

"If it was dark, oh, he was hit. Both of them."

"Trex, you'd actually kill somebody?"

He laughed. "Now how am I gonna get to heaven killing somebody?"

"You're playing, but I'm serious. You make me think you had something to do with that restaurant robbery and the dead guy."

"Lynn, I'm ready to try my hand in business management and shit."

She looked in the rearview mirror and changed lanes. "A businessman riding around with a gun?"

"Gun? I don't have a gun on me. I can't risk the cops

stopping us."

"What did you do with it?"

"I pitched it off when you caught the ramp to the interstate."

"What about your prints?"

He looked at his hands. "I won't have any for a few days."

She tilted her head against the headrest without responding.

"Let's look for a house in the paper tonight and lock it down with a deposit tomorrow."

"Trex, I have a job to go to. I told you, you have to get me back home before 8:30 in the morning."

"No more work; I'm taking care of you."

"How? Just tell me how, Trex. You said you were ready to divorce the streets, but you can't. It's been two years, and you said you haven't had a job since we broke up. Why do you—"

"Lynn..." He was searching for the best way to tell her. "I found some money in a...old sock."

"A sock? And that's supposed to do what?"

"Take care of us."

"Trex, don't play with me."

"I'm serious; I ran across some money."

"How much?"

He grinned. "Well, I have to split it with Rico and Tank; we found it together."

"How much?"

"Something like $622,850."

"Yeah, I believe you. My grandmother used to keep that much in her old sock all the time."

"Okay, I'm lying; it wasn't in a sock. But that's not important."

"And you didn't find any damn money, either. What is it you want me to do with the computer you were talking about? You were probably lying about that, too."

Trex licked his lips, leaned over, and kissed her neck. "I want you to show me how that Share-Link shit works."

"That's nothing as long as you know the system ID number of the computer you're trying to link with."

Trex stared at her. Now he knew what the file titled *System ID's* was for. He pulled at her shirt, looking down her cleavage. "When we get to my apartment, I got a *link* I wanna *share* with you."

Roc sat in the driver's seat of the Lexus; It was facing the street as usual, and Rico was in the house sound asleep. Roc turned the key in the ignition and the cellular phone lit up. He dialed Tremaine's number and listened to the ringing amplified through the speakers.

"Hello."

"Tremaine, this Roc."

"Roc, tell your daddy to forget it."

"I'm on Tank's car phone; my daddy is in the house sleep."

"You got me on a speaker phone?"

"Yeah, in the car."

"Take me off of that thing. Who are you in the car with?"

"By myself. I was gonna drive over to your house so my daddy could get mad at me."

"Roc, that's crazy. Why do you want to make your daddy mad?"

"Because I asked him why he keep making you mad,

and he said you wouldn't understand."

"*I* wouldn't understand or *you* wouldn't understand?"

"Me."

"So what does that have to...Boy, you better not drive that car."

"I know how to drive. My daddy showed me how last year, and Trex let me drive his car when he in it with me."

"Roc, I'm not playing with you. Get out of that car and take your daddy those keys, or put them back where you got them from."

"If you drive over here and get me, then I'll get out. If you say no, I'm driving over there."

"Roc, I know your daddy is putting you up to do this."

"Tremaine, I promise, my daddy is in the house sleep."

"Then why do you want me over there?"

"Because I like you, and I want you to like my daddy."

"I already like your daddy; your daddy can't even prove that he likes me."

"But he do."

"Why didn't you try this hard to get Chelsea and your daddy back together?"

"My momma say my daddy ain't no good."

Tremaine laughed. "She's right. So why do you want me with a no-good man?"

"You real nice, and you can make him be a good man."

"Roc, listen to me. I love you like you're my child, and I'm glad you like me, too. But maybe you're too young to understand that your daddy isn't satisfied with one woman."

"Yes, he is."

"No, he's not, Roc. He's still messing with Sequerria, and he's probably still messing with Vera Hunt, too."

"That mean I can't be around you no more?"

"No, that doesn't mean that, but I'm not coming over

there to be treated like cancer by your daddy no more."

"Well, I'm on my way over there."

"Roc, you remember you promised me that you wouldn't curse around me?"

"Yeah, but I didn't curse."

"I know, you kept your word. And do you remember when you promised me that you will do what older people and grown-ups ask you to do?"

"I can't remember when...I—"

"Yes, you do. Now get out of that car and take those keys back inside. Do that for me, Roc. Please?"

"Okay."

"I promise I'll call you sometimes, Roc."

"I'm going in the house to wake my daddy up and tell him to take me home."

"Why, Roc? I thought you were staying for the summer."

"It ain't even fun over here. You're the only one that like to do different stuff with me. Sequerria ain't shit."

She laughed. "I'll let you get away with that one, Roc."

"I'll call you when I get back to my momma's house."

"Roc, don't go home. Your dad loves you, and he wants you to stay for the summer."

"I don't care. I'm still going home; ain't no fun over here no more. I'll call you when I get home."

"I love you, Roc."

"I love you, too." Roc terminated the call, removed the keys, and went inside to wake his father.

"Dad, I'm ready to go home."

Rico cracked open an eyelid. "Go home? What's wrong?"

"Ain't no fun over here. All you do is sleep and be gone all the time. And you always arguing with Sequerria, with her big-ass mouth."

Rico sat up in bed. The child had just crushed him with the truth.

"My momma say I could stay with you all year if I came home on the weekends, but I don't want to. I wanna go home." Roc sat on the bed. "And you can keep the thousand dollars."

Rico hated to cave in to the child's decision, but... "Get your clothes together; I'll take you home."

CHAPTER 10

Hundred Proof entered the house with a newspaper. "Guess who made front page."

Caston stretched and yawned, feet kicked up on the arm of the sofa. "What did I do this time?"

"Not you. Dan. He's suspected in the murders of your wife and daughter and the police that was killed in the car."

Caston swung his feet to the floor. "Let me see that."

Hundred proof passed the paper to him. "*Dan Kapata of 2816 Lander Lane...*"

Caston looked up at Hundred Proof. "You're kidding."

"No, but the bad news is you're still the main suspect in the murder of that Hansen cop."

Caston began reading.

"I took Kayla home this morning and her husband pulled up as I was leaving."

"What did he say to you?"

"I never gave him a chance; I drove away. I told her we'd have something for her to smoke anytime she wanted to spend the night. She said she'd like to come back tonight."

"I don't think so. Not for me anyway. I got a special date tonight." Caston continued reading.

"Where's Roc?" Trex leaned against the side of Rico's wide-screen TV.

"No more Roc, Trex. I took him home."

"I thought he was staying for the summer."

"He was; problem is *I* wasn't."

"What the hell you talkin about?"

"Forget it."

"You must be on that shit or something. Your main girl left you; your damn son left you."

"Stay out my business. Did Lynn figure that computer shit out?"

"Yeah. She's sitting out there in the car."

"What did she say about it?"

"I gotta let her explain it to you." Trex opened the door and waved for her to come inside.

Rico hugged her. "Trex didn't tell you he tried to kill hisself when you left him, did he?"

"I would believe you if you had said he tried to kill everybody else." She smiled and sat on the sofa. "I like the big TV."

"It's cool, but I need a theatre now."

"Man, damn all that. Ask her about the Share-Link shit."

"Trex got a point. What the deal with the computer?"

"Last night I was telling Trex that there's a file with a

list of twenty-eight system ID numbers in it. Each ID number belongs to a computer. If you're online while one of those computers are, too, then you could access their files."

Rico sat on the coffee table. "So we need online service. How do we find out who the ID numbers belong to?"

"She already pulled that up in another file—all businesses—like the white...like the guy said who sold you the computer."

"What kind of crime are you and Trex trying to pull off? I know it's got to be a crime."

"Lynn, how do we find out...How do we get inside the business files of Novelty Bread?"

"Easy. Whenever you catch Novelty's computer online, you'll automatically receive a hyperlinked e-mail message."

"Oh, that sounds like something I can handle."

"The computer that Trex had me messing with had probably most of Robert Mayes's information stored in RAM, whoever that is."

"What the hell..." Rico smiled at her.

"That's random access memory. That's just the memory stored in the computer. But if you boot the hard drive up, I bet you'll find all the files to those twenty-eight businesses already there."

Rico turned toward Trex. "Why didn't you hook the hard drive up?"

Trex walked to the door. "Let me mute this conversation for a minute."

Rico and Trex walked outside and stood in the front yard. "Mark said the hard drive has nothing in it but the shit relating to Computer 411." Trex's eyes shifted to one of Rico's neighbors who was on a riding lawn mower. "Me and you looked through some of those files and Mark was right."

"But we didn't look through all of them. You know they probably used a bullshit name for the business files—a throw-off."

"I'm taking Lynn back to my apartment, and she can look through all of that shit."

"Don't worry about it. I'm only going after the account with the most money. Mark made that easy for me by giving up the Robert Mayes ID."

"So, why did you lie?" Greenburg sat across the conference table from Sequerria. "You know I could have your ass locked up for a while, don't you?"

"That cop lied on me, talking about we had sex."

"That's not the point. You said you never talked with him on the phone, but his cellphone records show me otherwise."

"We didn't talk about none of that stuff his card friends told you about." Her eyes roamed about the interrogation room.

"Do you know John Caston?"

"I...The man from the news? The one that killed the cop that you keep askin me about?"

"Yeah. You know him?"

"No. I saw his picture on the TV, though."

"You said you were with your boyfriend, at the house, at the time of Hansen's death."

"I was."

"Does he know Hansen or Caston?"

"I don't know but I doubt it."

"Why is that?"

"Because I never saw him around neither one of them."

Greenburg got up from the table. "I don't know how yet, but I'm sure you and your boyfriend set up a diversion for Caston to—"

"This shit is crazy. I told you—"

"Save it. I'm locking your ass up for obstruction of justice—impeding my investigation by lying about the phone call."

Detective Jim Neely walked up the driveway. He removed his sunglasses, admiring the neighborhood.

Tank closed the hood on the Suburban and met the detective. "Who are you lookin for?"

"I'm Detective Neely, and I'm looking for Mr. Ernie Adams."

"Make it fast; I got shit to do."

"This past Friday a call was made to a computer shop using a cellular phone."

"Keep going."

"Records show that the cellular service is in your name. Your carrier has records to show that the service is being used from a Lexus LS 400, which is also in your name."

"What the hell you want me to do?"

"The owner of Computer 411 was murdered eighteen to thirty minutes after the call."

"And you're here to ask me how I could have possibly made the call when I was at work, right?"

"No. I'm pretty sure your brother, Rico Adams, had the car."

"So? What does a phone call have to do with a murder at a shop?"

"Well, he said he never called the computer shop."

"Then you just reached a dead end. He let's everybody

use that phone; the weekend minutes are free."

"Thank you for your time, Mr. Adams."

Roseanne Kapata watched her husband through the thick Plexiglas partition. She thought she would have been able to touch him during her visit, but she should have known that his maximum-security status would keep them physically apart. She picked up the receiver when he walked up to the partition.

He picked up a receiver as well and studied the small visiting booth. "Hello, babe."

"Hi, Dan." She mustered a smile. "How much longer will they have you locked up?"

"Rose, it might be a while." He lifted his top lip and removed a flat, folded piece of paper. He gave a hand gesture for her to keep talking, and he unfolded the paper.

"Do you have a chance to see the newspaper in there?"

"No, but my lawyers say they'll keep me posted."

"The lady that ran into the back of the bread truck told the police that she was pretty sure the passenger was a black guy."

"How does she know?"

"Says the trucked pulled out in front of her, and her headlights lit up the whole passenger side. She couldn't give a description, though."

Dan pressed the note against the partition.

Call L.C. at the nearest payphone. Tell him 1.5 for freedom. Give him the .5 account number to get started. Roseanne nodded her head.

Dan chewed the note and swallowed it. "Can you handle the transfer?"

"Yes, but I would rather give him the account number and let him do it."

"Whatever's better for you. Is Perry home?"

"No. He says he'll come to see you on Saturday."

"So, John hired some black guys to steal my trucks."

"The lady only saw one black guy. She doesn't know anything about whoever was in the first truck or the driver of the second."

"The son of a bitches better hope..." He decided to keep the threat to himself. "Listen, let's end this visit. I need for you to get started on that as soon as possible."

Roseanne left the county jail and drove toward a convenience store. She knew that her husband had no other chance at freedom. Her phone call to Philadelphia would be his only hope.

Roseanne sat in the Mercedes, waiting for her electric garage door to open.

John Caston was pressed up against the side of the garage in the dark. He heard the Mercedes pull in. He crouched and duck-walked in behind the car, waiting for the garage door to close.

Roseanne got out and headed for the side door of the house. She turned and gasped at the sight of the rough-looking white man. "How did you get in here? Get the hell out!"

Caston calmly walked up to her and rested the barrel of the handgun between her breasts. "Open the door and go inside."

Roseanne unlocked the door and entered the kitchen. "What do you want?"

"I wanna keep this crime down to a minimum. A classic case of rape with a twist. Take it all off."

"Please..."

"I'm sure my wife and daughter said the same thing. Take your goddamn clothes off already!"

Roseanne began unbuttoning her top, her eyes holding water now.

Caston safely assumed that no one else was home because he had rung the doorbell earlier and had not received an answer. He watched her come out of the shirt. "If you wanna live, you'll have to move faster than that."

She unbuttoned and unzipped her Jeans. "Don't kill me, please. I didn't have anything to do with your wife and daughter, and I'm sorry."

"Come on, pants off."

She kicked off her shoes and pulled her jeans off one leg at a time.

"Not bad. You must be, what, forty-three, forty-five?"

No answer.

Caston waved the gun at her. "To the bedroom, honey. And don't waste any time taking the bra and panties off when you get there." He followed her through the house, admiring her slightly overweight shape.

Roseanne reached the bedroom and began removing her bra.

Caston kept the gun trained on her and began undressing himself.

Roseanne turned away from him and worked her panties down to her ankles then stepped out of them.

Caston reached out and squeezed her ass with his free hand. "This might be more fun than I expected." He took off his boxer shorts and stood before her, his erection revealing his approval of her. He walked up to her and threw his free hand around her waist, pressing their naked bodies together.

She closed her eyes and did not put up a struggle.

Caston released her, closed the room door, and got in Dan's big bed.

Roseanne glanced at his erection again. She couldn't help the feeling of curiosity.

"If it'll make you feel better, I don't wanna kill a woman. I'm not like your husband. I just wanna screw you real good so you can go back and tell him." He waved her over with the gun. "Put up any resistance and I'll have to consider shooting you."

She stopped at the bedside and wiped her eyes.

"Have a seat."

She sat on the bed.

"No, no. Not there. Sit there." He pointed the gun at his penis.

Roseanne hesitated for a few seconds then climbed on top of him.

Caston smiled. "What are you waiting for? Put it in."

Roseanne wrapped her hands around Caston's erection and held her position. *Much bigger than Dan's.* She licked her lips and pulled her body down, bringing her face near the erection.

Caston leaned up and watched her. "Be careful; both guns are loaded."

She grabbed his free hand with her other hand then took the head of his erection into her mouth. She squeezed his hand, and her head bobbed slowly.

Caston was enjoying himself but he remained aware and cautious. The woman seemed to be enjoying herself, and this worried him. This was too easy.

Roseanne stopped and looked up at him—his erection still in her mouth, her eyes no longer holding water—then continued bobbing.

Five minutes later she stopped again and pulled herself back on top of him. She used one hand to guide his erection inside her.

Caston watched her large breasts swing and bounce as she rode his erection. He felt a climax trying to steal his entertainment, so he stopped her.

"Am I doing something wrong?"

"Hell no. You're doing something too good." He grabbed a breast and pulled her closer.

Roseanne kissed Caston as if they were newlyweds. She felt the butt of the gun against her back, but she knew that she was keeping herself alive. Now it was time to see how far he would go. She pulled her mouth away from his and carefully turned her body around. She took his erection into her mouth again, this time from the sixty-nine position.

Caston couldn't believe how intimate his rape act had become. He spread her thighs further apart and parted the hairs, gun still in his right hand. He smiled then kissed the pink folds. Two minutes later he wanted to get on top of her. They repositioned themselves, and he entered her as she lay on her back.

Roseanne looked in his eyes. "I know you don't believe me, but I'm not going to report this to the police."

"I think you will, but this is like a misdemeanor compared to the shit they're after me for." He kept humping on top of her, gun still in his hand; it was resting on the pillow beside her head.

"Would you be mad if I didn't tell Dan?"

"Very mad. I'd be so mad that I'd come back to screw you again."

She was meeting his humping with vigor. She threw her arms around his waist and held him against her. She could feel him climaxing. She moaned and used all of her strength to pull him deeper. Roseanne faked a climax, too.

CHAPTER 11

"Therefore...feeding your *neighbors*...is merely a parable." The preacher's index finger marked his place on the page, and his eyes shifted to the white man who was now entering the all-black church.

Louis Carrielli appreciated the brief attention of the congregation. He walked up the aisle and settled in a vacant spot between a huge old lady and a teenaged boy.

"You'll note that...God...had laws for the Old Testament, which were stricken in the New." The preacher removed his glasses and leaned forward, resting on the podium. "Folks, there's so much going on today, it wouldn't surprise me if the Lord saw the need to guide us with one more testament."

Some of the congregation laughed, but most of them added *amen*.

Carrielli checked his wristwatch. He was glad that he

wouldn't have to put up with the godly shit for long. Twelve more minutes to go. Because the county jail was only twelve hundred yards away, he'd calculated the church to be perfect for the diversion, though he still wondered just how many policemen his actions would draw from the jail.

Two clean-cut lawyers from Boston, Massachusetts—at least their ID's, bar numbers, and relevant papers suggested so—entered the detention center, each carrying a briefcase made of light-weight, ABS plastic, set in top-grain leather. One of the interior compartments had been concealed by an additional ABS wall, housing an M-16 and two handguns.

The lawyers stopped at the thick window that shielded an officer who would greet them from the other side of a countertop.

"Good morning, gentlemen. Who are we here to see today?"

"Ah, yes, we're here to see our client, Dan Kapata."

"You two must be the big-time fellas from Boston here to replace the Delvin brothers."

"I wouldn't say that we're big-time." The taller lawyer smiled.

"I'm going to need to see your ID's and your bar licenses."

They placed their cards in the window tray.

The desk officer studied the cards then made a phone call.

The shorter lawyer—though he was easily six feet tall—checked his watch and began making conversation with his partner while they waited. "So, you think the prosecutor really wants to go to trial in that Carver case?"

"I doubt it. Wouldn't make sense. He's trying to get more out of the deal."

Two minutes later the desk officer was off the phone. "If I could get you gentlemen to sign here." He pushed the clipboard to the other side of the window tray.

Both lawyers scrawled a signature, and the clipboard was pushed to the officer.

"There's an officer down the hall sitting on his tush at the metal detector; he'll get you guys squared away."

The lawyers arrived at the metal detector and exchanged pleasantries with the hall guard.

"I'm going to need to get a quick look inside your briefcases."

The lawyers placed their briefcases on the table beside the metal detector and cracked them open, revealing pamphlets, documents and manuals.

"Okay, that's fine. You can leave them there." The hall guard stepped away from the table. "If I can get you guys to walk through for me, you'll be all set."

The lawyers walked through then retrieved their briefcases from the table. Through the electric gate ahead, they could see a man and a woman sitting in the control room. The floor-to-ceiling structure was forked by the hallways and boasted a conventional look in the new detention center. The uppermost portion of the structure was all glass at 360 degrees. The electric gate opened, and the hall guard escorted the lawyers to the left of the control room. The lawyers were led upstairs.

On the second floor they stood in front of the cameras, waiting for the control room to buzz them through the second floor gate.

At exactly eleven o'clock, Louis Carrieli stepped out from the pew and walked toward the pulpit. He could feel the turning heads following him.

He was nearing the pulpit, and two deacons were walking toward him.

"A lot of times we go and sin without much worry, because Jesus...has already forgiven—"

Carrielli rushed to the pulpit.

The church fell silent. No fanning. Nothing. Then an infant broke the brief silence with a high-pitched cry. The mother's bottle calmed the infant.

The preacher faced Carrielli. "Can I help you, sir?"

Two deacons and an usher continued toward the pulpit.

Carrielli grabbed the flexible microphone. "If anyone tries to leave, the preacher dies!" He produced a handgun and aimed it at the preacher's forehead.

The church members let out screams and gasps. Some rose, some shrieked in their seats.

"Everybody, take a seat!" Carrielli's peripheral vision caught an usher creeping toward him. Carrielli drew another handgun from his waistband, swung it around, and shot the usher in the neck.

The church roared, the majority shrinking and ducking behind pews.

"There will be no favoritism. Everybody, take a seat!"

Several babies were crying. The restless congregation would not rise from their seats.

With a gun in each hand, Carrielli threw one arm around the preacher's shoulders, gun resting against the man's temple. The other arm waved a gun in a sweeping range as he began walking down the aisle with the preacher.

An eight-year-old boy lashed out from his seat next to

the aisle and kicked the gunman on the calf.

Carrielli redirected the gun, dropping its aim between the child's eyes, preacher still under control. Carrielli's reflexes were as if the left and the right sides of the brain were operating two minds. He'd always thought of himself as a reactionary genius. He abruptly withdrew the gun from the child's head and continued out the door with the preacher.

The taller lawyer walked up to the steel door from inside the client-attorney visiting room and tapped on the window.

One of the guards approached. He looked inside and saw Dan at the table with the other lawyer. They appeared to be arguing.

"Our client says one of his ankle cuffs are too tight. I'd like it loosened just a notch."

The door was unlocked and the three guards entered the room. Dan's attitude toward the other lawyer made the guards feel as though he might have to be restrained. They listened to him curse at the lawyer and pound his fist on the table.

The taller lawyer closed the steel door.

The guards found themselves to be the only men in the room without firearms.

Dan aimed his handgun at one of the guards. "Wasn't a trick; the damn cuffs are too tight. Toss those keys over."

The guard complied without hesitation.

The taller lawyer glanced through the door window. "Wouldn't it be nice if you guys could make it home and still have a job to return to tomorrow?" His eyes shifted from one guard to the next. "Be sure to follow my instructions; you'll thank me when it's over. Otherwise, you'll die and be forgotten."

"I can't get my youngest daughter to stop being afraid of the deeper waters." The white woman in the control room watched several monitors.

"You have two on the second-floor gate." The black man watched another set of monitors, and he noticed a guard standing with one of Dan's lawyers.

She pressed a button to open the gate. "So how did you get your daughter so comfortable with swimming?"

"My wife and I started her in a pool when she was much younger."

After taking the stairway, the lawyer and the guard walked by the control center and waited for the first-floor gate to open. They stood by the gate, talking as if they were associates. The electric gate opened.

"Two more on the second-floor gate."

She pressed the button again, this time for the taller lawyer who was escorted by another guard. "Why couldn't they all leave at once?"

"Lawyers are so smart they don't have any common sense." They laughed until he noticed the shorter lawyer standing in the path of the first floor gate. He pressed a button to effectuate the hallway intercom. "Sir, you can't obstruct the gate; you have to let it close."

The lawyer paid no mind to the intercom. *What's taking so damn long?*

"Wait a minute!" The woman turned in her swivel seat. "We have an orange jumpsuit headed for the first floor. He's in the stairwell."

Dan had caught up with the taller lawyer and the

guard on the stairs. They bolted down the stairs, allowing a guard to lead the way.

The intercom was useless. "Stop blocking the god-damn gate!"

No response.

The alarm sounded off.

The black man opened the door to the control room and yelled at the lawyer. "Hey, asshole? Can't you fuckin—"

The lawyer fired three successive shots and watched the man fall out of the control room.

The woman screamed.

The desk guard, who had checked the lawyers in, retrieved a gun from underneath the countertop.

One of the hostage guards came out of the stairwell and into view; Dan and the taller lawyer were only a few feet behind him.

The alarm continued, summoning staff from all over the three-story building. Twelve guards were rushing toward the control room from the right. The other side of the fork revealed eight guards trying to catch up with the orange jumpsuit.

The desk guard burst out of a door, forty feet behind the lawyer who was obstructing the gate.

The taller lawyer, approaching the first-floor gate with Dan, saw the desk guard spring out of a doorway. The taller lawyer fired two shots through the gate.

The desk guard got off two wildly aimed rounds, crashed to his knees, and fell backward.

Every approaching guard came to a halt—none of them possessed firearms.

Dan, the taller lawyer, and their hostage guard met with the other lawyer and the other guard at the first-floor gate. They sent the two hostage guards down the hall to join the others who were at bay.

The taller lawyer cracked open his briefcase and removed an M-16 assault rifle. He could easily rip through the guards if they decided on a bold stampede. He dropped the briefcase and held the weapon with one hand as if it were a large pistol. Without the extension of the barrel, and with no woodstock and carrying handle, the gun weighed only 4.4 pounds now.

"We've overstayed our welcome and we should leave." They backed away, rushing for the exit. He tapped the trigger with the M-16 aimed upward. Five rounds sprayed at the ceiling.

The guards flinched and held their positions.

The taller lawyer gritted at the guards. "Your objections have been overruled."

Dan and the lawyers rushed outside, and a bulletproof Mercedes Sedan was waiting near the exit. They got inside and the driver stomped the gas pedal. The big Mercedes was attacked, to no avail, by the multiple gunshots from two rifles in the distance.

A few churchgoers had watched Carrieli as he tore out of the parking lot, the Porsche fanning at the rear end, the preacher in the front passenger seat. They had informed the police that the red Porsche was moving south on Route 901. A total of nine police cars raced down the highway—seven of which had come from the county jail. More cars were on the way.

Carrielli—now riding a Suzuki motorcycle—traveled north on 901 and smiled when the line of police cars blew by him, heading south.

The Mercedes sedan cruised at sixty miles per hour. The driver was allowing the five police cars to catch up.

The taller lawyer watched three of the police cars gain ground on the Mercedes. He sprouted from the moonroof and emptied the M-16 magazine, ripping through the windshields, hoods, and rooftops.

The leading police car veered off the road; the second slammed on brakes, hanging a sharp right. The third police car smashed into the side of the second car.

The Mercedes picked up speed.

A half-mile later, the Mercedes slowed to make a right turn. More police cars were further behind, and the drivers could clearly see the Mercedes make the turn. The Mercedes stopped fifteen yards from a helicopter and a motorcycle. The four men poured from the sedan and ran for the helicopter, stooping for the loud, whipping blades.

Louis Carrielli watched each man board the helicopter. He elevated the aircraft, tilting it forward, and the jailbreakers were whisked away.

The five men were in the den of a Pineville, North Carolina house. Carrielli inhaled the scent of the marijuana. "So why did you want the first cop dead?"

Dan handed over a suitcase. "He was a threat to the bread store."

Carrielli opened the suitcase and nodded at a million in cash.

"He stops by the store one day to buy a few things. Me and Arnold were running the store that day; we were waiting on one of our workers to return. The son of a bitch started asking questions about how we got the money to start such a nice business. On top of that, he started dropping by nearly every day trying to make conversation."

"Makes sense to want him dead, but why didn't you handle it yourself?"

"The plan was to pay Caston to kill the cop, then I'd kill Caston the next day. You know the rest of the story."

"You realize I kinda took this job as a favor to you?"

Dan laughed. "Yeah, a favor that cost me a million and a half."

Carrielli retrieved the marijuana joint from the taller lawyer. "Your lawyer fees were $450,000, and say hello to your hundred-thousand-dollar chauffeur. I didn't even charge you for my labor in stealing the helicopter from the tour guide."

Dan smiled at the driver of the Mercedes. "Good driving."

The taller lawyer waited for the marijuana to make a full round. "So does anybody know about this place—I mean, nothing is in your name—"

"Listen, kid, if anybody shows up here you just follow me. This place has been me and Arnold's getaway for fifteen years, and nothing is connected to me or my brother."

Carrielli passed the joint to the driver. "Yeah, it took me, Arnold, and Dan nearly six weeks to dig an underground trench deep enough to hold a tube 105 inches round and pieced together for 197 yards."

Dan smiled. "The grass is greener on the outside, and there's light at the end of the tunnel. Literally."

They all laughed, and most of their worries were gone.

Dan got up from the chair and gazed out the window of his Pineville hideout. "The cops are still looking for Caston, but I need to find him before they do. It's the least I could do since I couldn't pay any last respects at Arnold's funeral."

"Yeah, and I'm sorry about Arnold. We had lots of fun back in our Mafia days."

"I received a partial fax seconds before we were trapped inside the store. I think one of the guys working with Caston was cut out of the plan or something." Dan paused. "I got a name but the fax went dead."

"What was on the fax?"

"*Rico Adams is a double-crosser. At this very*...and then it got cut off."

Carrielli got up and walked to the window. "What do you say I send my crew on back up north and you and I shake Rock Hill up with an unforgettable hunt? One last run before we get too old for the fun."

Dan looked his friend in the eyes. "I think that just might help Arnold to rest in peace."

CHAPTER 12

Robert Mayes rubbed his clean-shaven face. He wore braids in his hair and occasionally adjusted his non-prescription bifocals. He retrieved his ID from the hotel's front desk attendant.

"Your suite comes with many complimentary services." She passed him a pamphlet of the Quadra Casino. "If you need anything else, Mr. Mayes, feel free to ask."

"Thank you." Mr. Mayes was followed by the bellboy to the elevator. He stepped inside and waited for the twenty-year-old white guy to get in with the luggage cart.

The bellboy stepped inside and the doors closed.

"So what do they call you?" Mr. Mayes extended a hand.

"My friends call me Clockwork, but my real name—"

"I like that. Why do they call you Clockwork?"

"Started a long time ago with my first job. Everybody

says I'm never late for anything."

"They're just pumpin your damn head up. That ass get stuck in some damn traffic, what do you do, get out and run just to preserve the name?"

The bellboy laughed. "No, I guess I'd have to be late."

Mr. Mayes entered his suite, admiring the décor of the room. He looked back and saw the bellboy waiting at the door. "What are you standing in the hallway for? Bring your ass on in."

Clockwork pulled the luggage cart inside. "We don't enter rooms unless it's at the occupant's request."

"Shut the door and have a seat."

Clockwork closed the door and sat in the cushioned chair that boasted an antiquated look.

Mr. Mayes sat at the edge of the matching sofa then reached down to feel the plush carpet. "What kind of tips do you get around here?"

"Twenty, fifty, and sometimes a hundred."

"You're just throwin up big numbers, thinking I'mma tighten you up. How much does this hotel pay you a year?"

"About twenty-two thousand."

"Damn, they got you *depending* on a tip. Wanna work for me?"

"What do you do?"

"I own a big company in South America, but I want you to work for me while I'm here to gamble at the hotel's casino for the week."

"Will I have to quit my job?"

"Hell no. And I'll pay you twenty grand at the end of the week. Cash."

"This isn't one of those hidden camera shows, is it?"

"No. I make money not family videos."

"What do you want me to do?"

"Real simple. First I want you to get the word out over the entire hotel about me, Robert Mayes, the confident gambler, otherwise known as the Crapless-One."

"Is that all you want me to do?"

"Nope. Not for no damn twenty grand. Stick around; you're about to come up like vomit."

Robert Mayes was wearing a tailor-made suit and a pair of hand-made crocodile shoes. He adjusted his bifocals and stepped up to the front desk of the casino carrying a briefcase that contained lots of money. He placed his ID on the counter. "Let me get some chips, four hundred grand."

The blonde, busty attendant accepted the ID and began entering information into the computer. "How's your stay so far, Mr. Mayes?"

"Shit is good. So far."

"And how will you be paying for your chips?"

"Cash."

She returned the ID and called security. "Someone will escort you to a private room where your money can be counted."

"Money-counting machines?"

"Sophisticated. Very fast and accurate."

Fifteen minutes later, Robert Mayes returned to the front desk of the casino area without his briefcase. He gave the attendant a ticket.

She smiled, signed the ticket, and gave him the yellow copy. The pink copy was placed in her register, and the white copy was placed in a chute capsule. She dropped the capsule in a vacuum beneath the countertop and pressed a button next to the vacuum opening. A quiet suction. The capsule disappeared. "What chip quantities would you like, Mr. Mayes?"

"Five at twenty grand each and the rest at fifty grand."

She entered the denominations into the computer and waited for the capsule to return with the chips. She smiled at him again.

"I know they pay you to keep that smile and to act friendly, but don't you get tired of that shit sometimes?"

She laughed. "I don't want to answer that one."

"I see it on TV all the time. You gotta deal with the rich, snobby, arrogant-ass folks—white and black."

"Most of the customers are nice people." That smile again.

"Only because you don't have to deal with them more than five minutes at a time."

"Well, are you rich and snobby?"

"I'm rich, but I'm only snobby toward people who are richer than me."

The capsule arrived in the vacuum chute. "Well, I hope you win a lot of money; you seem like a nice guy." She removed a ticket from the capsule for him to sign."

"And I hope you meet more rich people like me; you seem like a nice woman." He studied her smile and was impressed; it appeared genuine. He signed the new ticket and received eleven chips. "What's the policy against casino workers receiving tips?"

"Um, it's not a problem as long as we don't solicit them."

He pushed a twenty-thousand-dollar chip across the counter. "This is for your troubles with all the assholes you got to deal with this year."

She stared at the chip then shifted her eyes toward one of the cameras without moving her head. "This is...not a good time."

He retrieved the chip. "Why didn't you say something? I ain't tryin to mess things up with your job."

"For tax purposes and management suspicion, it's better if I receive that kind of tip when my shift is over."

Clockwork hadn't used those exact words, but he'd explained it well. "Find me in the hotel somewhere, whenever your shift's over, and I'll convert this to cash for you, under the table, but this time it's for that stupid-ass management you got to deal with."

That smile again.

Mr. Mayes sat in the Jacuzzi watching the flat-screen TV.

A knock at the door.

"Who is it?"

"Christine."

Christine? The desk attendant? He looked at the wall clock. Then stepped out of the Jacuzzi dripping wet. He grabbed a large towel and wrapped it around his lower waist. Mr. Mayes walked to the door and cracked it open.

"This looks like a bad time for you." She saw him without the bifocals, and he appeared to be naked.

"Not really. Come on in." He stepped aside and opened the door.

She walked in trying not to look at him.

"Have a seat. You in a rush?"

"No, but I thought you might have checked in here with a roommate at least."

He examined her from a few feet away. Her blonde hair was styled different now. No more casino uniform. She wore a small T-shirt to highlight her large breasts. Tight

115

jeans and Nike running shoes. "How long have you been off from work?"

She still didn't turn to face him. She took a seat in the same cushioned chair that Clockwork had used earlier.

He closed the door.

"I've been off since an hour after you left the desk...maybe five-thirty. I was really scheduled to be off today; I was just filling in until Danielle showed up."

He walked over and sat on the sofa that was directly across from her and propped his feet up on the well-polished coffee table, legs crossed at the ankles.

Her eyes shifted away, pretending to be interested in some of the hotel amenities. "I didn't think you knew my name when I was at the door."

"I saw it on my receipt." Plus Clockwork had given him the run down on the lowest-paid people in the hotel and casino. "I was in the Jacuzzi when you knocked; I didn't expect you so early. That cash won't arrive at my room until about ten tonight. We can talk for a while if you want, or you can come back."

She finally looked at him. She kept her eyes focused on his face and was struggling to keep them from dropping. "What do you want to talk about?"

"White people, black people, employment, crime, children, social life, morals, sex, personalities, and whatever you wanna talk about. Now, where do you wanna start?"

She laughed. "I don't know. That's a hard one." Her eyes shifted down briefly.

"Pick one."

"Okay, white and black people."

"Both, at the same time?"

"Why not? Seems like a good topic to start with."

He removed his feet from the coffee table and propped

them up on the end of the sofa closest to her. He laid his moist back flat on the sofa and talked with her while staring up at the ceiling. "Check it out: one question at a time. I'll ask you something I always wanted to know about white people, and you ask me a question you always wanted to know about black people. What do you think?"

That smile again, but this time he did not see it. She watched him stare at the ceiling. "Good idea, but you go first."

"And we got to give absolutely truthful answers—even if it hurts."

"I promise." She sat back in the seat, turned for comfort, and threw both legs over the left arm of the chair.

He cleared his throat. "Do white people really believe Jesus was white?"

"We're only talking about the ones I've been around or know, right?"

"Yeah, for every question."

"Jesus was...I guess so. I...even...Is he not?"

He laughed. "Your turn."

"Um, why do black people call each other the N word if the word is so bad? I know they sometimes do it in a friendly way."

"My grandmother said folks today just don't know or care about the pain that word gave birth to. They ain't understanding of the pain, so the word don't mean shit to them."

She pondered. "Your turn."

"Why is it that white people over here try to run shit in other countries?"

"I guess it's to stop other countries from getting powerful enough to run shit over here."

His facial expression suggested that she might have

made a good point. "Your turn."

"Why is it that black people try so hard to be accepted yet strive to be so different?"

He sat up, resting on his elbows. He stared at her and twitched his mouth, searching for the perfect answer.

"I'm sorry; I didn't...If that question—"

"No, no. That's a good-ass question." He sat up further and pulled his feet to the carpet. He patted the cushion on his right. "Come sit here."

She got up from the chair, walked over, and sat on the other side of him.

He propped his feet on the arm of the sofa again and leaned back, resting his head on her right thigh.

She smiled, not knowing how to react to such a move.

He grabbed her right hand and placed it on his bare chest. "We don't really give a damn about being accepted by white society; we just wanna be able to co-exist with all races."

She stared at the bulging area of his towel but shifted her eyes when he looked up at her.

"Your turn."

She hesitated. "The rumor about black guys being...well-endowed...is that true?"

He raised from her thigh and felt the braids in the back of his head. Still intact. "You never been with a black guy before?"

"No." She hiked her eyebrows.

"First I'mma show you the answer." He unfastened the towel at the waist side and exposed a full ten-inch erection then fastened the towel again. "Then I'mma give you the answer after I get you to help me with something. But if you're thinking about that shit the hotel tramp took Kobe through, you might be better off trading stocks with

Martha Stewart."

CHAPTER 13

Robert Mayes was entertaining the huddled crowd with rhetoric. He was at the crap table with fans that he had not met personally. He had already won $150,000 and was now placing another bet for fifty thousand dollars. The house was betting—against seven other players—that Mr. Mayes would not make his dice point of six. When all bets were closed the house nodded at him.

"Can the Crapless-One make his point?" Robert Mayes grinned.

"*No shit!*" Most of the onlookers and gamblers could keep up their cheering and crowd participation as long as Robert Mayes was winning.

He let the dice fly. The first one stopped rolling, landing two points. The second die banked from a corner, landing four points.

The crowd cheered.

He adjusted his bifocals. "Anybody wanna get me a damn drink?"

Maybe ten people offered at once—seven of whom he had won money for.

He had already sipped champagne with Christine earlier. "I'm just fuckin with y'all. I ain't tryin to get drunk so damn fast. I'm going to make everybody who bet on me rich."

More applause.

"And now, folks, this will be my crapless stunt of the evening. I'm placing a bet of five hundred grand with the house."

The crowd grew more excited. Most of them would also place larger bets, jumping on the same bandwagon that had made their pockets heavier.

The house man took on all bets. When the bets were closed, he gave the shooter that familiar nod again.

"Would you rather die tonight or get killed in the morning?" Robert Mayes studied the smiling faces in the crowd. He shook the dice in his hand. "The answer to that catch-22 question will surprise even yourself."

The crowd laughed, enjoying the foreplay.

"Can the Crapless-One make his point?"

"*No shit!*"

He let the dice fly but did not look this time. Instead, he looked in the faces of a few of the betting players. He watched their expressions reduce to gloom. He now had a good reason to smile, but he'd save it for later.

"The gentleman has thrown a seven and craps." The house man collected all the chips.

"I fucked up, people. We'll try again tomorrow." He smiled.

Some returned the smile, some laughed. Who cares?

They were used to throwing money around.

Robert Mayes strolled over to the attendant's desk, looking disappointed.

Danielle, another blond with stand-up breasts, typed his last name and room number to call up certain information on her screen. Her manager often told her that the customers who were quick to gamble must be accommodated before their minds could change. "Is everything going well, Mr. Mayes?"

"Shit's fucked up right now. I'll try my luck at the Black Jack table."

"I thought you were doing well over there at the crap table."

"I won two hundred grand but lost it back plus three more."

"You really had that crowd."

"You know how it goes; everybody roots for the good guy."

She smiled. Not as radiant as Christine's.

"Listen, I'm waiting on a transfer from my bank to my casino account. Could you find out if that's ready for me? The manager said he'd let me know something as soon as the transaction came through, but I can't understand why it's taking so long."

She looked at the computer monitor. "Your suite accommodations included a laptop and online access." She retrieved a pamphlet from a countertop display and gave it to him. "This should give you all the information you'll need to check the transfer. And if you'd like, I could send someone up to your room to help you."

He scanned the contents of the pamphlet. "I think I can handle this. Good looking."

She blushed. She thought he had just complimented

her on her looks. "Thanks."

"Tell you what: I'll go get my shit together; you get ready to set up another five hundred grand in chips—all fifty-grand pieces."

"I'm ready when you are."

"First I wanna try my hand on the Black Jack table."

After losing fifty thousand dollars at the Black Jack table, Robert Mayes was approached by the manager.

"Mr. Mayes, the transfer is complete, and you're all set."

"Well that's good timing, Mr. Allen. So I guess the Black Jack table didn't break me after all."

The manager smiled. "There are a few more papers you'll need to sign whenever you're ready."

"Thanks. I appreciate the way you guys handle things around here."

"We're glad to have you. If there's anything I can do to make your stay more pleasing, just give me a call."

"Now that I have a bigger wallet to gamble with, I'm gonna try to empty the casino." Mr. Mayes laughed.

Orville Allen joined him in laughter. "I think I should comp your three-day stay and send up a nice bottle of champagne."

"That's a good way to keep me here and an excellent way to get me back."

Robert Mayes heard a knock at the door. He got up from the small table in the bedroom and walked to the living room area. "Who is it?"

"Clockwork."

He looked at his wristwatch then opened the door. "Come on in."

Clockwork stepped inside. "How'd it go?"

"How the hell did *what* go? The hell you smiling about?"

"With Christine?"

"I didn't fuck her, if that's what you wanna know."

"No, I mean about the offer you were supposed to make her for the extra twenty thousand."

"Oh, she likes it. Follow me." He walked to the bedroom area and sat at the table. "Sit down. I wanna show you something."

Clockwork sat at the table and watched Mr. Mayes peck at the keys on the laptop.

"You know you showed up two minutes early?"

"That's why they call me Clockwork."

"I'm saying, your ass wasn't on time—it wasn't really *clockwork*."

"I got off at ten, and you asked me to be here at half past eleven."

"You sound like a damn robot. *Half past eleven.* You ever fucked Christine?"

"No way. I've never seen her give anyone the time of day—not as far as relationship-wise. She's nice, though."

"You look too young for her."

"Probably. She's around thirty, but I don't know if she likes older guys or younger."

Mr. Mayes turned the monitor toward Clockwork. "This is my casino account."

"That's a lot of money. A little more than 5.6 million."

"This was a transfer from one of my company accounts."

"You're not going to gamble with all of that, are you?"

"Depends on my luck. I read some information on the internet about the Quadra Casino. They claim they can cash-out up to ten million dollars on any given night."

"That's true."

"How the hell's that possible? They don't look like they're doin that goddamn good to me."

"I'm sure you know the catch to their cash-out policy."

"What catch?"

Clockwork laughed. "They're gonna want ten percent of anything you cash out."

"Oh, yeah, I know that. I'm saying, they keep that type of shit around here?"

"I really don't know much...I don't know *anything* about how much money they keep on hand, but there's been some talk about the Quadra having some kind of affiliation with the biggest casinos in Las Vegas."

"So they probably get other casinos to help come up with the cash—"

"And give them a small percentage of the ten percent profit."

Mr. Mayes adjusted his bifocals.

"Nobody knows anything about how the casino handles its money—at least not a low-level employee."

"I got a question for you?"

"Shoot."

"How many people walk out with large sums of cash?"

Clockwork thought about it. "Are you planning on robbing the casino?"

Mr. Mayes laughed. "Hell no. You must be on that shit. Didn't I just show your crazy ass one of my six accounts? I just transferred damn near six million dollars and you think I need to rob for a living?"

"No, I wasn't saying—"

"I wanna know if people cash out big around here."

He shrugged. "Few thousand dollars is about normal, I guess. They really don't have a need to carry hundreds of thousands on them, and nobody wants to just give away free money to the casino—don't forget the ten percent—unless they're gambling."

Mr. Mayes got up from the table. "Time to put your ass to work—"

The room phone rang.

"Hello?"

"Yes, may I speak with Mr. Robert Mayes?"

"Speakin."

"This is Danielle. Your chips are ready."

At 1:51 a.m. Robert Mayes slammed an open hand down on the Roulette table. "Who the fuck y'all think y'all fuckin with?" He looked at all the customers standing around the table then pointed an index finger at the house man. "They must pain...They must be paying you a lot of damn money!" He picked up his glass and found it empty. He dropped it on the floor, breaking it, then picked up a glass of liquor that belonged to the white man standing closest to him. He drank the four ounces in one shot then walked off with a slight stagger here and there.

He arrived at the attendant's desk and met a different busty white woman—Danielle's shift had ended. The woman's red hair was short and the style seemed to fit her. Mr. Mayes slammed his fist down on the counter, startling her. He knew there were many eyes following his every move now. "Cash me out! I'm sick of this shit!"

She had already pulled his file up on the screen. "Is everything all right, Mr. Mayes?"

"What kinda fuckin question is that?"

She took a step back; his evil look was menacing.

"I done...I done made...placed ten bets on that damn Roulette table—all of them fifty thousand each—and ain't won a muthafuck-fuckin-thing." He adjusted his bifocals.

The manager, along with two security employees, walked up from behind Mr. Mayes. "Is there a problem here?"

"Ha! A muthafu— You goddamn right." He turned around to see whom he was cursing at. *The manager and his do-boys.* "Am I the only one to notice that weak-ass set up? Every stupid-ass game in here is rigged!"

"Mr. Mayes, I'm going to have to ask you to leave the casino area; I think you've had too much to drink."

"Ain't never in my life been drunk...What the...Get my muthafuckin money up! That's what you do!"

The manager turned to his security workers. "Escort Mr. Mayes to his room or out of the casino. Anywhere except the casino."

"He says he wants to cash out." The desk attendant looked at Mr. Mayes for approval.

"I can always find plenty of respectable casinos that...that...they should be happy to get my money without cheating me out of it."

The manager checked his watch.

"I don't expect you to admit the shit. Cash me the fuck out! I'm takin my business to the MGM Grand." He stuck his tongue out and wagged his head at the manager.

"Mr. Mayes, I assume you're aware that a cash-out would give this establishment ten percent of all monies handled."

He laughed. "I respect that. How else could you afford

to pay all these cheats?" He laughed again.

Robert Mayes was in his suite punching numbers on a small calculator. He was waiting for the manager to call him down to the money-counting room—with escorts of course.

A knock at the door.

He looked at his watch and walked to the door. "Who the hell is it?"

"Clockwork."

He opened the door. "It's 4:32. Your ass is thirty-two minutes late."

Clockwork hurried inside. "Did you ask to cash out?"

Mr. Mayes closed the door. "That was hours ago."

"One of the guys from security told me all about it. He said you were drunk, though. Is that why you pitched the chip to me when you saw me downstairs?"

"I thought you said you was always on time. Your ass—"

"I told you, the guy was telling me about how drunk and loud you were. He said management was preparing a lot of money for you."

"That don't explain why you're late."

Clockwork walked over to the chair and leaned against it. "He says he has some help from the outside on the way." He hesitated. "He wants me to show them who you are and help watch for the type of vehicle you get in."

"What did you tell him?"

"I told him I'd do it, but you know I won't."

"I don't really know that shit. You been knowing him longer than you knew me."

"Why do you think I'm here telling you this stuff?"

"Not because of the six-figure salary I promised you at my company, or the twenty grand I promised you for this week. I just tossed you a fifty-thousand-dollar fuckin chip."

"I think they're trying to steal whatever amount you plan to cash out. I think I'd have a better future working for your company."

"I don't know about that, but at least you'll have a future." He stepped closer to Clockwork. "You think they got guns?"

"He didn't give me any details; didn't even suggest that he was trying to steal from you. He tried to make it sound as if he was providing extra security for you."

"Might not look like it, but I got some good-ass security already—"

The room phone rang.

"That's probably the manager, ready with the cash-out. Stay tuned; this is where you really make your money."

CHAPTER 14

Jason sat behind the wheel of the stolen BMW. His partner, Larry, sat next to him, chewing gum and looking down the barrel of a handgun.

"That's probably not the best way to check your ammunition." Jason glanced over at the Quadra Casino.

"Who is this Clockwork fella, and why couldn't Terry come out and show us what the drunk guy looks like?"

"Terry's in there working. He's not going to take a chance on being linked to this." They watched the slim white male cross the street, headed in their direction.

Larry held the gun down between the door and the seat then lowered the passenger window. "Who are you, and what do you want?"

"I'm Clockwork. Terry sent me."

"Get in the back." Larry turned toward the back to push a case of CDs to the other side.

Clockwork opened the rear door and slid in. He closed the door and lowered the power window.

Jason looked back. "Put that window back up."

"But I can hardly see through the tint."

Jason used the main panel up front to raise the rear window. "There's enough lighting in front of the Quadra to put the sun out of business. I'm sure you can see the guy when he comes out."

"Terry said you're a bellboy here." Larry turned to face Clockwork.

"Yeah."

"Why are you the only bellboy here wearing loafers and...what, Dockers?"

"I'm not working; I've been off since ten."

"You really love your job, don't you?" Larry grinned at Clockwork.

"I checked in a suite here for a few days. My girl-friend—"

"What's up with the stupid questions?" Jason kept his eyes on the marquee area of the hotel.

Clockwork saw the three taxis pull up and park one after the other, just below the marquee.

"Tourisan Taxi?" Larry looked on, interested. "Who would use the cheapest taxi service in the city for a hotel that charges at least one thousand a day?" He turned to face Clockwork again. "Your manager must have given you one helluva discount."

Clockwork moved his right hand to the door handle. "It was a gift; somebody else paid."

Larry turned toward Jason. "I think I need some new

friends." He grinned.

"When I show you the guy, I have to get back inside. My girl probably knows I'm out by now."

"I don't know why Terry didn't just give us a description of the guy." Jason watched one taxi driver get out and head inside.

Larry tried to push a pinky finger inside the barrel of the gun. "He said the guy was going to some other hotel and casino and wasn't sure if the guy would change clothes, add a hat, or whatever. I agree with him; we're sitting too far off to notice detail like bifocals."

"But he said he was a black guy with braids."

"He might be a black guy with a hat when he comes out." Larry turned toward the back again. "He says you'd be able to recognize him."

"That's only if..." Clockwork opened the door. "He's walking with the bellboy and the taxi driver now." He got out and slammed the door.

Robert Mayes looked up when he heard the sound of the car door then turned to focus on other traffic. He had just discovered the type of vehicle that Clockwork had been in. He followed the black bellboy to the taxi that had been parked behind the other two.

The bellboy removed one of the large suitcases from the luggage cart and placed it in the back seat.

The taxi driver got inside and drove away with the suitcase.

The bellboy dropped an identical suitcase in the back seat of the next taxi.

The taxi driver watched for traffic then left the area

with the suitcase.

Robert Mayes and the bellboy stopped at the remaining taxi. He dug into his front pocket and pulled out a handful of hundreds. He gave all five of them to the bellboy. "Do me a favor, okay?"

"Name it."

"Do you know Terry? He's a security guy for the casino. He should be close by the—"

"I know him. He's working the upstairs floor right now." The bellboy hadn't paid attention to the fact that Mr. Mayes had suddenly lost his drunken speech.

"Good. Make sure you tell him that there's only one way to beat the cross...and that's that goddamn double-cross."

"I got it."

Robert Mayes shook the bellboy's hand and got in the back seat of the taxi, with a suitcase identical to the other two that were already gone. He closed the door. "I think you know where to take me. There should be a dark-colored BMW following us in a few. Try not to lose it."

"Gotcha."

Jason pulled out tailing the taxi that carried Robert Mayes. "Three different cabs. First time I've ever seen that one."

"I don't care about no other suitcase except the one he's got with him." Larry looked back at the hotel area one last time, making sure no one had pulled out to follow them.

The taxi turned south at a traffic light, two blocks away from the casino. They saw the taxi slowing down in front of the Lavish Tavern.

Robert Mayes rushed out of the taxi with the suitcase before the driver could bring the car to a full stop. He dashed across the street, hesitating only for the 5:20 a.m. traffic that would soon pick up. He was headed for the Tourisan taxi that was parked directly across the street facing north.

Larry looked across the street and saw the Tourisan taxi that Robert Mayes was headed for. "It's a fucking switch! Stop the car! Turn it around!"

Jason brought the car to an abrupt stop, and the car behind the BMW nearly tapped the bumper.

Larry opened the passenger door and began running after Robert Mayes. Arms pumping. Gun still in hand.

Robert Mayes looked back; he saw the man coming after him. *Straight muthafuckin fool.* He hadn't noticed the gun yet. He opened the rear door of the taxi and jumped inside. "Drive! Go!"

The taxi driver smashed the gas pedal.

Robert Mayes ducked down in the backseat when he heard the gunshot that broke the driver's window. He pulled the .45 from his waistband and raised himself, looking through the back window at the gunman who was still coming. "Get me to the third cab and you get a damn good—" He heard all the horns blowing. He turned to face the front. The taxi driver was gone, but the car was moving thirty-five miles per hour and approaching a red light. Robert Mayes lunged from the back seat to take the wheel and found the driver bent over as far as the passenger seat.

He glanced back and saw the gunman still coming.

The taxi scraped the side of a limousine, but he pulled the vehicle back to the right. Robert Mayes's eyes shifted to the dead man's foot. "Get your muthafuckin foot off the gas pedal!" He saw the Nissan low-rider truck coming from the left. Not much could be done. He shook his head at the thought and jerked the wheel to the right.

The low-rider truck skidded twelve feet.

Robert Mayes braced himself by gripping the wheel even harder and turning his head away.

The low-rider smacked the front corner of the taxi, sending it in a half spin toward the right.

The taxi's ass end slapped the bed of the low-rider and continued to roll—although much slower—toward the casino again. The dead man was still on the gas, so Robert Mayes grabbed the heavy suitcase and rushed out of the rear door before the taxi could pick up more speed.

Larry was not far behind. He saw the black man jump from the taxi. He fired another shot at the runner.

Robert Mayes ducked and made it across the street, wobbling and carrying an extra 123 pounds. He tripped over the curb in front of the Encore Health Resort and dropped the suitcase on the sidewalk. The dead taxi driver crashed into something. *Told you to get your damn foot off that...* He looked up and saw the gunman rushing his way. He drew the .45 and squeezed three times.

Larry fell to the street.

Robert Mayes scrambled to pick the suitcase up then ran toward the BMW that was pulling around the wrecked low-rider at the traffic light.

Jason saw his partner fall. He whipped the car around the congestion at the light and was driving up to the body in the street when he saw the black man running in his direction.

Robert Mayes ran harder. The weight of more than 4.6 million dollars was punishing his left arm. He fired one shot through the driver's window of the BMW. The tinted window disappeared and he saw the driver fall out of sight. *Now, how the fuck did Caston do that shit?* He made it to the driver's door, car still moving, and the driver sprang up, surprising him. He had missed the driver but had hit the headrest. He fired again, hitting the driver in the chest.

He glanced at the flashing blue lights in the distance; the sirens were closing in on him. Most traffic had stopped. He jerked on the handle, but the driver's door was locked. The BMW was veering off the road. The suitcase was tiring his arm. The BMW toppled a parking meter and slowed more. He ran around to the other side of the car and finally noticed the spectators further down the sidewalk.

The BMW came to a stop; the driver was on the brakes, somehow thinking it was helping him to hold on for life.

Robert Mayes ran up to the front passenger door but was out of time. He ducked when he saw the police car stop at the intersection. He opened the passenger door and threw the suitcase to the floor. He tucked the gun in his waistband then reached over to pull the driver out. The driver was still alive but helpless. He tugged on the half-dead man and glanced up at the intersection again. He saw the white Acura NSX making a left, headed in his direction. The driver had disobeyed the officer who was standing in the street holding up traffic.

Robert Mayes released the dying man, grabbed the suitcase, and ran out in the street to meet the NSX. The driver stopped and Robert Mayes heard the trunk snap free. He saw the traffic cop running toward him. He pulled the handgun and fired once in the cop's direction; he hadn't really aimed for him. He saw the cop peel off toward the sidewalk. He threw the suitcase in the trunk of the NSX then rushed for the passenger seat. He saw that the driver was now in the passenger seat, so he ran to the driver's side.

The policeman fired twice, both rounds entering the side of the NSX.

The passenger ducked and remained low.

Robert Mayes shot back three times—this time aiming for the cop—but couldn't stick around to find out if he'd hit. He opened the door, got inside the NSX, and scarred the street in first gear. "What took you so damn long?"

Christine remained in her cowering crouch. "You were supposed to get out of a taxi, and I was supposed to be waiting across the street in your rental, remember?"

He blew by the Quadra Casino and paid no attention to it. "Get up and watch my back." A police car shot by, headed in the other direction. He glanced in the rearview mirror and saw two police cars.

She turned in her seat to face the back. "The police that passed us is turning around."

"Why in the hell am I driving? I don't know shit about Vegas."

"Why are black people...always harassed by the police?"

"I was saving that question for you." He slowed to make a left turn at the yellow traffic light. "Why did the white girl come back to give the black man a ride?"

"I was coming to the Quadra; I thought you had stood me up." She turned to face the front.

"With the sex or the extra twenty grand?" He swerved around an old van then dipped back in the lane.

Christine clinched the door handle and kept her other hand pressed against the dashboard. "Both."

He checked the rearview mirror and saw the leading police car making the turn at the light. "Hold on." He made a sharp right turn, tires crying and hopping several inches. He picked up more speed. "You never asked me why I'm running from the cops."

"I already know why. You don't want them to catch you."

"And they say blondes ain't nothing but boxes of rocks."

"I'm brunette. I dyed my hair to get the job at the Quadra."

"They don't hire brunettes? Hold on." He made another sharp turn, this time a left, ignoring the red traffic light. The tires cried again. The oncoming Chevy Blazer skidded and grazed the side of the NSX then came to a full stop in the middle of the intersection. Other vehicles skidded to a complete stop.

Christine still had her eyes closed, head facing down, feet planted, holding on.

He glanced at her. "Open your eyes, and get ready."

She looked up. "Ready for what?"

"Pop the trunk."

"The release handle is on your side."

"Damn, I knew that."

He felt for the lever with his left hand, found it, and pulled it. "When I make the next turn, as soon as that building puts this car out of view for—" He checked the rearview.

No police cars.

"We got to get out of this car." He made another sharp left, running a stop sign, but this time nothing was crossing the intersection. He shifted gears and drove until he saw a Toyota Camry about to pull out on his right. He slowed the NSX and whipped it to the right, coming to a full stop, blocking the path of the Camry. "Get the suitcase." He jumped out and threw himself across the hood of the NSX then rushed up to the driver's side, pointing the handgun.

Christine was struggling with the weight of the suitcase. She couldn't even drag it over the lip of the trunk.

Robert Mayes opened the driver's door on the Camry. "Get your big ass out, get in the white car, and disappear!"

The huge white man worked himself out of the driver's seat and walked around the front end.

Robert Mayes shuffled backward, keeping the gun trained on the man. He rushed to the trunk and snatched the heavy suitcase. "Girl, get your weak ass in the Camry. This time, you drive."

CHAPTER 15

She pulled in to the parking lot of Laymen's Inn. Robert Mayes raised the back of his seat. "Drive to the back and park near the yellow Mazda MPV."

"Is this where we're staying?"

"No. The cops is gonna be looking for Robert Mayes. I got a room here in that name."

"They wouldn't know about this hotel, would they?"

"Not until somebody at the front desk heard about me on the news. I'm sure every Tourisan cab driver is talkin about Robert Mayes to the cops right now."

She parked in a vacant space two cars down from the minivan. "Where are we going?"

"Another hotel near the interstate. Something in your name." He got out of the car and picked the suitcase up from the passenger floor.

She got out and walked over to the minivan. She

looked at the sky. "It'll be daylight in a matter of minutes."

He carried the suitcase to the minivan and stood beside her at the passenger door. "You look worried about something."

"I'm not worried. I have a lot of questions for you, though. I'm not talking about the black-and-white questions."

He slid the side door open and pitched the suitcase inside. He turned to her and moved his face in closer to hers. He licked her lips until her mouth opened. He pulled her tongue with his lips while massaging the tip with his tongue. He released and pulled back. "We gotta go. You're still the driver."

Christine drove the minivan on the interstate. She was driving east but had no idea where Robert Mayes wanted to stop for a room.

"Why are you so quiet? You said you had a lot of questions." He was sitting on the floor in the back area.

"What's your name?"

"Why can't it be Robert Mayes?"

"Because Robert Mayes—the real one—probably doesn't have a braid missing from his head. He probably doesn't really give tens of thousands of dollars away. He probably doesn't seduce white girls. He probably—"

"Christine, this shit isn't over yet. If I'm not really Robert Mayes, what makes you think I should tell you my name?"

She kept her eyes on the long stretch of interstate. "When you and I were in the room at the Quadra, your style and conversation moved me. But I knew you were up to something ever since then."

"Why, because I'm black?"

"Save that black shit! Wasn't I there when you needed

me?"

"Let me straighten up two things for you: I was gonna get away even if I had to take that BMW. And furthermore, you didn't show up to rescue me; you showed up thinking I had jumped the fence on you."

"You're welcome. Don't forget that I saw you at a scene where a body was lying in the street. When you came to get in the car, carrying that heavy-ass suitcase, with God knows what in it, I could've driven off when I saw that gun in your hand.

And I woulda shot the shit out your momma's daughter. He did not respond.

"But again, you're welcome."

"Why did you think I was up to something when we was in the hotel?"

"When your head was on my lap, I could tell that your hair was short. I knew the braids weren't real because there was hair underneath covering your scalp."

"Looks good from a distance. I didn't plan on being that close to somebody."

"So, where are you from?"

"South Carolina. A city called Rock Hill."

"Married?"

"Nope."

"Girlfriend?"

He hesitated. "I don't even know. Next question."

"Children?"

"One. Love him to death but need to spend more time with him."

She thought about his last answer. "Is there any room for me in your life?"

"I think you just made room."

"I don't mean for one day or one night."

He was looking through the windshield. The sun had ran the darkness off. "Why do you want somebody like me? You don't know me. You met me thirteen or fourteen hours ago."

"And that risk is no bigger than the ones you took coming out here. You're attractive, rough on the outside, and seductively smooth with a woman."

He laughed. "My thirteen-year-old son is better than I am at that."

"The way you talked to me in that casino, I knew you were far from boring. I knew you had guts."

He absorbed all of the compliments. "Okay, you're probably the sexiest white girl I ever met. Ass like a black woman. I'm thinking the titties are fake but, damn, the muthafuckas look good. A little danger don't freak you out, and you kiss good."

"But?"

He thought about it. "But you got one more test to pass."

Christine entered the room at the Best Western hotel; Robert Mayes followed closely with the suitcase. He closed the door and flung the suitcase on top of the bed.

She pulled the T-shirt off. No bra. Plump breasts. Flat stomach.

He stood near the door watching her.

She unzipped her jeans and took her time pushing them down to her lower thighs. She stood holding the jeans with one finger through a belt loop. She looked down at her bare crotch.

"So it's true. White girls don't wear underwear?"

"I was wearing underwear when I came to your room earlier."

"Don't mind me; take it all off." He walked toward her. "I been out playing in the streets. Give me *ten minutes* to get out the shower." He stopped only inches away from her.

She released her pants.

He cupped a hand between her legs, feeling the smooth crotch. "All I need is *five minutes* in the shower."

She stood on her tip-toes and licked his mouth. "Did I do it right?"

"We'll work on it until you do. He looked down at her breasts. He bent down and kissed a nipple. He opened his mouth wider and sucked while dragging his tongue around the areola. He released the handful of crotch flesh and stepped back from her. He gave her a strange look then shifted his eyes back to her breasts. He lifted her breasts with both hands. No scars. He lifted her arms and still found no scars. "Is that how all implants look and feel now?"

She gave that luring smile again. "You were wrong. These titties are real."

He backed away. "Get in the shower with me."

She leaned against the wall and kicked her shoes off. She pulled each foot through the jeans then followed him to the bathroom.

He ignored her presence while adjusting the temperature of the water. He undressed and grabbed a face cloth and a new bar of hotel soap from the countertop. He stared at her shapely body in the doorway. "Turn around one time for me."

She turned and gapped her legs.

He shook his head. "You *gotta* have some black in your family, somewhere close down the line." He walked up to her and tried to push the nearly vertical, curving-to-the-left erection down far enough to place between her legs—no penetrating yet, though. He had to squat for the task.

Christine looked down and saw the head and part of the neck of the erection. She closed her legs together, closed her eyes, and threw her head back.

He placed a hand under her chin and guided her mouth to meet his. They sucked and pulled at one another's lips and tongue. He stopped. "Open your legs and let me back out. I gotta hit this water so I can beat the brakes off the cat in the box."

They were in the shower. He stood with his hands pressed against the shower wall while she washed his back.

"Turn around." She waited.

His head was directly under the jet spray. "Hell no. If I turn around again I'mma end up going deep up in you. I'm saving up for the bed." He stepped farther under the shower head to rinse his back.

She stepped closer and reached around, grabbing his erection. She jerked on it twice with the soapy hand then pressed her body against his. "Is this what you meant by black and white people co-existing?"

"No. But, *damn*, this ain't bad." He turned the water off and stepped out of the tub. "Come on. No drying off." He walked to the bed area and pushed the suitcase to the floor.

She was right behind him.

He pulled the covers off the bed, leaving only the sheets. He got in the bed and lay on his back. He cocked a pillow behind his head. "Now bring all that to me."

She climbed in bed from the foot and crawled toward his erection. She stopped, kissed the tip, then continued crawling upward. She kissed his stomach. His chest. His lips.

"Stand up over me."

She stared at his lips then stood in the bed, a foot on each side of his waist.

He looked up at the bald crotch. He wanted it in his mouth so bad. *Another time.* He straightened his erection from horizontal to vertical and held it. "I want you to take it all but don't move around on it."

She squatted and brought her vulva to the tip.

He pushed upward to let his erection catch the opening then placed his hands under her ass to help control her drop. He watched her take more than half with no problem.

Christine was still lowering her squat. The closer she got to sitting flush on top of him, the more her face contorted. She kept closing her eyes and dragging her head from left to right.

He pushed once to meet her and heard her moan.

She opened her eyes and gave him an angry look.

"You there now. Just sit still, hold your knees, and look at me."

The position was uncomfortable for her, but it only hurt whenever he pumped.

"Don't move."

"Trust me, I'm not."

"Can you feel this?" He made his erection jump.

That smile again.

"You have any kids?"

"No."

"Don't worry; I got you a beige, bad-ass little boy coming right up."

She laughed.

"You don't like that? I can make his ass come out gray."

She laughed again.

146

He locked his hands behind his head.

"So, what happens after this?"

"What do you want to happen?"

"I want to come to South Carolina with you."

"And then?"

"Maybe I should rephrase. I want to live in Rick Hill."

"That's *Rock* Hill. But I don't even know how much longer I'mma stay there."

"Tell me the truth. You just don't want a white girl."

"Something like that. But it's not what you think."

"Then tell me how it really is."

He stared at her navel. "If I woulda met you when I was dead broke, things would be different. Your color wouldn't matter. But I got a lot of money now."

"I don't see how that could—"

"Okay, Serena is fuckin with a white dude right now— all that ass and fuckin with a white dude. If she wasn't rich, just an average black woman struggling to get where she's at, you think he would want her?"

"I don't know the answer to that."

"The answer is no. Blacks are born in the struggle together. If I can overcome the struggle, or at least get an advantage, I'm taking another Black with me." He made his erection jump.

She smiled. "So you're...pro-black and against the white man but not completely against the white woman?"

"No. It's...The shit is complicated. Black people ain't worth a damn, either. They'll testify against one another; they'll kill each other; and they hate to see another Black rise most of the time. But my parents was black, so it just seems normal that my main woman be black, too."

She was at a loss for words.

"How old are you, Christine?"

"Twenty-nine my next birthday, three months away."

He made his erection jump again then watched her smile. "While I'm up in you, it's probably a good time to let you know—"

"Please don't tell me you have a disease."

He laughed. "Nothing that I know about." He made it jump again. "Christine, I know you have family out here."

"That doesn't mean I can't come out and visit them."

"Listen, instead of the twenty grand I promised you, I'm giving you $180,000 in cash before you leave this room. Now you don't have to dye your hair blonde just to get a $22,000 job."

"What if I use my money to move to Rock Hill? Maybe start a hair salon for you to get those braids done right."

"You realize your smile is keeping my dick hard?"

She laughed.

"I can't stop you from moving to Rock Hill."

"Will I be able to see you?"

"You don't want that." He made it jump. "Sometimes I can be possessive like an apostrophe."

"I don't care. I don't want to see anyone but you." She looked down between her legs. "This is all I need."

"I was tryin to tell you, while I'm up in you, it might be a good time to let you know that I'm fuckin with another woman back in Rock Hill." *Actually two or three.*

She stared at him and felt it jump. "Will you have time for me? That's all I want to know. Even with your black women, can you make time for me?"

He took a deep breath and released. "Ain't no mutha-fuckin question." He lifted his head and freed his hands. He spread her knees further apart. "But I want you to stay in Vegas for a few months. I want you to take your ass to work at the casino, and I want you to show up for your shift at two."

"Anything else?"

"Yeah. Turn around and get on your knees, but don't let it come out."

She shifted and turned until her back was facing him.

He planted his hands on her waist and followed her to her knees, trying not to let it slip out. He was now on his knees behind her. He grabbed her ass with both hands and pulled back until his erection rested at the edge of her vent. He held still and watched it jump. He pushed deep inside of her. He pumped several times, watching her ass shake. He turned away; the sight would retard him, and he'd have to start over. *Fuck that; I gotta see this.*

Christine clinched the sheets and bit her bottom lip. She spread her knees further apart, tooted her ass up at him, and laid her breasts against the sheets. She felt him stop. But the thing jumped. And jumped. And jumped.

CHAPTER 16

Tank picked Rico up near a shopping plaza in Atlanta, Georgia. He pulled out of the parking lot, and they were headed for the interstate in the Suburban. Rico sat in the front passenger seat. He was no longer wearing braids or glasses. "You won't believe half the shit that happened to me."

"You probably right, not even the shit they had on the news. How much money in that damn bag back there?"

"It should be about 4.4 and some change. No way in the hell I was gonna count all that shit."

"Maybe now you can stop that petty street shit."

"What happened since I was gone?"

"I told you, some cop named Greenburg wanna talk to you."

"Fuck that. I didn't have no business saying shit to that other cop. The muthafuckas don't know shit unless somebody get to talking."

"You just gotta know what to talk about. It's always good to know what your opponent knows."

"I already told you; they don't know shit." Rico leaned forward and pushed the AC vent upward.

"Grandma called; Roc, Vera, Tremaine, and Sequerria called. She said—"

"What did Tremaine want?"

"*Goddamn*! You putting Tremaine before your son and grandma?"

"Don't play with me. What did Tremaine say?"

"She says she need to sit and talk with you and Roc. And Roc said he want all his damn money."

Rico laughed. "That little fucka is sharp as...He set the whole thing up."

"Sequerria is mad because you sent me to bail her ass out of jail before you left. She been calling your number so much, the phone raised the room temperature."

"She's lucky I even bailed her out. I'm done with her, and I'm letting her know when I get home."

"Oh, and Yvonne called." Tank signaled then changed lanes.

Rico smiled. "I got a job for her. Might make her sister of the year."

"Remember hearing about the white man that killed the woman, her daughter, and the cop?"

"Before I left they wasn't sure if it was Caston or the guy that own the bread store."

"Well, the one that own the bread store broke out of the county jail. They say he had at least four other people to set the shit up for him, including some guy named Carrielli. The cops been looking for Carrielli for years, and he killing muthafuckas in Grandma's church, right beside the county jail."

"I'm glad Dan escaped."

"Why?"

"That's the muthafucka who gave us the millions. I'm rootin for the bad guy."

Tank checked the mirror, signaled, then switched lanes. "What happened to the Acura?"

"You said you saw it on the news—"

"The one you drove out there...Mark's Acura Legend."

"I was out of that car soon as I left the bank. I rented the minivan and parked it; I rented the NSX and parked it at another hotel."

"On the news they said the man who shot the cop in the groin area was picked up by some blonde. The man from the Camry carjacking said you had a blonde, too."

"Christine Everson. Damn white girl built like a black woman. She was at the desk in the casino."

"I'm surprised you didn't fuck her."

"Then you ain't really surprised."

"You fucked her?"

"Fucked her good. Especially when she got it back up the second time."

"Why you didn't bring her with you? I coulda hit that."

"I gave her 180 grand in all and she was—"

"Lookin at CNN's side of the story, you shoulda gave her a half-mill."

"I'll mail it to her, out of your cut."

"You knew her less than a day, and she helped you get away with murder, theft, assault, car jacking, and some more shit. How did you pull that off?"

"She...I killed the two dudes before she showed up. She didn't know I had stolen money in the suitcase. The rest of that shit happened after she stopped to pick me up."

"So she didn't know what the fuck she was getting into?"

"Right. But she didn't panic when she got caught in the cross."

"I like her." Tank pushed the CD in.

"I do, too. She's planning on moving to Rock Hill in a couple of months."

Tank turned off the CD player before the music could start up. "How the fuck she know about Rock Hill?"

No answer.

"Don't tell me you gave that damn girl your name."

"Knowing my muthafuckin name don't prove I was in Vegas."

Tank looked at Rico with hacking eyes. "That's some...Man, you...straight up dopefiend move. That comes from doin all that petty shit with Trex."

Rico didn't want to respond.

"You fell in love with a goddamn white girl in a half a day? Your ass is goin to jail. You just don't give a fuck."

"What are you crying for? You get a third of everything in the suitcase, and she don't know shit about you. I didn't do a goddamn thing to jeopardize you. I don't need no approval from nobody to trust my own judgement."

Tank's turn to remain silent.

"I respect your concern with the big-brother shit, but don't forget, little brother the one who filtered the money through the casino in the first place. If I fall to some prison shit, I promise I won't even take an enemy with me."

"Finished?"

"Yeah. Run your mouth."

"First, you need to calm down; you act like you can whip my ass."

"I can sneak your big ass while you're driving."

"And I'll run this muthafucka off the road and kick a may-knot in your ass."

Rico laughed. "What the hell is a may-knot?"

"The swelling may go down, then again it may not." They laughed. Tank returned to the serious issue. "A white girl gave you some pussy and got you out of bounds. Why didn't you...Why do you want her in Rock Hill? You catch hell with Tremaine, Sequerria, Vera...What happened to Vera? I ain't seen her in a minute."

"She complain too much, and that keep my dick limp."

"Can't be worse than Sequerria."

"But Sequerria got the fattest ass, so I put up with her a little bit longer."

"The white girl supposed to push them out of the picture?"

"Hell no. I already told her I got a woman. She's still with it. So maybe I'll have her to get a house, and I can fall up in it whenever I feel like it."

"Didn't you tell me you was tired of cheating?"

"Nope. I told Trex that shit. He's the only one that coulda told you."

"But you did tell me you really don't want none of them except Tremaine."

Rico looked at the CD player. He turned it on again. "I'm keeping Tremaine and Christine."

Tank shook his head. "If Christine don't send your nothing-ass to jail."

Hundred Proof lay on the dirty carpet with his head resting against the couch. He'd been drinking but was not drunk yet. He looked over at Caston who was watching a morning game show. "Hey, if Dan has people willing to break him out of jail, why'd he hire you to get Hansen?"

"If I knew where he was I'd ask him. Just before I put one in his head."

"Don't you wish you'd slept with his old lady more than once now?"

"Too risky. I could never trust her."

"But it's been ten days now, and she never reported you to the cops. I haven't heard anything about it in the news."

"I don't need her; we got Kayla to bang around whenever we want."

Hundred Proof took a drink from the bottle of liquor. "The police will probably keep a good eye on Roseanne until they catch Dan."

"He's not stupid enough to go near that house."

"Hell, I don't think she'd go to wherever he's hiding, either."

"He'd better not; the goddamn cops...would be all over his ass." Caston sat staring at the TV, though it was far from his mind. "I think Roseanne knows where Dan could be hiding, though. Maybe she won't try to see him for now, and maybe she won't tell the cops, but I bet you she knows where he might be."

"How would you know? You already said you don't trust her."

"I think I can make her talk."

"Well, you better think of something real good; the cops must be watching every move she makes."

"This might be my chance to prove, once again, that cops are only human." Caston looked at the bottle in Hundred Proof's hand. Now that his friend was finally drinking again, he thought he might be able to get more help out of him.

Hundred Proof took another drink from the bottle. He opened the newspaper. "You ain't been in the headlines in a while, but you're still making the newspapers."

"Let's hear it."

"*Sources say authorities learned about John Caston's involvement in the murder of Officer Les Hansen from a discarded phone number.*"

Caston squinted his eyes at Hundred Proof. "A phone num—" He ran his hand through his hair. "Have Kayla's ass here when I get back."

Sequerria was past the stage of ringing the doorbell; she was beating on the door now. She looked back at the Lexus parked in Rico's driveway. "I know your black ass is in there!" She walked up to the Lexus and looked inside through the front passenger window. She was looking for anything that might suggest the presence of another woman. Her eyes shifted to the Volvo 740 that was passing the house. Through the light tint she could see the driver and passenger—two white men—looking in her direction. *Silly-ass cops ain't got nothing better to do.* She flipped a middle finger up.

Dan Kapata smiled and kept driving.

Carrielli looked at Dan. "Was that for you or me?"

"For me."

"I thought it might have been for me; she was closer to me than you."

Dan stopped for the stop sign at the top of the street. He looked in the rearview mirror. "That Escort is pulling off in the other direction."

"Turn around and follow her."

Mrs. Bea sat in a rocking chair, on her front porch, with a fly swatter in her hand. She watched the Suburban pull up and park on her lawn.

Rico got out of the truck from the driver's side. "Hey, Grandma."

"Come on here up on this porch so I can go across your head."

He laughed and leaned against the front end of the truck. "Now why would I come up there when you already told me what you gonna do?"

"If I got to get up, I'm subject to tear your ass up for old and new."

He grinned and walked up to the steps. "You know I love you, right?"

"You don't love Jesus, and he made you. Get you a seat and sit down."

He picked up a rusty, iron milk crate from beside the steps and placed it on the porch. He turned the crate upside down and sat it beside his grandmother's rocking chair.

She grabbed his ear and pulled him closer.

"Grandma, that hurt!"

"Get me a switch so I can cut your ass." She released his ear.

"What did I do?"

"You know that crate is for my flower plants."

"But it wasn't shit in that crate."

"I put the plants in the backyard, away from this hot sun. And what I told you about cursing?"

"You said I could curse when I move out; I moved out seventeen years ago."

"You still ain't too old to get an ass-cuttin."

He laughed. "Okay. I'm through cursing." He sat on the crate and rocked back to lean against the old wooden house.

"Give me some money to pay my light bill and get my scription filled."

"You always tell me I won't work in a pie factory; what make you think I got money?"

"My great gran say you promised him...you owe him two thousand dollars. You done stole some money from somewhere?"

"Why I gotta be a thief? I'm a good street hustler."

"Street my foot. I need a hundred and seventy-five dollars."

"I ain't got it. I'll be broke when I scrape up Roc's two thousand dollars. You might have to get it from him, since he told you all his business."

She turned and slapped him across the chest with the fly swatter.

He pushed from the wall, laughing and wiping his shirt. "Grandma, why you hit me with that nasty-ass fly swatter?"

She laughed, too. "Boy, you better be glad I ain't able to kick you in your ass."

He rocked back against the house again.

"Why didn't you bring my great gran over here with you? School out; you could let him spend a few days with me."

"I'm going to pick him up when I leave here. Me and him both spendin the night. How about that?"

"The Lord gone punish you for lyin so much."

"I ain't lyin. And I'mma give you a thousand dollars before I leave."

"Ooooh, the Lord will sho bless you."

He smiled. *The Lord just don't know what He wanna do.*

"Where's that pretty gal at?"

"Which one? I don't mess with nothing but pretty women."

"You know which one I'm talkin about. Nate Nicholson's granddaughter."

"Tremaine? I ain't seen her in almost two weeks. I been out of town, Grandma. I was checking on a job out West. Took me four days to drive out there and four days to drive back."

"You don't need no job that you got to drive that far to get to. I know you ain't thinkin about movin out there."

"No. It wasn't like that. I got paid by taking something out there and bringing something back."

She watched a fly circle and land on the banister. "Bet not be haulin nobody's drugs for them." She leaned forward and swatted the fly.

"No drugs, Grandma."

"Yeah, Nate's granddaughter came over here and talked with me for a while."

"What did y'all talk about?"

"She told me y'all ain't gettin along too well. I told her I'd put a switch to your ass when you came over here again. That thing tickled her to death." She laughed.

"Why you can't put a switch to her ass? She could be the fault."

"Cause she ain't the fault. You all time doin something you ain't got no business doin. You think you the only one God made with feelings?"

"Grandma, that ain't got nothing to do with it. Why did Tremaine say we wasn't gettin along?"

"I didn't ask her; that wasn't my place to ask. But she

said you treats her any kinda way."

"I don't put my hands on her, and—"

"But you don't know a good woman when you see one. And I bet you seein five or six different women. Same thing got your daddy killed. And wouldn'ta been that way if your momma hadn't died having you."

He sighed. "That's why I don't hardly come over here; you like fussin all the time."

"Well, give my money that I need, and bring my great gran over here. You can gone about your business."

"I ain't goin nowhere. I came over to spend some time with you and to give you some money for your birthday."

"When my birthday?"

"Your birthday is today."

"Now the Lord sho gone bless you for that."

"Tank said he was gonna give you a thousand, too."

"I don't wanna take Tank's money; he work too hard for it."

"Grandma, you won't believe what I went through to get mines."

"Nothin. You said you ain't did nothin but some drivin."

They sat in silence for a minute, watching the birds, flies, cars, and the mailman who had bypassed the residence. "Grandma, I got a question for you."

"Well, ask me, and take me to Kroger so I can buy me some groceries."

He hesitated. "I met this white girl who...got me out...stopped me from gettin in some big trouble." More hesitation. "I gave her something for her help, but she likes me, and I don't know...I like her, too."

"What about Nate's granddaughter?" You through with her?"

"No. I'm tryin to keep both of them. I know you don't like that, but I'm just asking you how you feel about black and white people co-existing."

"I don't know what that fancy word means, but my granddaddy was a white man that I never saw before. Tell her to come and sit and talk with me. I'll tell you if she ain't no good. But with that black gal that you treat so bad, you'll miss her when she gone."

He closed his eyes and smiled, still leaning against the house. "When she's gone, I know a little hustler that I can pay to get her back." He watched his sister Yvonne pull up in her husband's truck. He got up and ran off the porch to meet her before she could get out.

Yvonne lowered the truck window. "Hey, Grandma." She waved.

Mrs. Bea smiled. "I'm glad you came; you can take me to the store. Your stankin-ass brother don't wanna help nobody do nothing."

Yvonne laughed.

Rico leaned against the roof of the truck. "What the hell you wanted with me, fat girl?"

"No, that's phat thize to the men with good jobs."

"Let me find out you're chasing the head dishwasher at Wendy's."

"Please, stay away from those drugs. I wanted to know if that rumor about your girl, Vera, was true?"

"What rumor?"

"They say she's messin with Tanisha—lickety split."

"I don't know, but I hope that shit is true. I tried to talk her into that a while ago, but she wouldn't go for it. Why do you ask, you tryin to get a few licks in?" He laughed.

"Move, boy, get out the damn way. It's too many men

in the world for that." She opened the door and got out. "Your son spent the weekend with me. Where the hell was you at?"

"It's a business world; get your own. Wanna make a thousand dollars?"

"That's a stupid question. Damn right."

"Good answer. Look, tonight I want you to go over to Sequerria's house and tell her enough shit about me to break us up. Act like you're talking behind my back. Can you handle that?"

"She'll be through with your sorry-ass before I even get over there. I can even get her to kill you if you throw in another thousand."

"No, thanks, I'm on a budget."

CHAPTER 17

"Yeah, but I'm through with his lying ass." Sequerria turned the stove off and switched the cordless phone to the other ear. She listened to her ex-boyfriend's I-told-you-so lectures about Rico. She poured the scrambled eggs from the frying pan to her plate. "The police was askin me if I know anything about him stealing those bread trucks. He never told me about it, but I wouldn't put it past him." More listening. "He sent his brother to bond me out, and I ain't seen him to let him know."

The doorbell rang.

She headed for the door. "His pager ain't even in service no more. Hold on." She pulled the phone away from her ear. "Who is it?"

"Detective Ellis Pittman."

"Why y'all keep harassin me?"

"I'd like to ask you a couple of questions about Rico

Adams."

She raised the phone to her ear again. "I'll call you back. The damn police just won't leave me alone."

Sequerria flicked on the porch light and looked through the peephole. She saw the detective's head facing down; he was writing something on a palm-size notepad. She opened the door and stood with her arms folded under her breasts. "Why y'all keep coming around here fuckin with people?" She noticed the new cut in her screen door.

He snatched open the screen door and rushed inside, grabbing her neck with one large hand. Then both.

She had no time to think. Instead of kicking and slamming her knees against him, she clawed at his hands for air then banged the cordless phone against his head.

Dan Kapata kicked the door closed with his foot then flung Sequerria on top of the living room coffee table, smashing it to the floor. Before she could gather herself, he pulled out a sleek, black handgun. "Whatever your relationship with Rico, you better pray to God that you got the power to get him over here."

Rico rang the doorbell and waited. Roc stood beside him looking down at their new sneakers.

She opened the door and stepped aside.

Rico and Roc entered the house and invited themselves to the sofa. "Me and Roc spendin the night at my grandma's house tonight. Today is her birthday."

"I wish you would have told me; I could have bought her something. She's a real nice lady."

"Roc, go in the den and watch TV for a few; I need to talk to her about something."

Roc got up from the sofa.

"Roc, sit back down." She looked at Rico. "Whatever you want to talk to me about, Roc probably needs to hear it, too. I wanted to sit down and talk with you and Roc together."

Roc threw himself back on the sofa with a smile. "Y'all sound like y'all gonna get mad again."

Tremaine smiled at Roc. "I'm not gonna get mad at your daddy, Roc. I just want you to hear this promise he's about to make me."

"You get on me about lettin his little ass curse, but you want him to hear our grown-up conversation?"

"Rico, Roc is the only reason I keep giving you all these chances. I just want him to hear some of the promises you make. That way, the next time we fall out he'll know that it's because you broke a promise."

"What make you think I'm here to make you a promise? I might wanna discuss how I be hittin that thang from behind when we—"

"Roc, go in the den for me, baby. Your daddy won't do right."

Roc smiled even harder. He knew what his father was talking about. He got up again and walked to the den where the TV was on.

"Why do you do that? Why do you talk like that around that boy?"

"I usually don't talk sexually explicit around him, but you didn't leave me no choice."

Her lips conveyed a cynical gesture. "Please. Listen, everything in the past, let's just leave it there. I'm willing to start over and do whatever it takes to make you happy. I hope you can say the same." She got up from the recliner, walked over, and sat beside him on the sofa.

He leaned against her and lapped her cheek like a

puppy.

She pulled away, giggling, and wiped her cheek against the shoulder of her T-shirt. "Don't try to get me hot. I'll tell you what I want out of this relationship, and you tell me what you want from me. You wanna go first?"

Rico lowered his head and scratched it.

"And why did you shave so low on your face?"

He rubbed the four-day stubble. "Just tryin something. I'm letting it grow back."

She grazed her manicured fingernails across his face and chin. "Who's going first?"

"I better get my shit off first; you might want something that goes against what I want."

"Then go first, Mr. Selfish." She grabbed his hand and massaged it.

"The first thing I want is for you to quit your job and move in with me."

"Quit my job? Your street hustles don't carry enough benefits. You just borrowed rent money from me last month."

"I wanna start a business that me and you can run. I scraped up enough money to get it going."

"I'll move in with you, but don't expect me to quit my job."

He propped his feet on the coffee table. "How many other women can I see?"

She squeezed his hand. "Boy, don't play with me."

"Tremaine, you're a beautiful woman. You might not believe this, but I hate to see you mad or upset."

Her eyes rolled with disbelief.

"I mean that. I don't like to cheat on you; I hate sneaking and hiding."

"Then why do you do it? You don't hate it; you just

hate getting caught."

"No, I hate it. But to be honest, that don't mean I don't wanna mess with another woman."

She stared at him.

"I just don't wanna sneak around with it." He waited for a response.

Nothing.

"Now, you asked me what makes me happy. We're just talkin right now."

"So you're still trying me with that lesbian shit? That will never happen—"

"No, no. That ain't what I'm saying."

"That's what I understood. How else can you mess with somebody else without sneaking around?"

"I'm just saying, I would want you to know about the other woman; I wouldn't feel like I was cheating."

She released his hand, leaned closer to him, and wrapped her arms around his neck, pulling him closer to her. She kissed him on the lips. Her eyes began to carry water. "It seems like I'm not enough for you." A single tear ran. "All I want is you. I wish I could make you feel the same way about me. Instead, you come over here to stab me and sew me up in the same damn sentence."

"Tremaine, I love you as much as I love my son. I never cared about another woman like that before. But if I had another child, you think that means I don't still love Roc? Is Roc enough son for me? How can—"

The pager sounded off.

He checked the pager and saw Trex's home number and code.

"I called your pager and it was out of service."

"I cut it off, switched carriers, and got a new one. The cops been tracing numbers back to my shit and gettin nosy."

He leaned up and grabbed the cordless phone from the end table. "When I find out what Trex wants, we're gonna pick up where we left off."

Tremaine got up and headed for the den to join Roc.

Trex picked up on the first ring. "Studio."

"You just interrupted a family moment. You fuckin with my quality time."

"Yeah, I was having some quality time with Lynn till your box-of-rocks-ass woman called my sister, trying to get in touch with me."

Rico pulled his feet down from the coffee table. "Who?"

"Sequerria. Unless you got a box of rocks you didn't tell me about."

"What the hell does she want?"

"She said she wanted you to come to her house; it's real important."

"I ain't fuckin with that girl."

"Sound like something was wrong with her...like she wanted to cry."

"That's that weak-ass shit. She's doing anything to get me in her face."

"I don't even like your girl. You know we don't get along. She talk a lot of shit, but this the first time she ever sounded...humbled—like them bible muthafuckas."

Rico laughed. "I been with the girl a thousand times, and I ain't never seen her cry."

"Well, call her, and tell her to stop tracking me down to find you. I was eatin pussy when my sister's voice started talkin to me on the answering machine. You know that's fucked up."

"So she had you call Sequerria. Then you—"

"No. She had Sequerria on the three-way."

"You know what? I'm going over there just to let her know that it ain't gonna work between us. She's just in the way with the plans I got." He stared at Tremaine's wall clock. *Yvonne is probably...Damn.*

"I don't trust her. She was mad at you, and you know the cops been trying to question you. She probably put the cops on your ass in the first place."

Tremaine entered the living room again.

Rico pursed his lips for her. "I might be wrong, but I don't think she'll do that to me, Trex. I'm gone."

"Where are you callin me from?"

"Tremaine's place. Why?"

"Wait twenty minutes and I'll meet you at Sequerria's."

He heard the call end then replaced the handset. "Is Roc ready to go?"

"He's asleep. I didn't wake him up."

Rico got up and approached her. "I'll wake him. He's too big for me to carry. I gotta make a couple of stops before we get to my grandma's house."

"Are we finished with our discussion?"

"We can be if you don't disagree."

"I might always disagree, but your grandmother told me something that I might as well try."

"Oh, you can't listen to Grandma; she's still stuck with the ideas of the old days."

"Tremaine grabbed his hands. "She said she used to let her man do what he wanted to do as long as he took care of home. She said there ain't a man alive who won't get tired of running around. She said if I could hang in there until you got tired, I got myself a man that's worth growing old with."

He reeled her closer. "It's always good to listen to old people; they'll tell you some good shit."

She hugged him, but she was uncertain about their

future.

Yvonne parked behind Sequerria's Ford Escort. She got out and walked toward the front door. She wondered whether she should have left the truck running. She reached the front door and pressed the doorbell.

Silence.

She looked around. The neighborhood was quiet; it seemed like a peaceful area, but Yvonne knew better. She rang the bell again and followed it up with a knock on the door.

Nothing.

She finally gave up and returned to the truck. She would try again in the morning. Hell, maybe even later on tonight. After all, a thousand dollars were at stake.

Rico stepped out of the Suburban and barely closed the driver's door; he didn't want to wake Roc. He walked to the front door but before he could ring the doorbell—

The door opened. She smiled. "Come in. Why did you leave the truck running?"

"My son is in the back sleep. I can't stay long. I just came to straighten some things up with you."

"I thought you cut me off. It's been a while."

"You got a man inside?"

"No. You think I would answer the door in a house coat if that was the case? I just got out of the shower."

"Listen, I just stopped by to let you know that you won't have to worry about me cheating and fuckin around no more."

"What happened, you fell in love? Got somebody

pregnant? Got AIDS? I can't believe you're just getting out the game—the game you invented." She stepped outside on the porch and looked around.

"I didn't get out of the game; I decided to change the damn rules." He heard a noise inside. "I thought you said you didn't have company."

"I said I didn't have a man inside."

"Don't tell me you got that ugly-ass dog running around in there."

"No. You remember you told me to try something, and I told you I would think about it?"

"Try what?"

"Look inside and see."

Rico lowered his eyebrows, staring at her. He stepped past her and stuck his head in the door. He could faintly see someone sitting on the sofa. His hand searched the wall and flicked on the light switch.

Tanisha Bowens sat on the sofa completely naked.

Rico looked back at Vera Hunt on the porch.

Vera smiled and opened her housecoat, exposing her nakedness to him. "You said you was on your way over here to tell me something. Wanna go inside and talk about it?"

Rico's head turned from Vera to Tanisha to Vera again. "Hold everything. Don't nobody have no fun till I get back. He stared at the Suburban. *Damn.* "Y'all go ahead and have fun. I gotta make another stop then spend some time with my son and my grandma. Today's her birthday."

Vera opened her housecoat again, stepped to him, and kissed him. She pushed her tongue inside his mouth.

Rico closed his eyes and grabbed a breast. He released and stepped around her. "I need to leave before one of y'all end up sitting on my face and the other on my dick." He headed for the truck. "I'll be back tomorrow. Have Tanisha over here." He looked back.

Vera flashed at him again.

He shook his head, got in the Suburban, and drove away.

Rico parked the Suburban curbside at Sequerria's mailbox. He looked back to see if Roc had awakened.

The child was sleeping peacefully.

He stepped out of the truck and eased the door shut. He walked up the driveway, glancing inside the Ford Escort, then hesitated when he saw the police car crawling from the top of the street. He turned around and headed for the Suburban.

Dan Kapata saw his target hesitate and turn around. He rushed away from the window and opened the front door.

Rico turned when he heard the door open. No time to react to the sight of the white man rushing out of Sequerria's house. The first bullet tore into Rico's left forearm. Before he could crouch or fall, a second bullet made contact with a front rib and entered his body. Rico fell to the concrete at the rear of the Escort.

Dan moved swiftly toward the back of the Escort. He would not be satisfied until he could get off a couple of close-range headshots.

The policeman picked up speed and activated the siren.

Dan stopped when he saw the blue lights and heard the siren. He fired twice in the direction of the police car then ran for Tank's Suburban.

The policeman stomped the brakes and ducked behind the dashboard. He peeped up and saw two entry holes in the windshield.

Dan threw the Suburban in reverse and backed away.

Trex was on the gas. He had heard the gunshots a block away. He slowed to make the turn onto Sequerria's street when he saw the Suburban speeding his way in reverse.

The rear end of the Suburban crashed into the front end of his Camry.

Dan threw the truck in drive and sped away.

Trex turned the key in the ignition again. He wanted to catch up with Rico in the Suburban, but the Camry wouldn't move. The engine kept delivering a mechanical laugh at him.

CHAPTER 18

Louis Carrielli walked out of the front door of Rico's house. He stood on the steps and looked up at the moon. The damn thing had been following him. He cut across the lawn and walked up the street. He could see the Volvo parked below a street light, sixty yards off. Seemed like a much longer walk than before. He could hear sirens in the distance; he could picture the vehicles racing toward their destination. Carrielli glanced at the house again. He knew that those sirens would soon have a reason to travel to this side of town. Leaving a grenade in Rico's refrigerator was just a backup plan. He thought Dan was having all the fun.

John Caston peered in the darkness from the corner of the house, nine houses down from Roseanne's. He could see two undercover agents parked across the street in the black Bonneville. He knew that he was too far away to hear Roseanne's Mercedes if it ever pulled out of the garage. So he kept watching the Bonneville.

Hundred shoulda made the call by now. Caston crawled on the ground to the next house. He could see the fenced-in yard ahead and knew there was a dog on a chain farther down. He heard the Bonneville engine start but before he could turn around and peer from the corner, the black car had left the spot. He could hear it speeding, clearly farther and farther away from Roseanne's house.

He crept to the front corner of the house and watched the Bonneville swing a left at the stop sign. Caston stood contemplating for nearly ten seconds then darted to the street. He ran to Roseanne's house and stopped for rest next to the garage. He was short-winded for a forty-seven-year-old. He walked behind the house to get to the other side. He stopped.

Movement inside.

He had thought for sure that the agents had driven away tailing Rosanne.

Goddamn Hundred didn't even make the call. Caston had no idea as to when the agents might return; didn't understand why they had hurried off in the first place. He walked to the front corner of the house and scanned the area. He approached the front door and rang the doorbell, aborting his plan to break in now. It was time to test her interest for him.

"Who is it?"

He recognized her voice. "John."

"John who?"

"John Caston."

Silence.

The door opened.

He held the handgun behind his back, looking at her through the storm door. "You gonna invite me in?"

She unlocked the storm door. "I didn't think you'd ever come back."

Caston entered the house and tucked the gun back in his waistband. "Are you kiddin? I told you I'd come back to screw you if you didn't report me or tell Dan."

She closed the door.

"You here alone?"

"Yeah. I got the craziest phone call not too long ago."

"Crazy? How do you mean?"

She leaned against the door. "Somebody called and asked me to drive to the skating rink parking lot and wait for Dan."

He raised an eyebrow, pretending to be interested. "Turn the light out; the cops gonna come back to watch this house again as soon as they realize no one's gonna show up at the rink."

"Do I take everything off again?" She swiped the light switch.

Caston could see her silhouette. He moved closer to her. "We'll get to that. For now, I need to know something about that lunatic husband of yours."

"First, I wanna know what took you so long to come back."

The room was almost silent. A television in the background. The sudden movement of the hand could be heard. The barrel of a handgun could be felt against the stomach. The first shot ripped flesh, tissue, muscles. The next shot was unnecessary—but it happened anyway.

Roc heard the two shots then looked up to see what was going on. He watched his father fall to the concrete behind Sequerria's car. He moved closer to the side window and remained crouched as if he could be seen through the tinted window. He felt the sensation somewhere at the top of his nostrils; he was about to cry. Two more shots were fired, and now the white man was running toward the Suburban. Roc lowered himself face-down on the floor from the back seat and closed his eyes.

The driver's door opened.

Roc heard the man jump in and slam the door. He heard the gears shift, and the truck jerked away in reverse. Roc lay still and quiet; he could imagine the man looking over the shoulder to steer in reverse. The tears fell, but he pressed his lips together and kept his eyes closed. He felt the truck turning, so he gripped the bottom of the driver's seat.

The truck crashed into something.

The impact threw Roc against the back seat, loosening his grip on the driver's seat, rocking him forward again, banging his head against the back of the driver's seat.

Dan had no time to investigate whatever was in the back floor. He checked the rearview mirror again and saw the police car gaining. The blue lights and siren brought too much attention. He saw another stop sign up ahead but couldn't afford to make the turn without slowing down. He kept the pedal to the floor. The Suburban was fast, but it was not likely to outrun the police car.

Dan kept the gun in his right hand, both hands on the steering wheel, then pulled one hand over the other making a sharp right.

The truck tipped. Balanced on two wheels for four seconds.

Dan clinched his teeth, trying to will the truck down on four wheels again. The truck seemed to fight against his will, winning easily. The driver's side of the Suburban fell to the street and skidded.

Dan had made the turn, but the rear end of the truck tried to swing a three-sixty, still on its side. The truck finally stopped moving, but the wheels were still spinning and the windshield was facing the police car that was approaching. Dan had to act fast. He struggled to position himself then fired a single shot through the Suburban's windshield, hitting the hood of the police car. He watched the car veer to the side of the street and come to a stop. Dan managed to turn his body around in the front area of the truck. He unlocked the passenger door and had to push it open. The door was twelve times heavier now.

The policeman was out of the car, crouched behind the driver's door, waiting to shoot anything that comes out of the Suburban.

Roc was in an awkward position. He was resting with his upper back, his neck, and his head against the back passenger door. He had drawn his knees close to his chest, but he knew that his new sneakers could be seen from the front area.

The heavy door would not stay open for Dan. He pulled himself upward to crawl through.

Two bullets hit the door.

Dan ducked back inside. He examined the door but found no holes in it. He cracked the door open again and fired three shots at the street light. The last shot was good. It was darker now. He ducked inside again and hesitated. He looked at the police car again. He heard more sirens. They were coming to get him. *Fuck it*. He opened the door and pulled himself upward again.

Two more shots, breaking the window.

He flinched but continued crawling until he was out.

Two more shots in the door.

Dan knew now that the police was too far off; none of the bullets had made an exit through the inside door panel. Dan reached around the bottom of the door and fired three blind shots.

The policeman ducked.

Dan let the door slam shut then jumped to the street, running.

Roc rolled out of his awkward position. He could barely see the running man through the rear window. He heard another exchange of gunfire. He crawled to the back door of the truck and waited until the white man had cut between the two houses. Roc pulled the back door handle and pushed. The door swung open and thudded to the street. Roc poured out of the back and hauled ass.

The sirens were swelling.

The policeman was approaching the Suburban with caution. He had heard the noise that came from the back of the truck. He was quick. He saw a runner moving to the left. He fired once.

Roc hit the ground.

Trex had heard the Suburban when it turned on its side. He was jogging toward the scene with a gun in his hand. He slowed to a walk and stuffed the gun in his waistband—he was nearing the police car. He looked back and another police car was coming. The ambulance was in the area. Another police car arrived ahead on the intersecting street.

The Suburban was in view now. *Damn, I don't need this*

gun on me. The police car rushed past him. Trex wondered whether Rico had been shot after throwing the Suburban on its side. He looked back and saw the ambulance turning onto Sequerria's street. *I know Rico didn't shoot the damn girl.* He turned to see another police car arriving near the Suburban. Then another. More porch lights were on now. People were coming out of their houses. Trex glanced downward to make sure his shirt was still concealing the gun. His eyes shifted toward the closest parked police car. The sweeping motion of a bright search light caught his attention. He looked at the holes in the windshield of the police car but continued toward the scene.

The tall black police officer noticed Trex approaching, so he decided to meet him, hand on the butt of his firearm.

"What's going on, officer?"

"There's been some shooting and an accident." The police officer assumed that Trex was a resident of the neighborhood. "I'm gonna have to ask you to stay behind—"

"Hold up...That's..." Trex could see Roc now. "That's my damn nephew right there!"

The police officer glanced back at the child who was being escorted to the front seat of a police car.

"Roc, what's up?"

Roc turned and saw Trex standing thirty yards away with the policeman. He released the door of the police car and ran over to Trex, leaving the escorting policeman behind.

"Roc, what happened?" Trex studied Roc's watery eyes, saw the tear trails, and wondered about the dirt and grass on his clothes.

Roc fought to find a starting point and struggled to suppress his crying. "A white man killed my daddy at...at Sequerria's house." Roc had held it long enough. This time he cried out loud.

Trex dropped to one knee and hugged Roc. He took a deep breath and quietly exhaled.

The escorting policeman and his partner arrived.

For just a moment, Trex couldn't hear anything. No voices. No crying. No barking dogs. He pulled back from Roc and stared at him. "What happened to you?"

Roc sniffled, wiped at his eyes, then got the crying under control. "That white man...white man took the truck while...I was hiding in the back. Then he flipped it over and ran...and I...and I got out and ran, too. Roc looked back at the escorting policeman. "Then that...that crazy mutha-fucka shot at me...and...and I fell."

CHAPTER 19

Tank stopped the Lexus in his grandmother's driveway and tapped the horn. He watched the old lady come out carrying a purse, wearing a T-shirt and sweat pants. He leaned over and opened the door.

Mrs. Bea got inside the Lexus and closed the door. "Tank, don't you be drivin this car too fast."

"Yes, ma'am." He backed the car out of the driveway and drove off.

"Tank, don't you tell me no lie. Why that man come after Rico?"

Tank hesitated. For the first time since he was a child, he thought about lying to his grandmother. "I don't..." Couldn't do it. "We stole some trucks from him and found a lot of money hid inside. I don't know how he knew Rico had something to do with it."

"That ain't like you, Tank, to be doing the stuff Rico

get into."

"I know, but, Grandma, it was a lot of money in them trucks."

"Tank, you always worked for what you wanted. You don't have to steal nothin from nobody."

"I try to work to have the stuff I need, but I ain't always good as you think I am. I just try to stay out of *stupid* trouble."

"Well, you see what trouble can get you. And why the man had to kill Sequerria if he come after Rico?"

"Grandma, I can't answer that."

"Lord knows I'm glad that man ain't notice my great gran in that truck of yours."

"Me, too. I talked to Trex this morning, and he asked me how you was takin it."

"I like that boy. Trex got good manners and...He don't get into none of that mess with you and Rico, do he?"

Tank laughed. "Yes, ma'am, when he need the money."

"Lord, I don't know what to say. You know why y'all like that, don't you? Nobody don't come to church with me no more."

Tank glanced at her. "Grandma, you just saw the deacon get shot in your church not too long ago. Bad luck happen to everybody."

"And that's the same deacon who was stealin money from the church."

Tank poked out his bottom lip. He couldn't win.

"Who that other man got killed last night? They say he got something to do with the man that shot Rico."

"Some white man name John Caston. They say he went to Dan's house to do something to his wife. Dan is the man who they believe shot Rico. His wife shot John Caston twice in the stomach."

"I don't know what y'all done got yourselves into. That white man ain't through shootin and killin folks till he get his money back."

"Grandma, I don't see giving the money back as an option."

She could see the tall hospital building seemingly competing with other buildings in height. "Tank, it hurt me to hear you talk like that. I didn't raise neither one of y'all that way, but I thought you had a bit mo sense than your brother."

Tank saw no need to respond. They rode in silence until reaching the parking lot of the hospital.

Christine was in her apartment reading a Cordless Sims thriller, which she'd downloaded for free, called *In Rare Form*. She was curled up on the sofa; her roommate, Traci, a black dancer for a Las Vegas night club, was watching CNN. Christine glanced at the TV then looked at Traci. "Remember you said if the author was giving this book away for free, then it can't be worth much?"

"Yeah. So what's it about?"

"A gutsy killer is trying to find this young boy and the boy's mother. The young boy is trying to find an important package that his dad hid before he was killed."

"I'll read it next. Any woman in there built better than me?"

Christine laughed. "You're too competitive over physical appearance. It's only a book."

"Vegas is extremely competitive, and you know—"

"Wait a minute!" Christine had heard the name on the news. She thought. She grabbed the remote from the sofa cushion and increased the volume. The reporter had been talking about Dan Kapata, a small business owner who had allegedly killed a police officer and who had also broken out of jail. Christine caught the tail end of the news break—the reporter's talk of Rico Adams being shot twice and hospitalized. She then learned that Rico was in fair condition after his surgery. She had no idea of whom the Sequerria woman was—the woman who had been killed by a single shot to the temple.

Traci sat upright on the love seat now. "Where did that happen?"

Christine ignored the question. She placed the printed ebook on the coffee table and got up from the sofa. "I just remembered...I have to check on some out-of-town property."

Roc and Mrs. Bea were sitting in room 409; Rico was still sleeping; the heavy sedatives had him resting well.

"Grandma, how long my daddy gonna sleep?"

"Don't nobody know that but the Lord, baby. Just be thankful you still got your daddy."

Roc grabbed one of her hands. "Grandma, why you don't wear no rings?"

"I used to wear that stuff a long time ago. When you get my age, a lot of the things you like right now won't mean nothing to you no more."

"So I ain't gonna like Nikes when I get old?"

Mrs. Bea looked down at her Reeboks. "You might like your shoes, but you won't feel the same way about them."

Roc pulled his foot up in the chair to tie his sneaker. "My daddy got a friend name Blue that own a store called *Superstar Jewelry*, but my daddy don't even wear jewelry.

Did my daddy get old, Grandma?"

She smiled. "No. Don't waste no time tryin to figure your daddy out; I believe that's why I'm so old now." She laughed.

Roc laughed with her, though he hadn't understood the humor.

"What your momma say about your daddy gettin shot and you gettin shot at by the police?"

"She was up here before y'all came. Her and Aunt Yvonne. She said she was coming back tonight. My momma asked me why I ran out the truck."

"And what you say?"

"I told her somebody kept shootin at the truck before the man got out. I wasn't gonna stay in that truck."

"I don't blame you, baby. I woulda ran, too."

"My momma cursed the police out who shot at me. She was mad because he brought me home, too, instead of lettin Trex bring me."

"I thought Tank said his truck tore up Trex's car?"

"But when my momma was cursin the police out she didn't know, and I wasn't gonna say nothing to her while she was mad."

Mrs. Bea got up and walked over to Rico's bedside. "Reek, I'll get Tank to bring me back up here after lunch. Grandma gotta go and take her insulin, you hear me?" She knew he wouldn't answer, but the gesture was so grandmotherly.

Tank was standing in front of the lobby window on the fourth floor. He was watching different types of vehicles enter and leave the parking lot.

Lynn and Trex sat in the lobby reading different sections of the newspaper.

Tank turned and faced them. "Did anybody call Tremaine?"

Trex and Lynn looked at one another.

"Let me see your phone, Lynn. She's at work now." Tank extended his hand.

Lynn dug into her purse and pulled out a cellular phone.

Tank saw his grandmother and Roc coming toward the lobby area. "Never mind. I'll call her from the car; Grandma is ready to go."

Trex got up. "We're going back in to sit with him."

Tank met his grandmother. "You ready?"

"Yeah. I want you to bring me back sometime this evening."

"He might be sitting up by then."

"Unc, can I stay here with my daddy?"

"Boy, you been up all night. Don't you need something to eat and some sleep?"

"Me and my momma got some breakfast from McDonald's this morning."

Tank palmed the top of Roc's head. "Boy, it's after one o'clock; you need something else to eat. Trex and Lynn is staying; me and you are coming back in a few hours. Earlier than that if Tremaine can't get off from work."

Trex walked over. "Grandma, me and my girlfriend coming to sit with you and watch *Sandford & Son* one day next week."

"Trex, she seem like a pretty good gal. You treat her good, you hear me?"

"Yes, ma'am." Trex hugged her. He really liked the old lady. "I'll call you whenever he wake up."

Roc approached Lynn. "You and Trex gonna stay here

till I get back?"

She smiled. "We won't leave your daddy up here by himself, Roc. We don't have anything else to do until you get back."

Rico's eyes finally opened.

Tremaine got up from her seat and approached his bedside. Trex and Lynn joined her.

Rico's eyes scanned the room. Helplessly watching the white man run to the truck was the last thing he'd remembered before passing out. He looked at Lynn. Then Trex. Then studied the tears in Tremaine's eyes. He knew something was wrong. He closed his eyes. "Arrrgh!" The pain cut short his attempt to give a good yell. Water soon filled his eyes, and he gripped both sides of the bed.

Tremaine panicked and pressed a button to call the nurse.

Trex moved in closer. "Rico, Rico! Calm down, the doctor's on the way."

Rico released his grip, shut his eyelids tight, and pressed his lips together. He shook his head.

An elderly nurse entered the room. "Does he need anything?" She hurried to his bedside.

Tremaine, Trex, and Lynn stepped aside to give her room. Tremaine wiped at her tears. "He's in a lot of pain. He woke up and started groaning."

The nurse placed her hand on Rico's forehead. "Mr. Adams, are you okay?"

Rico opened his watery eyes and stared at the nurse. "I just want my son back."

Trex and Lynn were walking to her car in the hospital parking lot. Tank had called her cellular to let them know that he was near the hospital again.

Vera Hunt pulled up beside them in a Honda Civic. "Trex, how is Rico?"

Trex stopped. He saw Tanisha on the passenger side. *Damn, that girl still look good.* "He's straight now, Vera."

"What room is he in?"

"Room 409." Trex turned to Lynn and smiled.

"Thanks, Trex." Vera drove off, looking for a parking space.

Lynn pushed Trex. "What did you just do? Rico doesn't mess with her, does he?"

"No. Not while he got a cracked rib and a damaged liver." He smiled again.

"Trex, why did you do that?"

"Do what? She was gonna get the information from the front desk anyway."

"Tremaine might whip that girl's ass."

"Well, the least we could do is go and watch the shit." She pushed him again.

Christine Everson got out of the rental car, a Mitsubishi Gallant, and saw the couple. She wondered whether either of them knew Rico but decided not to ask.

Tank and Roc arrived again in the Lexus. He slowed the car for the white woman to cross. "Damn, that white girl looks good, Roc."

"Bet you won't say something to her, Unc."

"Boy, you must don't know who you hangin with." Tank lowered the window, and the heat rushed inside. He picked up a little speed and cut her off before she could cross to get to the main entrance.

Christine waited for the Lexus to pass.

"Excuse me, but my nephew wanted me to say something to you, and I didn't think that was such a bad idea."

She smiled and waved at the child on the other side. I'm sorry, but I'm really in a rush. My grandfather's ill."

"And I'm sorry to hear that. My brother's ill. You wanna go out later to get a few things off our minds?"

"No, thanks. Sounds like a date, and I'm already taken." She began walking around the car.

"Sounds like you got something against a black man. I don't fuck with no white women anyway; I was just pumpin that head up."

She ignored Tank. From the rear end of the car she saw the boy in the passenger seat looking back at her. She smiled and waved at him again.

Tank watched her as she headed for the entrance door. "Roc, that white girl got a fat ass on her."

"You'll like her if she go on a diet?"

Tank laughed. "I'll be disappointed if she did that."

Tremaine was in the bathroom washing her hands when she heard the knock at Rico's room door. She walked out and stood beside the hospital bed. "Come in."

Rico lay with his back raised. He studied Vera as she entered the room, Tanisha close behind.

Vera stopped at the foot of the bed. "You look good. How do you feel?"

"You look better, and I feel...like I might live."

Another knock at the door.

"Come in." Tremaine took a seat in the chair beside the head of the bed.

Christine entered the room as a brunette with a stylish haircut, wearing tight jeans to highlight her shapely curves.

Rico stared at her until he was sure of whom she was. "Come here."

She displayed a friendly smile for the women then walked around to the window side of the bed.

Tank and Roc entered the room. Tank stared at the white woman and figured it out.

Rico saw Roc for the first time since the back seat of the Suburban. "Man, bring your tough-ass here and give your dad a hug."

Roc rushed up to the side of the bed, stopping in front of Tremaine's chair. He leaned over and hugged his dad.

Rico fought the pain; he held onto Roc with the arm that was not bandaged. "Roc, listen."

Roc pulled back and looked at his dad.

"I be on some tough shit all the time, and I haven't told you I love you in a few years. So even if it's gonna be a few more years after today, I just want you to know that your daddy love you more than everybody on the planet."

Roc smiled. "I be on some tough shit..." He glanced at Tremaine. "...tough stuff, too, and I love you, too."

Tank walked up to the white woman. "Now, I know damn well my brother don't look like the grandfather you came to see."

Christine smiled then turned to Rico. "I couldn't resist coming here to make sure you were okay."

"I like that, and I appreciate it." His eyes shifted to Vera. "I appreciate everything. Even more now. That's why I hate to ask three of the finest women to put your skates on and stay out of my life unless you really need something from me." He looked at Tremaine. "I want you to stay. I owe you for puttin up with all the bullshit."

CHAPTER 20

Dan and Carrielli sat in the backyard of the North Carolina house, drinking can sodas and listening to country music on a portable radio. "Maybe the grenade was bad. Sometimes that happens." Dan sipped more soda.

"I don't think so. The minute that refrigerator is opened...Let's bet on it."

"That's not a good bet. He's still in the hospital; it might be a couple more days."

"So what's the plan now? I know you've got enough money in one of those offshore accounts. You thought about Brazil or some other nice spot?"

"I don't have that much left, but that might not be such a bad idea." Dan stared at the picnic table. "I was wondering why the cops are always nearby whenever I pull a trigger."

Carrielli laughed. "Face it, Dan, you've lost your

touch. Things have changed, and we don't plan like we used to."

"Rose told the cops Caston raped her two weeks ago."

"Why didn't she say something before?"

"She knows how I feel about a rape. I've told her before, a long time ago, that I would lose my interest in her if she was ever fucking around or even raped."

"You're a harsh guy."

"Is that coming from a guy that killed a preacher? Hallelujah!" Dan laughed.

"I let the preacher live; that was a deacon. You're trying to make me out to be a monster." They laughed.

"Then again, I don't know why she didn't report it earlier; she still ended up reporting it."

"Don't worry yourself about that. At least she killed Caston for you."

Dan sipped more soda.

"This is a nice house, but I think you need to get out of the country."

"What about you? You're wanted for two jailbreaks and three attempts. You think this country doesn't watch America's Most Wanted?"

"I already got my plans together. I'm leaving this country. There's too much crime here. You know I'm a peaceful guy, Dan."

"I'd like to make sure the grenade takes care of Rico before I leave. I did a half-ass job on him."

"Don't be so hard on yourself. Take a break. Take a vacation. Have faith in the grenade, or come back to the country in, say, two or three years, and track him down again."

"You know I hate to postpone something like that. He's a goddamn threat."

"He's no fucking threat. The cops will stay glued to his ass. I don't mind taking the risk with you, but we'd have to renegotiate the financing."

Dan thought about his son, Perry, who was now living in Tennessee. "Give me a few days. Let's see what happens."

Rico, Tank, and Trex were in the hospital room trying to put things together. Trex got up and walked to the window. "How the fuck did Dan know you had something to do with his bread trucks?"

Rico was about to respond but held his words when the white man entered his room without invitation.

Tank and Trex decided to meet the man.

He held up a badge. "Please, no standing ovations. I'm Detective Greenburg, and I have a few questions for the patient."

Tank and Trex stepped aside but kept their eyes on him.

Rico watched the slender detective. "Mr. Detective Greenburg, why is it that your ass can't knock like everybody else? Don't you need one of them muthafuckin search warrants to come up in my room?"

"It's a state-owned building. But I don't want to depress you with the complexities of the law. I'm here—"

"Complex your ass up out my room. Can't you see I got enough company?"

Greenburg turned to Tank and Trex. "You gentlemen mind if I have a word with him alone?"

Tank and Trex looked at one another and burst out laughing.

Rico cleared his throat, gaining the detective's attention again. "You must be still into that Perry Mason shit. Ain't no damn crime scene in here. My peoples ain't goin no damn where. Say what you got to say, then put your fuckin skates on so we can laugh and talk shit about you when you leave."

"Then that explains it. These two guys must be your help, since you don't mind them hearing what I'm here to question you about."

"I'll call that fat-ass nurse in here; that don't mean she helped me with shit."

"A fax was retrieved from a wastebasket inside Dan Kapata's bread store on the morning of the robbery. You know, the trucks you stole from the guy that shot you."

No response. Rico simply stared at the detective with a smirk.

"You wanna know whose name was on the fax?"

"You was doing good till you fucked up the general line of questioning between a cop and a suspect...I'm guessing you see me as a suspect."

"You're about to make a point?"

"Yeah. Don't count on me answering questions that you ain't already got the answer to. Why the fuck would I help you investigate *me?*"

Greenburg walked closer and sat in the chair beside the head of Rico's bed. "It must have slipped my mind." Greenburg got a closer look at Rico. "The 5.6 million that you squeezed through the Vegas casino...that was brilliant. How's that for investigating a suspect?"

Rico resisted shifting his eyes toward Tank and Trex. He thought about Christine. *That's what I get for fuckin with a box of rocks.* "PCP, LSD—what the fuck are you on? I don't gamble, and I don't fuck around no casinos."

Greenburg smiled and got up from the chair. "Now

isn't that something? Funny, I didn't hear you say you don't fuck around with no bread trucks." He placed a business card on the seat cushion. "If you happen to stumble across a million in cash, call me." He headed for the door. "A trial would only make things worse for you." He nodded at Tank and Trex. "Good afternoon, gentlemen." He left the room.

Trex walked over and locked the door.

Tank approached the bedside and sat in the chair now. "That was fast. Too damn fast. You just kicked the white girl out less than three hours ago."

Trex walked up. "All I need is her name and address. I'll ride a *bicycle* to Vegas just to teach her some good shit."

"Calm the fuck down; everybody is moving too fast. Maybe it ain't the white girl."

Tank shook his head. "You don't even believe that your damn self. Nobody else knew. That big-ass mouth of yours is just—"

"Man, it's too late for that bullshit. I told you, I can go to Vegas and get—"

"Trex, that don't solve shit." Rico rubbed his forehead. "The damn cop already got his foot in my ass."

"What's your point? You act like the crooked-ass cop can't get it, too. I ain't playin about this shit! I don't play the fuckin radio!"

Tank shot Trex a look of contempt. "And what if the cop already told somebody else about what he's—"

"Slow down. Just think about this shit for a minute. Tank, is that the same cop who was looking to ask me some questions when I was gone?"

"Same muthafucka."

"Okay, a different cop was asking me about some phone calls and my connection with the computer store before I went to Vegas."

"So." Tank shrugged.

"And you know they found Mark's Acura in a mall parking lot in Vegas. They connected the car to Rock Hill. They probably wanna question Mark but can't find him, so they match the black guy in the casino and bank photos with the only black guy they can connect with the computer shop, since the Acura is owned by somebody that worked at the shop."

Tank nodded. "So, you think Greenburg is just guessing?"

"Not really guessing, the muthafucka got a little bit of sense."

Trex looked away. "That white girl must have some good-ass pussy; she ain't even on the list no more. You really don't think she crossed you, do you?"

"Maybe. But I gotta look at all angles. If the cop mixin guesswork with homework, he probably ain't told nobody because he expect to get a million out the deal."

Tank looked at Trex. "This shit is big-time. We can't run it like you handle that petty shit."

"You can call my prior crimes petty, but I used big ideas to beat the cross every time."

Tank laughed. "Name one big idea you ever used, Trex."

"All you have to do is check with Joe Dobbs, and you'll see my skills."

Rico's eyebrows lowered. "Joe Dobbs? Didn't they pick him up for robbing Gadden's and killing Westwood in the parking lot."

"Yeah." Trex grinned. "I'm the one who got him to put his prints on the knife handle. I ain't selfish; I let him get the credit for the robbery and all that shit."

Rico knew that Trex was serious. "I asked you did you

rob Gadden's, and you said you didn't."

"And I'm stickin to my story. Joe Dobbs, the mutha-fucka who used to be a police informant, gettin all the credit. I just talked Eric Westwood, the muthafucka who got away with killing his momma, into going in to rob Gadden's."

Tank looked at Rico. "I like the boy's motives."

Trex rubbed his hands together. "Stop fake breakin; you like the damn idea, too."

Rico watched the ceiling, contemplating from his reclined position. "The doctor said my liver was just nicked. I could be out in a few more days."

"The doctor told me ten days."

Rico smiled at Tank. "Then stay your ass in here for ten days. But I'm leaving in a few." He looked at his band-aged arm. "I wish I knew who Dan associated with. Then again, I know the police probably sweatin his people and his contacts like the sun."

Trex walked to the window again. "Well, we got plenty money. The names Kapata and Carrielli can't be hard to find. We can put the press game down on anybody related to them fuckas."

I thought you promised Lynn you was through with the streets." Rico waited on a slick response.

"Fuck the streets; I'm talking about running up in houses."

"Wait a minute." Tank paused. "Greenburg said he had a fax, acting like your name was on it."

"What about it? You think he's just shootin me a bluff?"

"No. The damn Acura had a mobile fax in it. That's how he might be—"

"And faxes leave numbers that show where the fax

came from." Trex looked at Tank.

Rico's eyes shifted from Trex to Tank. "I don't know if mobile faxes do that, but it makes sense if Mark sent the fax."

"Tank, I thought you cut the phone lines at the bread store."

"Trex, you read the story in the muthafuckin newspaper yourself. They talked about the cut phone lines, remember? You think they shoulda mentioned my name or something?"

"You're right. I'm just—"

A knock at the door.

Trex looked at Rico, then he walked off to unlock the door.

Another badge. "I'm detective Jim Neely." His eyes cut past Trex to the patient in the bed. "I'd like to ask Mr. Rico Adams a few questions." He walked inside and stopped at the lower end of the bed.

"Why couldn't y'all just bring your asses in here at the same time? That way, you coulda saved both of us some time, because I ain't answering no questions."

"I understand that a couple of investigators spoke with you this morning about your run-in with Mr. Kapata, but I'm... really not concerned with that at all."

Rico smiled at the detective. "You ain't the first black man that didn't show me love. String your skates up, say what you gotta say, and roll the fuck out."

Neely laughed. "So, at least you know your rights. You have a right to curse in the hospital. I, on the other hand, had the right to look into Mark Aldridge's cell phone records for the Acura that was found in Nevada. Now, you wanna know what's really funny? The records show that a call from the Acura was answered by someone at your residence just hours before the bread store trucks were taken."

CHAPTER 21

Tank stood at Rico's mailbox collecting bills and junk mail. Roc stood beside him, his face turned away from the bright sun. "Unc, it's too hot out here to be reading mail. Get that shit and let's go in the house."

"You ain't got no key?"

"No."

"Then shut the hell up and let me read."

Roc looked back at the Lexus at the top of the driveway then turned toward the house. He saw some shade by the doorsteps.

Tank began walking toward the house, still reading. "Come on."

Roc followed. "Unc, Tremaine is gonna move in when my daddy get out the hospital this Saturday."

Tank crumpled the letter. "He need that. It's time to settle his wild ass down."

"Why you ball my daddy's letter up?"

"How you figure that's your daddy's letter? All that shit he got is in my name." Tank stopped at the doorsteps, searching for the right key. "Roc, you still can't remember answering the phone that morning the white man broke in the house?"

"I told my daddy I was sleep before that man came in."

"Well, if the man broke the window and woke you up, the damn telephone coulda woke you up, too." He stepped up to the door, unlocked it, and walked inside.

Roc was two steps behind. "The phone did wake me up, but whoever called didn't say nothing; somebody was playing on the—"

"Why didn't you say that when we ask you a few days ago?" Tank stopped in the hallway and turned to face Roc.

"Y'all kept asking me who called. I don't know who called."

"Man, we asked you did the phone ring before the man broke in."

"The phone didn't ring...soon as...before he broke in; it seem like it was a long time before that."

Tank thought about it. He wondered how Mark had gotten the private number. "I got to get your dad some more underclothes. Get what you need to get, and hurry up."

Roc headed for the kitchen. He stopped in front of the refrigerator.

Tank noticed that there were no messages on the answering machine. "Roc, go to the car and dial this number and see if the answering machine will pick up."

"I gotta fix something to drink first." He jumped up to grab the bag of Doritos from the top of the refrigerator. His arm pulled open the freezer side of the double doors. A cup of frozen yogurt fell to the floor.

"You get something to drink and you won't be able to handle the milkshake I was gonna get you from Burger King."

Roc picked up the yogurt, placed it back in the freezer, and closed the door. "I'll wait till we get to Burger King." He headed for the door with the bag of Doritos in his hand.

Tank waited for less than a minute, and the phone rang. After the fourth ring, the answering machine beeped, and Tank could hear Roc's message.

"Unc, hurry your ass up in there before I drive to Burger King and leave you."

Tank played the digital message back. It seemed to work fine. He gathered a few underclothes, stuffing them in a gym bag, then headed for the kitchen. He stopped in front of the refrigerator.

Roc tapped on the Lexus horn.

Tank looked up at the ceiling. *I know I'm forgettin something.*

Roc tapped the horn again.

Tank walked out of the kitchen and headed out the front door.

Roc sipped at his milkshake, watching the cars drive past the carwash.

Tank was vacuuming the front floor of the Lexus when the blue Celica arrived and parked at the next vacuum.

The black man got out of the Celica and walked over to Tank. "I see you still keepin the Lex clean."

"What's up, Chris? Somebody got to."

"Yo, I heard about your brother and Sequerria. That's

fucked up."

"Yeah, but he's coming through."

"You know I got them things for sale—nines, four-fives—and can get a pretty Uzi for a good price."

"I'm good. You know I know how to find you."

"Yo, when the last time you talked to Trex?"

Tank contemplated the answer. "I ain't seen that crazy muthafucka in about a month."

"Well, I don't know how to get in touch with him, but some niggas was down here askin about him. I figure they don't know it, but they lookin for the wrong mutha—"

"Asking what?"

"Where he lives, where he hang out, who he be with. They had a North Carolina tag plate, and they—"

"Where was they at?"

"Right here at this car wash. You woulda been here a hour ago, you woulda seen them."

"How many, and what did they drive?"

"A blue Cutlass, maybe 1981. It was two in the front and one in the back."

The vacuum gave out. "Anybody talked to them?"

"They asked me and Sylvia from Boyd Hill. I don't know who else; I left after I saw them talkin to her."

Tank rubbed his chin, staring at the vacuum hose. "Did it look like they wanted some problems?"

"Hard to say. They didn't make threats, but they wasn't on joke time, either."

Roc walked over slurping the bottom of the cup with his straw. "Chris, I saw your sister in the hospital."

"What up, Roc? Tanisha ain't in no hospital."

"She came with Vera to see my daddy."

"Oh. I was about to *say*."

Roc threw the cup to the concrete ground.

Chris laughed. "You just like your dad." He shook his head. "I heard the people talkin about you on the news, even though they didn't say your name."

"Well, how the hell you know they was talkin about me?"

"They say the man tried to get somewhere in Tank's truck, and Rico's son was hiding in the back. You the only son I know Rico got."

Tank stepped out of the car with the hose in his hand. "Roc, pick that cup up and put it in the trash can. And get your bad ass in the car."

Roc did as he was told. The tone of Tank's voice dared him to respond with the usual smart mouth and profanities.

Tank coiled the hose and hung it on the vacuum. He and Chris walked beyond Roc's earshot. "Roc is going through some shit right now. You gotta ignore that fly mouth."

"That's his style. I know he don't mean—"

"You say the dudes had a North Carolina tag. You know the plate number?"

"Nah. I didn't try to remember that shit. The state just stuck out at me."

"Good lookin out, anyway. If I see Trex, I'll let him know."

Chris made a gun gesture with his hand and twitched the thumb. "You sure you don't need nothin?"

"No, but you'll be the first to check with if I do."

Rico was standing by the window in his hospital room. The phone rang, and he looked over his shoulder at Tremaine.

She leaned over from the side of the bed and grabbed the receiver. "Hello."

"Is this the room of Rico Adams?"

"Yes it is. May I ask who's calling?"

"Dr. Lexington."

Tremaine carried the phone to Rico. "A doctor."

Rico took the receiver. "Hello."

"Rico, Rico, Rico. You apparently pray to a lot of gods."

"Well, I don't think no god is interested in personal prayers. What doctor am I speakin with?"

"Don't concern yourself with nametags; numbers are more important. Does the number 622,850 mean anything to you? How about 5,671,000?"

Rico stared at Tremaine.

"What on earth would a black guy want with that kinda money? Oversized rims for a car? Loud radio? Gold chains? A case of—"

"Man, what the fuck do you want? You got your shit off, but I bet you won't catch me slippin again."

Dan Kapata laughed. "I'm taking you up on that one. Unless you're interested in my offer."

"Offer your muthafuckin head, because that's what I'm after."

Tremaine's face held a look of confusion.

"If only I'd known that kid was in the truck with me."

"Listen, when I fuck you up, it won't have a damn thing to do with you shooting me. I'm fuckin you up for Sequerria and for even thinking about my son. Muthafucka!"

"Please don't kill me, Mr. Rico." Dan laughed again. "Can't we talk this over?"

Rico heard more laughter; it included another person in the background. "Keep sticking that neck out; I will get that ass, Dan."

"And I really hope you get well soon. But aside from

that, I think I have a way for you to get the property back to me that you stole. Do that, and we can call this war off."

"If I got anything that belong to you, then take it. Get it like Dracula." Rico walked up to the nightstand and slammed the receiver down on the telephone.

Tremaine stepped to him. "Why is he calling here? Can't they trace his call?"

"I heard static; he must be on a cell phone."

"You ready to tell me what happened between you and Dan?"

"We'll have the family discussion when you move in. But I don't think it's gonna be this Saturday; Dan probably knows where I live."

"I'm sure he does. He knew about your connection with Sequerria; he might know a lot more about you. But I still want us to live together."

"We will, but not right now, baby. I got the feeling a lot more shit is gonna jump off."

Trex entered the house and saw Lynn in the kitchen by the stove. He walked to the kitchen table and sat down.

"Are Tank and Roc gonna eat with us?"

"No. They're on the way to the hospital."

She turned the stove off and sat at the table with him. "What's wrong?"

"I don't know yet, but I'm sure you can help."

"I'm listening."

"Thomas, the guy you was fuckin with in Charlotte. You ever saw him in a blue Cutlass?"

Lynn thought about it. "Like an old model car?"

"Yeah. Maybe 1980 or somewhere around there."

"I've seen him in an old blue car before. What did—"

"Do you know whose car it is?"

"No. Some guy he hangs out with. Why?"

"I need to know your boyfriend's address."

"I thought you were my man."

"You know what I mean. Thomas. The Thomas guy."

"Trex, tell me what's going on?"

"I think your boyfriend is looking for me, and I wanna see what the fuck for."

"I...I thought you were through with all that street mess."

"I am, but I don't feel like the streets is through with me. I mean, ain't nobody got no business lookin for me, the world's number one street villain...retired street villain."

"I don't understand you. Almost a million and a half dollars later and you still got your mind on something stupid."

Trex sighed. "I need that address when you're finished protecting the guy who's probably looking to smash me."

"I'm not protecting him, Trex. I just don't want you to get in any trouble."

"And I love you, too, Lynn. Now give up that address; I promise I'll let you chastise me later."

"Come in."

Greenburg entered room 409. "You're alone?"

"No. Somebody's under the damn bed."

Greenburg's eyes shifted, and he could see that clearly no one was under the bed.

"I didn't call you for your company. You wanna talk or what?"

"Yeah. Let's take a walk to the lobby."

"Fuck that. You know I gotta shake you for a recorder

or a wire first."

Greenburg threw his hands up. "So long as you return the favor."

Rico walked closer and frisked him thoroughly.

"You seem well enough to leave this place."

Rico threw his hands up. "You do, too, but I see you rushed your ass over here anyway."

Greenburg smiled then pat-searched Rico's hospital garments.

They walked to the fourth-floor lobby and sat in the corner near an imitation tree-like plant. "You wanted a million in cash, but I want you to tell me what you plan to give me for that type of money."

"The gun that they found on you when you were in the driveway trying to die—there's nothing I can do about that."

"Then why did you bring the shit up? I don't have a record; possession of a handgun carries what, two, three days? Just tell me what's for sale."

"My help, of course. Right now, I'm probably the only cop who even suspects you in all that Vegas shit."

"And how did you get to be so damn special?"

"Well, I wouldn't call it special...Actually there's one other cop that knows, but, you know—"

Rico watched an old man moving along with the help of a walker. "This the last time I'm askin you, what the fuck is your million-dollar evidence?"

Greenburg hesitated. "The Acura, the money trans-fers—all of that came from Rock Hill. So did you. Me and my partner got a digital image constructionist working with a photo that comes from the Department of Motor Vehicles. Wanna guess whose photo?"

"No. I don't wanna guess; I just want you to keep talking till you satisfy me with your evidence."

"Alright. Working with your photo, the construction-ist can add on the bifocals and the braids; he can remove the necessary facial hair to get a good matching image of the casino photos and the Segron Bank photos."

Rico stared Greenburg in the eyes. "That ain't shit. What the fuck can that prove?"

"I don't think you want the jury to decide what that proves. Forget the theft, you got charges in Vegas that range from car jacking to murder. The gamble in the casino might have paid off, but you don't wanna gamble with a trial."

"Trials don't scare me. I always think I can win at whatever I do."

"Now there's a conflict of interest, because prosecutors feel the same way as you. And I have *never* met one who didn't cheat to win."

Silence.

"Most times I try to be honest as a cop, until I'm deal-ing with criminals." Greenburg smiled.

Rico smiled, too. He was thinking about Trex.

CHAPTER 22

The sound of the doorbell at two in the morning was followed by silence and contemplation. Thomas Baker watched the black man through the peephole. Thomas turned to his two partners in the apartment then gestured the number 5 and the letter O with a hand.

The doorbell rang again.

Guns were stuffed under sofa cushions and between the sofa crevices; drugs were whisked away on newspapers; and the scales were rushed to the kitchen.

The doorbell.

"Who is it?" Thomas knew the cop had heard the scampering inside.

The visitor held a badge up close to the peephole. "Lieutenant Dover, homicide division." He began adjusting the squelch on the two-way radio.

"It's two in the morning; what the hell you waking me

up for?"

"You can either step outside and answer a few questions concerning the homicide of Lynn Gardner or I can get a warrant to enter in a matter of minutes over the radio."

Somebody killed Lynn? Thomas understood now why the cops wanted to question him. He scanned the living room, making sure nothing illegal was in plain view. One partner was on the sofa; the one in the matching chair was channel-surfing a muted television with a remote. Thomas unlocked the door and opened it.

Tank never gave him a chance to step forward. He pushed Thomas backward with all of his strength, dropping the two-way radio, and drawing a gun on the guy on the sofa.

Trex had poured in directly behind Tank with a gym bag, aiming his gun at the man in the matching chair. Trex had been crouched to the left of the door, anxious to get inside. He pushed the door closed with his elbow and dropped the gym bag. "Everybody, get your ass on the couch, and keep your hands on top of your head. And I forgot to say police, freeze. Watch these damn criminals, Lieutenant." Trex walked down the hall and began searching each room.

Tank watched the other two men get situated on the sofa. When they were seated, he sat on the arm of the matching chair.

Thomas had recognized Trex. He looked at Tank. "I shoulda knew you wasn't a damn cop."

"Don't make no difference, I can still shoot like one from this close range."

Trex returned, grinned at the three men on the sofa, and stepped in the kitchen to scan the area. He saw the digital scale in the sink and returned to the living room, considering his next move.

Without warning, Mac, the sofa guy closest to Trex, was smacked on the forehead with the side of Trex's gun.

Every man on the sofa flinched.

Mac leaned forward, trying to stop the blood by pressing his hands against his forehead.

Trex tapped him on the back. "Take some of that blood to the other end of the couch. Trade spots with your man on the end."

Mac got up and walked to the other end.

4X hesitantly got up and traded seats, hands still on top of his head.

Tank watched quietly, knowing Trex would do something crazy.

"Now, who the fuck was driving that raggedy-ass Cutlass out there, looking for me, a violent-ass muthafucka name Trex?"

No answer.

Trex looked at Tank.

Tank smiled. "Hope you don't think I know who was driving."

"I don't know who the fuck told y'all not to talk to strangers, but I'm about to establish my presence up in this muthafucka." Trex headed for the kitchen again.

Tank heard Trex rambling in a kitchen drawer. "I don't know why y'all didn't answer that crazy fucka."

Thomas could feel the Uzi underneath the center cushion.

Trex opened another drawer and saw the cocaine. He ignored it and grabbed the largest kitchen knife.

Thomas imagined swinging the Uzi out from underneath, clearing the whole goddamn room in one grand sweep.

Trex entered the living room, turned toward 4X, and swiftly fed seven inches of the knife into his chest. Trex left the knife in the man's chest then took a seat on the love seat, propping his feet on the coffee table.

They all watched 4X struggle with imminent death as he gripped the knife in a failed attempt to remove it. He keeled over onto the arm of the sofa and continued to breathe but with much difficulty.

"Now, you see? Don't think I'm soft for not shootin him; he had a damn good reason for taking his hands down." Trex watched the dying man. "I might...uh...need to get that knife back when you're done playing with it."

Thomas looked away; he couldn't bear the sight of his best friend fighting helplessly for life.

"Let me try this again. Who was driving that blue Cutlass out there?"

Mac looked at 4X. "The guy that you just stabbed."

Trex looked at Tank. "Lieutenant, I want you to suspend that muthafucka's license." He turned to Thomas. "You came to Rock Hill to kill me? Where do y'all keep the goddamn guns at?"

"We don't keep guns in the apartment."

"You got probably two keys of coke in a damn kitchen drawer, and you tellin me y'all ain't got guns up in this muthafucka?"

"The guns make it federal."

"You're a fonky-ass lie; the feds make it federal."

4X's pager sounded off.

Trex smiled. "He's dead serious about that money, huh?" He got up and retrieved the gym bag.

4X released the knife and died with his eyes open.

Trex walked over and snatched the knife from the man's chest and kept stepping toward the other end of the sofa. He stopped in front of Mac. "Lead the way to the bathroom. We gotta get you cleaned up."

Mac got up, hands still on his head, eyes on the knife in Trex's hand. He headed for the bathroom with an eerie feeling that he was about to get stabbed in the back.

When Trex and Mac were in the bathroom, Tank got up from the arm of the matching chair, placed the gun on the coffee table, and retrieved the remote control. He sat in the matching chair and began surfing through the channels.

Thomas glanced at the gun on the table. He wasn't about to go for it; he thought it might be a set up. However, he thought this might be a good time to get the Uzi from under the cushion.

Tank watched the television. He could hear the beard trimmers running in the bathroom. The slightest movement of the man on the sofa was within Tank's peripheral view.

The scramble. Thomas urgently went for the Uzi.

Tank kicked the coffee table, banging it against Thomas's legs, sending the handgun to the floor.

Thomas pushed up from the cushion and snatched the Uzi.

Tank pulled a silenced handgun from the rear of his waistband.

Thomas now had possession of the Uzi but it was upside down and backward; the necessary time for re-handling could not be considered.

Tank shot him once in the shoulder.

Thomas let out a loud moan and dropped the Uzi on the end cushion.

Trex peeped down the hallway and saw Tank retrieving the large gun from the sofa.

"Keep doing what you're doing, Trex; I got this." Tank dropped the Uzi on the love seat. "Let me get that up off you. And don't yell out like that again; you got neighbors tryin to sleep."

Thomas leaned back, holding his shoulder just below the wound, and made a grieving face as the blood flowed. He clinched his teeth as if it would ease the pain.

Tank heard what sounded like someone falling to the floor, and he knew that the sound had come from the bathroom.

The trimmers had fallen to the floor and had gone silent when one of the batteries ejected. Trex walked from the bathroom with the knife in one hand, gun in the other, and stopped in front of Thomas. "Didn't I tell you to keep your fuckin hands on top of your head?" Trex rushed the knife into the right side of Thomas's chest and left it there.

Thomas let out another loud yell, easily waking two of his neighbors.

Someone banged on the wall from the adjacent apartment.

Trex gabbed him by the neck with both hands. "I finally got over the fact that you called me soft." He paused, watching the victim tug at his wrists. "This is for rollin up on me while playin the fuckin radio."

Carrielli wore a baseball cap and a hooded raincoat when he entered the convenience store. He had the hood pulled over the cap, with its drawstring tied underneath his chin.

Dan waited in the driver's seat of the Volvo at a gas pump. He could hear the rain beating down on the top of the gas pump island.

Carrielli placed a twenty-dollar bill on the counter. "I'm in the Volvo, pump number four." He walked toward the drink cooler.

The cashier slipped the money in his pocket. He knew a trick with pump number four. He could activate that pump without entering an amount into the computer. "Raining hard enough for you?"

"I love it. The rain is a good time to come out."

Dan saw the green light flash on top of the gas pump. He got out and started pumping gas into the Volvo.

Carrielli placed a case of beer on the counter and walked toward the back of the store.

The cashier checked his watch. "I don't think everyone loves it. When it rains like this, business gets slow."

Carrielli thought southern people were too social. He was still amazed at how the door of a convenience store stayed open to customers at this time of morning. He grabbed two boxes of Ritz Crackers and was looking for some squeeze cheese.

Tank and Trex pulled up to the front of the store in a stolen Mazda RX7. Trex looked at Tank. "You parked at the door of this muthafucka like we're legal."

"Better than parking on the side like we ain't. We can wait here till the rain slacks up. Go in and buy something, and take your time so we'll have a reason to be parked here."

"You must be crazy. I know you see all this blood on my clothes."

Tank shook his head. "You don't feel bad about stabbin them dudes?"

"No, but I woulda felt bad if they woulda found me

and shot my ass up in Rock Hill."

"You know what? I think you're goin crazy."

"No, you don't. You knew I was coming to take care of that before we left Rock Hill."

"At the time, I was hoping you wouldn't have to smash nobody but Thomas."

"When you finish stalling, get me a soda and a candy-bar—any kind."

Tank cracked the door open. "You know I got a mean interest rate."

Dan stopped pumping at $20.09. He had thought the pump would shut itself off at an even twenty. He saw the taillights go out on the Mazda RX7. His eyes cut to the right, and he watched the police car pull onto the lot.

Tank closed the door and stayed in the car. The rain was pouring harder now, but he could still make out the vehicle that had parked three and a half feet away from Trex's door. "Keep looking at me. I think a Pineville police car just parked beside us."

"You *think*?"

"Oh, it's a fuckin police car; I can't tell if it's Pineville or not. Get your ass out and ask him."

"It ain't gonna happen. I take your word."

Dan got back in the Volvo and pulled up on the driver's side of the Mazda RX7.

Carrielli saw the cop enter the store. He looked away and considered shooting the cop and the cashier, but there was no way to tell if there was another cop outside waiting. He saw the Volvo pull up to the front, headlights still on. He didn't know if Dan was trying to tell him something that he didn't already know. Carrielli could hear the cop and the cashier talking as if they had known one another for years. He looked up at the security mirror in the corner of the store and knew that the cop would not recognize him with all the rain gear on.

Tank and Trex watched the cashier and the policeman look in their direction. "What are you sittin here for? Pull off."

Tank gripped the handbrake. "I don't want the cop to get suspicious. I know the clerk probably told him that we haven't came in yet."

"How the fuck do you know all that? Back this car up out of here before we get in some shit."

Tank released the hand brake, and the Mazda rolled backward.

Carrielli brought four items up to the counter and gave the cashier another twenty-dollar bill.

"I'm gonna need to see some ID for the beer."

Carrielli removed the doctored driver's license from his wallet and gave it to the cashier.

The policeman watched Carrielli. "I don't think he can get a good look at you with that hood hiding most of your face. You could be a big nineteen-year-old." The policeman laughed.

Carrielli's eyes shifted toward the glass front. There was no one else in the police car.

Tank stopped the Mazda when a pick-up truck entered the lot and blocked his path.

The driver of the truck banged on the horn. "You can't just back out into the street, asshole!"

The policeman turned his attention toward the sound of the horn. "I hope that's not a fender bender. With my luck, it probably is."

Tank shifted the stick and drove toward the other side

to exit the lot.

The policeman rushed out of the store and displayed a hand that commanded the driver of the Mazda to stop.

Tank drove past the police, ignoring him.

The policeman got inside his cruiser.

Trex looked back and saw the blue lights pulsing. "Stop the car."

"I'm not stopping shit."

Trex jerked the handbrake up and opened the door. The car was still moving.

Tank shifted to neutral and stepped on the brakes.

Trex got out of the car and fired two silenced shots at the police car before it could back out of the parking space. One of the shots had hit the back tire. *Good enough.* He got back in the Mazda.

Tank quickly released the handbrake but was held up by a passing station wagon.

The policeman got out of the cruiser and returned fire, hitting the rear end of the Mazda three times; the fourth shot flattened the back tire.

CHAPTER 23

The driver of the truck backed out of the parking lot, in the pouring rain, and got missing.

Carrielli left the goods at the counter and rushed to the door.

Dan tapped the horn from inside the Volvo. "Get your ass outta there!"

The policeman was crouched behind his cruiser; he was waiting for some action from the Mazda. He grabbed his two-way radio and called for back up.

Tank made a sharp turn and parked on the other side of the store.

Trex opened the door and ran up to the corner of the store. He peeped around and fired another silenced shot, breaking the front passenger window of the police car.

Tank got out of the car and rushed up to Trex. "Hold

this end down; I'll go around back and come up on the other side of that Volvo. That might be our only ride out of here."

Carrielli watched the crouched policeman. He eased out of the store.

The policeman saw him. "Get back inside! Now!"

Carrielli kept moving on the walkway, headed for the Volvo.

Trex peeped around the corner again. He aimed at the leg of the customer in the hooded raincoat. He pulled the trigger twice.

Tank stood at the opposite corner. He glanced around the corner and saw the man in the raincoat fall to the concrete walkway. He hadn't heard a gunshot over the rain, but he knew it was Trex's work.

Dan watched Carrielli fall but couldn't understand why. He opened the driver's door and rushed toward him, gun in hand.

Tank had heard the car door open. He pulled back behind the corner then glanced again. The driver of the Volvo was scampering toward the body on the walkway.

Trex fired another shot, breaking the rear passenger window of the police car.

Tank hunched over and raced quietly toward the opened car door, hoping not to get hit by one of Trex's random shots.

Carrielli lay on the walkway in pain. He turned himself over, with Dan's help, then pulled a handgun from the large pocket of the raincoat.

The policeman raised and fired three shots at Trex's corner of the building.

Trex saw the Volvo rolling backward. He backed away from the corner of the store and ran wide.

Carrielli shot the policeman twice.

Dan saw the Volvo rolling backward, but he didn't see anyone inside. He thought the car must have slipped out of gear. He considered going after the car but the sound of the sirens snapped him out of it. He hurried over to the policeman and picked his gun up from the pavement. He crept to the corner of the store and fired two shots at whoever was on the side. He peeked around the corner.

Nobody.

He ran back to Carrielli, helped him up, and struggled to get him to the police car. The flat tire would at least get them out of the area.

Tank stopped the Volvo in the middle of the street. He leaned over and opened the passenger door.

Trex got inside. "What are you waiting on, Judgment Day?"

Tank drove away, headed for the interstate. "I saw the man in the raincoat fall; I didn't even hear the gun."

"I shot for the legs. I thought the cop was gonna rush over and try to help."

"That shit only happens in the movies."

"I was long gone and I still heard the cop let off four more shots."

"I can't believe you shot at somebody's legs."

"Shit, I thought if I woulda shot to kill, the cop would simply let the muthafucka lay there. Plus I thought that might be a woman, couldn't tell."

Tank drove cautiously, but the windshield wipers were a lot better than the wipers on the Mazda. "I'm glad I didn't have to shoot the driver or the cop."

Trex began rambling through the glove compartment. "Leaving witnesses ain't a good idea. I gets my shit off."

"Yeah, but I don't just kill a muthafucka just because I

got a gun. It's better to stay low-key in a crime."

"Low-key your ass; you better hope that driver can't describe your face to a sketch artist."

"The driver didn't see me. I didn't jack the car; he got out when you shot whoever was in the raincoat. I guess they was together."

Trex opened the console box. "Look at the good shit I found."

Tank looked inside the console and saw the two handguns. "This must be an undercover car."

"I think they was gonna rob the store, or maybe another spot."

Tank smiled. "Everybody ain't a criminal like you."

"Try not to hurt my feelings." Trex checked the clip on each gun. "Loaded." He slid the seat back and searched underneath with a hand. He pulled out an AK-47 assault rifle. "This look like some undercover shit to you?"

Tank glanced at the rifle. "No barrel, no—"

"Nothing extra. This muthafucka got broke down to a big-ass pistol that can cut through an elephant's ass." Trex stared at Tank.

"Either the rain is slackin up or it just wasn't raining that hard in this area."

"You know what? That was Dan Kapata and the other muthafucka who they accused of breakin him out of jail."

"You done fell out of the tree. The shit you saw in the glove compartment got Dan's name on it?"

"Hell no. But you remember Dan was broke out by somebody using a pistol-grip AK or whatever kind of machine gun."

Tank glanced at the gun again. "You know how many AKs is on the street? Even pistol-grip."

Trex looked in the back seat. It was empty. "It might

be a bunch of AK pistol-grips, but I bet it ain't no bunch of white dudes riding around in a Volvo with handguns in the console, a big AK under the seat, and something like a dozen clips in the floor in the back."

"Damn! That'll be some shit if we got Dan's ride."

"You think they're hiding out in Pineville somewhere?"

"Only if this is Dan's ride. But I thought they used an M-16 for the jail."

"The car is registered to somebody name Adreanna Blackmon. You know it must be stolen, but it don't make sense to ride around in a stolen car with all this shit in it."

"Unless whoever they stole it from ain't around to report it stolen."

"What state is the license plate?"

Tank shrugged. "Fuck if I know. And they probably was on the way to rob something—and I ain't talking about no damn convenience store."

"Maybe they was on the way to Rock Hill. Rico talked to Dan on the phone; they coulda been on the way to the hospital."

Tank did not respond.

Trex reclined the seat and yawned.

Tank pulled out a cellular phone and gave it to Trex.

"What...Where did you get this from? The apartment back there?"

"I bought it yesterday. It's a prepaid throw-away. Call Lynn and get her to meet us in the Waffle House parking lot in Fort Mill. Tell her to just park; we'll come to the car."

Trex dialed his home number; the phone rang twice.

"Hello."

"You don't sound like you was sleeping."

"I'm waiting on you to get in. I'm hoping you haven't done any—"

"Lynn, not right now. Get in your car and drive to the Waffle House in Fort Mill. If you leave when you hang up, we might get there at the same time."

"I'm on my way, but I'm telling you, Trex..." She held the receiver for a few more seconds then hung up.

Trex raised the back of the seat up. "What if a police car is in the lot?"

"We pull up to the cop and turn ourselves in. Kinda question is that? I just keep on going and stop at another spot."

"I wanna get everything outta this car and put it in Lynn's car. No tellin what's in the muthafuckin trunk."

"Call Lynn back and tell her to forget the Waffle House. Have her meet us at—"

"I'm dialing now. Meet us where?"

Silence.

"In the rear parking lot of the—"

"Lynn, forget the Waffle House." Trex looked at Tank.

Tank hesitated. "Tell her to stay by the phone; you'll call her back."

"I heard him." Lynn hung up again.

Trex was confused. "What the hell are you up to?"

"We're keepin the car and stashing it."

"What's the purpose?"

"I think the Volvo could make a good casket. It's coming fully equipped with Dan and his partner's prints."

Trex thought about it. "That's a nice-ass cross." He thought about it some more. "So, you agree this must be Dan's ride?"

"All this firepower up in this...muthafucka—don't nothing else make sense."

"Sometimes I wish I could kill certain muthafuckas twice."

Tank shook his head. "Boy, you're pitiful. When you get to hell, the devil might let you run that shit."

"He might as well, or he can get fucked up, too."

Rico and Roc were in the hospital room eating breakfast from McDonald's. Tremaine had dropped Roc off with the breakfast and had left for her appointment at the hair salon. Roc sat in the chair, legs swinging, sipping orange juice.

"I got a question for you, Roc."

"What question?"

"What do you wanna be when you get big?"

Roc placed the orange juice on the nightstand. "Make a lot of money."

"You can't just say that. What kinda job you wanna have to make money?"

"I don't want no damn job. You said I don't supposed to work for people; I'm supposed to have people workin for me."

"You're right. I said that. But before you can have people workin for you, how do you plan to get the money to get your company started?"

"From you?"

Rico laughed. "What make you think I got that kinda money. It takes a lot of money to get a company started."

"Well, you still owe me two thousand dollars. I can start a company with that."

"That ain't as much money as you think it is. But you got the right idea." Rico took a bite of the sausage biscuit.

"Dad, why you don't have no company?"

"Messin with too many women, and I didn't focus on

money when I was young like you. By the time I knew how to make money, I only used it to impress women."

"You did the same thing with Tremaine?"

"No. I met Tremaine in a grocery store. I was eating grapes and she was getting oranges. She asked me why I was stealing, and I said because I didn't wanna go through the trouble of robbing the store for no damn grapes. She laughed, and it was on from there."

"Well, why do you steal and you told me not to?"

"This the truth, Roc. I steal for two reasons...I mean, I don't steal no more. But I used to steal for two reasons: one, the money is faster—if you can find some good shit to steal; and two, I stole so you wouldn't have to."

Roc ate tater tots.

"You gonna be a businessman; you know what I want you to start working on?"

"What?"

"The way you talk. That means I gotta talk better, too."

"What kinda talk?"

"What they call proper English. Like, we can't be leavin the G off the end of our words all the time. See how I said *leavin*?"

"It shoulda been *leaving*."

"That's right. And you can't be sayin *shoulda*."

"It shoulda been *should have*."

Rico laughed. "You already know this stuff."

"My momma be tellin me the—"

"Your momma be *telling*."

"...be telling me the same thing."

"Good. When you're a businessman, it's good to know how to talk both ways. You can relate to more people, and more people can relate to you."

Roc sipped more orange juice.

"Now, let me teach you about investments—makin your money grow."

"*Making*."

"You got me. And that's part of your investment plan. Every time I say a sentence around you with improper English, I owe you a dollar. When you say one, you owe me a dollar. Deal?"

"Wait a minute, before we start. That mean we can't even curse no more?"

Rico stared at Roc and smiled. "Hell no! We won't take the shit that damn far." They laughed.

CHAPTER 24

"Come to the hospital alone. And bring an empty suit-case or shopping bag—something large enough to hold the money."

Greenburg lowered the volume of the receiver. "Who am I speaking to?"

"You got less than fifteen minutes to get there or else the agreement between you and the patient is off. Bring any company, it's off. Come wired, it's off."

"Do I come inside with the bag or wait in the lot?"

"Just get to the hospital; the man with the money will see your Pathfinder when you arrive." Trex slammed the receiver down on the pay phone. He got in Lynn's car and drove to the hospital.

Tank entered room 409. "You ready?" He walked up to

the window and studied the parking lot.

"Yeah. I ain't got shit to pack. Tremaine got my clothes in her car."

"I thought Roc was here."

"Tremaine picked him up about thirty minutes ago, and I'm glad."

"Why?"

"We got a little bet going, and he's fuckin me up with it."

Tank shook his head. "I don't even wanna know what it is. Let's go."

"I'm waitin on the phone to ring. Trex was supposed to call Greenburg to set it up; I know Greenburg gonna call me to check up on it."

"He won't call. He's on his way to get that money."

The phone rang.

Rico picked up and hesitated. "Studio."

"Did you send for me to pick up?"

"Of course I did. The shit is waitin on you. Hurry your ass up." Rico hung up. "I hate when you're wrong. You look so crazy."

"Yeah, but I'm rich, so I don't give a damn."

"Finish telling me about the Volvo. Trex told me a little bit a few hours ago, but he was talking in tongue, damn near, because Roc was here."

"Did y'all catch it on the news?"

"Yeah. They don't know much, though."

"The Volvo had a North Carolina license plate; we switched that with a South Carolina plate. We found two hand grenades under the driver's seat; the AK, the two handguns, the map of Pineville—all that shit was inside the car. We didn't find shit in the trunk."

"I hope y'all didn't handle the map."

"Didn't have a reason to. We put all that shit in a bag and stashed it. We looked at the map to see if they made any markings on it. They didn't."

"I wanna use a magnifying glass and some talc powder to check it for prints. That's why I hope y'all didn't handle the map with a lot of touching."

"Just on the edges where anybody would hold it. What the fuck are you gonna do with a fingerprint?"

"When people find a spot that they're trying to get to on a map, they usually finger the section. Might be a big area, but it's something to work with."

"Get out of here with that Sherlock shit."

Rico laughed. "Let's go." They walked out of the room. "That's some weird shit how you and Trex came across Dan."

"I wish I woulda knew that was him. I woulda shot till my finger cramped up."

"You know what? I think...I don't see no reason for Dan to need a Pineville map. That belongs to the jailbreaker from out of town. Pineville is a rock-throw from Rock Hill, and Dan probably knows his way around."

Tank stepped inside the elevator. "The cops think Dan is with Carrielli. So what if it is Carrielli's map?"

Rico entered the elevator and waited for the door to close. "That means our guess about them hidin out...hiding out in Pineville must be accurate."

"I don't think Dan is staying in Pineville after that shit at the Pineville convenience store. The cop identified him, and I know they thought they killed the cop."

"I don't think Trex need to be driving that Volvo around; they mentioned the style and color on the news."

"It's parked for the moment, and it's already downstairs in the lot."

Tremaine and Roc walked out of the designer shop with a decorated red velvet cake in a box. "Roc, I need you to sit in the back with the cake to make sure it doesn't move."

"I ain't never taste a red velvet cake before."

"Best cake in the world. We're gonna stop and get a gallon of ice cream and take it all to your daddy's house to surprise him."

"My daddy keep too much stuff in the refrigerator; that big box won't fit."

"I'll make room. Most of that stuff in there is probably bad now."

"We'll be there when he come home?"

"Yep. I'm trying to hurry so he won't beat us there."

Rico was sitting inside the Lexus when Greenburg arrived in the Pathfinder. He flashed the headlights. The sunny day reduced the effect, but he had still caught Greenburg's attention.

Greenburg parked several spaces down from the Lexus and got out, leaving the Pathfinder running. He had two folded plastic shopping bags in his hand and was dressed in summer clothes—shorts, T-shirt, sneakers, and a ball cap. He had a gun in the rear waistband of his jean shorts.

Rico saw him coming. He lowered the window when Greenburg was only two cars away. "Don't stop at this car; keep walking until you come to the Volvo about eight cars down. The money is in the back seat. Get it and keep going. And don't try to keep my fuckin suitcases." Rico raised the window and pulled off to circle the hospital.

Tank eased inside of Greenburg's Pathfinder and

waited for the signal.

Trex sat behind the wheel in the Volvo. He took a deep breath and released slowly. He watched Greenburg's casual steps.

Greenburg saw the Volvo, all four windows lowered. He saw the black guy inside with his head against the head-rest. A few steps more and he recognized the guy as Rico's friend from one of the hospital visits.

"Get in the back, get your money, and get the fuck on."

Greenburg walked to the driver's door. "Nice car. You and Dan share the same salesman?"

"Save the silly cop jokes. Get your shit so I can go."

Greenburg smiled then looked in the back seat. He saw the opened suitcase and the hundred-dollar bills. He opened the door to the back seat and sat inside, one foot still on the pavement.

"Close the damn door."

"I don't think so. This is fine." He opened one of his shopping bags and tried to grab a handful of the money. He discovered that only the top layer was real, somehow pasted to a large, single sheet of paper.

Trex turned and extended the silenced handgun to Greenburg's chest and fired three times.

Greenburg released the sheet of money and fell over, his head resting in the suitcase.

Trex retrieved the sheet of money from the seat. "You know you can't take this with you when you die." He put the sheet in the front seat then turned toward the back again. He pulled Greenburg's leg inside and closed the door. He raised the power windows, started the car, and waited for the Lexus to come back around.

Rico drove past the Volvo. He checked his rearview

mirror, noticing the Volvo pulling out to catch up.

Trex checked his rearview mirror and saw the Pathfinder pulling out. "And I thought you was a bad person, Greenburg. You ain't been dead two minutes, and you already got three cars in the funeral line—whatever you call that shit." Trex looked back at Greenburg and thought he saw him breathing. He held the handgun close to Greenburg's head and pulled the trigger. "You trying to make me out of a liar?" Trex placed the gun in the front seat. "Now, just so you won't think *I'm* a bad person, when I park this muthafucka I'll leave the moonroof open so you can get some air, and I'll even leave the radio on so you can lay back with *The Tom Joyner Morning Show* tomorrow. And that's being nice, because everybody already know...I usually don't play the muthafuckin radio."

Tank followed the Volvo. He watched Trex and wondered about him. Trex seemed to enjoy killing, and Tank thought Trex might be losing his mind or something. *I'm glad that crazy muthafucka is on my side.*

Rico waited on Trex and Tank to get in the Lexus.

Trex walked out of the woods first; Tank was only a few yards behind. Trex got in the front passenger seat and sighed. "Do you know how sleepy I am?"

"Real sleepy." Tank got in the back and stretched out as much as he could in the seat. "Wake me up when we get to the first restaurant in Rock Hill."

Rico drove off. He glanced at Trex. "It might be a few days before somebody goes inside the Charlotte apartment. I hope y'all spread the evidence just like I explain to—"

Tank yawned. "We ain't got to explain how we put your weak-ass plan in effect; catch that shit on the news."

Rico's eyes shifted to find Tank in the rearview mirror. "Put some close on your mouth before I put that ass out."

Tank laughed. "You must be crazier than Trex."

Trex turned to face Tank. "Shit, I got good sense. I ain't even close to crazy."

Tank sat up. "Trex, you just killed four muthafuckas and shot a fifth one in the legs in less than..." Tank looked at the clock in the dashboard—2:14 p.m. "Just say about twelve hours. And you ain't even fucked up about it."

"What do you want me to do, cry? You think everybody that kills is crazy?"

"I didn't say that. I said *Trex* was crazy. Plus you killed Westwood at the restaurant, Dave at the computer shop, and Mark in the country—"

"But name just one of them that I was supposed to let live."

"That ain't my point, Trex. Maybe all of them needed to die. You just seem like you enjoy the shit."

Trex laughed. "I do enjoy the shit. When a muthafucka cross me or somebody that I fucks with, I like gettin some get back. That don't make me crazy; that make me human."

Rico smiled. The conversation was entertaining.

"Everybody likes revenge." Tank yawned again. "But everybody don't get carried away with it."

"Sometimes I say some crazy shit; sometimes I do some crazy shit. I ain't crazy, though."

"You're right; you just said some crazy shit."

Rico laughed.

Trex looked at Rico. "What the hell is you laughing at? You smashed Norman in the country."

"And I'll smash a thousand more fuckin Normans if they break in on my son. I'll kill a muthafucka if they cross *you,* Trex. But me and you probably got different definitions for the word *cross*. To me, it means somebody is trying to kill you, get you locked up, or threatening your well-being."

"You kill for your reasons, and I'll kill for mine." Trex turned to Tank again. "If I didn't have a reason to kill somebody, could you name one other thing that make you think I'm crazy?"

Tank thought about the question, but he couldn't think of a good answer. "Probably not, but the pleasure you seem to get from killing tells me you're crazy as hell anyway." He laughed.

Trex looked at Rico. "I know you wanna laugh, too, you blockhead fucka."

Rico burst out laughing.

Tremaine parked the Honda in Rico's driveway. Roc got out and unlocked the front door using Tremaine's new key; Tremaine grabbed the box from the back seat. He stood on the small porch, holding the storm door open for her.

Tremaine entered the house and headed for Rico's kitchen.

Roc jumped from the porch and ran for the mailbox. He removed two pieces of mail from the box and studied the envelopes. One was addressed to his father but had no return address. The other was addressed to his uncle and was from the telephone company. Roc folded the mail and put it in his back pocket. He ran toward the front door, preparing to jump to the porch.

Tremaine dried her hands on the bathroom towel. She walked to the kitchen again and smiled at the box on the table. She stepped to the refrigerator and opened the right half of the double doors.

The electrical spark.

She had no time to perceive the pain, to reflect on her life, or to say a prayer.

The explosion punished the kitchen and threw a portion of her body through the large kitchen window. The wall separating the kitchen and the living room was destroyed, and the force easily smashed out the living room window.

Roc was attacked by glass particles and small debris. He fell to the ground, confused. He picked himself up and backed away, veering toward Tremaine's car. He watched maybe a fifth of the house burn intensely. He yelled for Tremaine. He screamed for Tremaine. He cried for Tremaine. He got inside the Honda and kept banging his fist against the horn. His eyes leaked. His nose ran. His cuts bled. He clinched his teeth and banged the horn even harder. "Tremaine, *please* get out of the house!" Someone would have to make the child give up.

CHAPTER 25

Tank sat beside Rico on the airplane. He had always known Rico to be afraid of flying, but this flight didn't really bother him. Rico seemed to be sleeping peacefully next to the window. Tank nudged him. "Wake up. The pilot said fifteen minutes to landing."

Rico pulled away from the window and shifted in his seat. He sighed and wiped the corner of his eyes with a thumb and an index finger.

Tank passed him some cashews. "Try some."

Rico began eating the cashews one at a time. "I had a bad-ass dream."

"About what?"

"I dreamed Grandma was at Tremaine's funeral...and she cursed me out in front of everybody."

"But Grandma ain't even mad at you; Roc is the only one mad."

He pondered. "I know, but Grandma got a good reason to be mad."

"Maybe Roc do, too, but Grandma can sympathize with your loss. Roc is only thinking about the friend that *he* lost. And he think it's your fault."

"I called him everyday for the last eleven days and Chelsea said he won't even get on the phone."

"Let him have his way for a while. He just want you to feel bad as hell right now."

"Oh, so he thought my crying at the funeral was bullshit?"

"Nope. He probably didn't think it was enough punishment for you."

Rico stared at the remaining cashews in the bag. "I'll probably hurt inside over Tremaine for a long time, but I know I woulda went nuts if Roc woulda been in that house with her."

"Stop thinking about crazy shit. Get your mind ready for this meeting or else get your ass ready for prison."

Matt Christensen wore an expensive suit and carried an Italian leather casing with a laptop computer inside. The hostess of the Beverly Hills restaurant escorted him to the table.

Tank and Rico stood and greeted the young white man. They were the only ones in the restaurant wearing casual attire.

Matt sat the new leather casing next to his seat. "Gentlemen, let's talk business."

They all took a seat. Rico used two fingers to summon a waiter. He'd seen that gesture in a movie.

Matt only ordered wine. The discussion began after the waiter walked away. "You guys picked a nice restaurant, the Opulent Eve."

Rico looked around. "I read about it in a magazine. I thought you might like it."

"Oh, I do like it, but you can't always go by the stuff they put in mags."

Tank smiled with a toothpick between his lips. "Not even the shit we read about you?"

Matt laughed. "Especially the shit you read about me."

Rico feigned a laugh. "Mr. Christensen, we—"

"Please, call me Matt."

"Matt. We appreciate you takin...taking the time from your busy schedule to meet with us."

The waiter arrived with Matt's wine. He nodded at Tank and Rico then walked off again.

Rico leaned forward. "Are you familiar with the Robert Mayes scheme at the Nevada casino?"

"Only what's reported on the news. But my friends and I talk about that all the time."

"The cops think I'm connected to that scheme."

Matt stared at Rico. "How so?"

"They think I acted as Robert Mayes." Rico smiled.

"I don't understand. How can I help?"

Tank pushed Rico's compact disc across the table. "Everything is explained on the disc. We also—"

"Almost everything." Rico sipped at his wine. "We want you to freestyle with the digital images, we're still waiting to get a few more photos for you to work with."

"What do you mean by *freestyle*?"

"You know, whatever you think is best."

Matt stared at Rico. "You don't look like the Robert Mayes guy to me."

"Maybe I will at trial. I heard the cops was workin on my—working on my DMV picture."

"Have you been charged yet?"

"No. But I probably will be any day now."

Tank pulled the toothpick from his mouth. "Let's talk about your fees."

"I'd rather not. Let's talk about how much publicity the trial might receive." Matt smiled. "I have a new product nearly perfected. The attention could help us both."

Rico's eyes shifted to Tank then back to Matt. "It still seems fair to talk about the fees for your trouble."

"So far there's been no trouble; a discussion of the fees can wait. I just want to know how much time I have to work with the images."

"Well, like I said, I ain't even been charged yet. The state will end up working with the feds because the crime was federal. Whenever they decide to charge me, a trial should be within three to six months."

Matt finished off his glass of wine. "Give me a few weeks; I should know by then a fair price range."

Dan and Carrielli sat in the living room of the Pineville residence watching the news. Carrielli's left leg, wrapped in gauze just above the knee, was propped on the ottoman. He stared at the bandage. "Now everything is starting to make sense. The bullets plucked from the police car match those found in the shooting in the Charlotte apartment, so I'm sure they'll match up with the two you took out of my leg."

No response. Dan listened to the news anchor. A photo of Rico was being displayed on the screen as well as a photo from the Segron National Bank.

"If Rico is responsible for that Casino shit, then he could be the brains behind the bread trucks. Maybe he actually hired Caston."

"That sounds likely, but I hate to give that black son of a bitch so much credit."

"You think the cops really just want him for questioning?"

Dan looked at Carrielli. "Let's hope so. I'd hate for them to jail his ass before we could find out where he's staying."

"I'm still wondering how we ran into the other black guys at the store without..."

Dan got up when he heard the vehicle arriving. He barely parted the curtain, saw the Dodge Intrepid, then sat in the leather seat again.

Carrielli released his grip on the handgun in his waistband. "Perry?"

"Yeah. We can finally stock up on a few things."

Perry Kapata inserted a door key and opened the front door. "Anybody happy to see me?"

Carrielli smiled. "Only if you're sure the cops weren't watching you from Tennessee."

Perry closed the door. "You don't have to worry about that. My dad taught me all the tricks." He walked up to Carrielli and extended a hand.

Carrielli shook his hand.

"It's been a while, but I've heard so much about you recently."

"From your old man over there or the television?" Carrielli laughed.

"Both." Perry turned and walked toward his dad.

Dan stood and hugged his son. "I was worried about you. We expected you to arrive yesterday."

"After more than a hundred miles of driving I couldn't tell whether I was being followed. I thought I was, but I wasn't sure."

"So you turned around?"

"No. A woman I'm seeing had already driven my Intrepid to a hotel near the Georgia state line. I spent the night with her and switched cars with her at three in the morning."

Dan nodded with approval.

Perry sat on the sofa next to Carrielli. He looked at the gauze on the injured leg. "Can you walk at all?"

"Yeah, but it's sore as hell. Maybe two more weeks and I won't need the crutches."

Perry looked at Dan again. "Dad, you're in a lot of shit. What are your plans?"

"I'm not through with Rico yet."

"Rico? Is that the guy that you shot when you took the Suburban?"

"That's him."

Perry turned from Dan and stared at the curtains. "I can't believe you're worried about some petty loser. Mom told me everything you told her when you were in jail."

"Perry, the money—"

"You had nearly two million in the bank, dad. It makes no fucking sense."

"Perry, I was responsible for managing several million dollars for company executives. I gained that trust. That means a lot to me. Rico made the main offshore account disappear. There's no way I can just forget about that."

"Hey..." Carrielli gathered his crutches. "I'm going out back and enjoy the sun by the picnic table. Let you two have your father-and-son chat."

"Perry, I paid a million and a half to bust out of jail. These things are going to set me back for a while."

"Come on, Dad, I know you better than that."

Carrielli was up and moving toward the back door.

"Look, Perry, Rico Adams is the reason your goddamn uncle is dead. If me and Arnold had not been trapped inside—"

"I understand, and I'm sorry about what happened to Uncle Arnold."

Carrielli made it outside and closed the back door. He worked his way toward the picnic table.

Perry walked to the kitchen and saw Carrielli using the crutches. He returned to the living room and sat on the arm of the sofa. "And how could you pay him all of that money? You used to tell me about how close you were back in the days."

"It's business, Perry. Nothing is for free."

"Well if there's a price on friendship, who really needs it?"

"I watched him pay most of the money out to the three guys that helped him."

"And you fell for that? Dad, you're losing your..." He searched for a word but quickly gave up. "You're not thinking straight. You need to get rid of that extra weight in the backyard, first of all. Then, you need to move out of the country like mom said you had planned to do once you broke out of jail."

"Have you talked with your mother lately?"

"Yeah. She's fine. She said she made the whole thing up about the rape incident, thinking that was needed to justify killing the Caston guy."

Dan pretended to be interested in a commercial.

"So, what's the plan? You should leave the country and let me worry about Rico and what he did to Arnold."

"The cops will probably be all over him whenever—"

"I'm not even concerned with killing him now. I'd even wait several years then go after him. You taught me to be patient, but I don't think you are anymore."

"I didn't mean the cops were watching him; they're looking to question him about the theft that was pulled off in the Vegas casino. He could be in prison soon."

"So, the cops are helping you with some of your problems. Get out of the country, dad. If the cops leave anything for me, I'll clean it up. Rico is history either way."

Dan sighed. "What about your mother?"

"Start your life without her. Face it, Dad, you fucked up. But you still might be able to get situated again in another country, and you might be able to talk mom over a few years from now."

"I'm down to almost four hundred grand."

"You could live well with that. And you could also help me by setting up an account. I have some real estate proceeds in a corporate account. You could handle my offshore account for me." Perry glanced at the back door. "Where's Carrielli's share of the money that you paid him?"

"Why?"

"I think I can talk him into giving it back."

"No, you can't. And even if you could I wouldn't feel right accepting it."

"Is the money here?"

"Yeah, but I don't want—"

Perry got up and headed for the back door.

"Perry, the man deserves that damn money."

"If you hadn't told me that he was a good friend all those years, I would agree with you." Perry opened the back door and walked out.

Carrielli smiled as Perry approached him. "You and your old man work things out?"

"Mostly, but we still have one problem."

"Something I can help with?"

Perry sat at the picnic table across from Carrielli. "It's not quite a financial crisis; it's more like a money dilemma, but I believe you can help."

"What do you need?"

"First, I need to know why a friend would charge another friend in need. If those old Mafia stories were true, then you owe my dad for saving your life a few years after I was born."

Carrielli laughed. "That's true. Your dad did save my life...in 1982. But I had saved his life twice *before* that." Carrielli laughed again. "So, really, it's like I'm responsible for saving my own life."

Perry turned and looked at the trees. "Are you two friends or not?"

"I sure as hell hope so after what we've been through."

"Then give me the money back so I can help my dad get going in another country. I'll pay you back later—with interest."

"I'm wanted, too, Perry. Your father—"

"You've been a wanted man for the past eleven years. You have a lot of money, and you're not thinking about leaving the country."

"Perry, your dad has money in the bank. He could survive. I don't think his needs are any better than mine."

Perry traded stares with Carrielli. "So, I can't change your mind?"

"I don't think so."

Perry calmly pushed away from the table and got up

from the picnic bench.

Carrielli didn't like the nerve of Perry. He knew that Dan hadn't sent Perry to talk for him.

Perry lifted his shirt and removed a handgun from his waistband, aiming it at Carrielli's face.

Carrielli did not panic; he didn't have time to panic.

Perry pulled the trigger, disturbing the peace only slightly with the .22 caliber handgun. He had drawn the attention of no one on the outskirts of Pineville—except his father. Perry shot Carrielli in the face again before he could fall out of the picture.

The reactionary genius fell to the grass.

CHAPTER 26

Rico was greeted at the door by Chelsea. She invited him inside, and he sat on the sectional sofa.

"Where's your man?"

"None of your business. Did you rob that casino?"

He laughed. "None of your business."

She couldn't help but laugh. "Fuck you, Rico."

"Not right now; I got shit to do. Where the hell is my son?"

"He's upstairs. He's still mad at you." Rico got up from the sofa and rushed upstairs to Roc's bedroom. He eased the door open, without knocking, and saw his son lying across the bed asleep. Rico stepped over a dictionary and turned off the small television. He ripped a thin strip of paper from a tablet on the dresser then crept over to Roc. He gently twirled the paper near Roc's ear canal.

Roc swatted at his ear but was still sleeping.

Rico jerked the paper away. He smiled at Roc then toyed with his ear again.

Roc swatted again. He opened his eyes and looked up at his father. "What are you doin over here?"

"The hell you mean? And you owe me a dollar for dropping that G on *doing*."

Roc sat up in the bed. "I saw your picture on the news. You stole all that money from the casino?"

"I wish you wouldn't ask me shit like that. You know I don't like to lie to you."

"That means you took the money?"

"Yeah, I took the money, Roc."

"You goin—going to jail?"

"Probably. But they won't get that damn money back. I just wanna make sure you have everything you need. It don't matter what happen to me."

"But I don't want you to go to jail. Can't you just give all the money back?"

"No. It don't work like that. That's why I wanted to talk to you before I go to the police station."

"Why don't you run and live in New York somewhere?"

Rico palmed the back of Roc's head. "If I run, I'll always wonder how my trial woulda turned out."

"You owe me another dollar for the word *woulda*."

Chelsea knocked and entered.

Rico watched her approach Roc's bed. "Now if your man come home and catch your ass in the bedroom with me, I don't wanna have to scramble his egg."

Chelsea threw up a middle finger and ignored Rico. She sat on the opposite side of the bed. "Roc, I thought you were still mad at your daddy."

Rico held a fist up at Chelsea's face, and she batted it

away. "We was doing good; why did you have to bring that up?"

"Because Roc need to understand that he was wrong." Chelsea looked at Roc. "Tell your daddy about the letter."

Rico watched Roc. "What letter?"

Roc smiled and hesitated. "The letter I got out the mailbox at your house when me and Tremaine went there."

"I found the letter in the dirty clothes basket." Chelsea looked at Rico. "It was unopened, so I put it in my room on the dresser until you could come get it. Don't you know your bad-ass son went in my room and opened it after I asked him about it?"

"Who was the letter from?" Rico turned to Roc then to Chelsea.

Chelsea shrugged. "No return address and no name on the letter. It came somewhere from Arizona, according to the postmark. You got your little trick bunnies all over the world."

"Be nice if I could read my own damn letter and keep you two out my video."

"One of your hookers says she respect the fact that you chose to put Tremaine and Roc first in your life. From the letter, I could tell that you dissed her. She must be ugly, because you don't turn nothing down but the volume."

"Roc, go get my letter."

Roc headed for Chelsea's bedroom.

"It ain't in my room. Go downstairs and get it out of my car."

Rico waited until the door was closed. "Chelsea, I told you this before, but I want you to know how much I appreciate what you do for my son."

"You know he would still be mad at you if it wasn't for that letter."

"I woulda worked it out."

"Well your ass going to jail now. How do you plan to work that out?"

"You won't have to ever worry about money for him. He's set for life."

"Rico, what the hell...The boy needs his daddy. What the hell do you plan to do about that?"

"If I'm gone, I think he's strong enough to depend on his momma for five or six more years. He'll be a man in no time."

"Rico, I always like the fact that you were never selfish. You always have to be the one to look out for the people you care about—"

"Then explain why you left me?"

"You know why I left your sorry ass. I didn't want to be in your female committee."

"But you wasn't only a member, you was the president." He laughed, and she punched him in the shoulder. They could hear Roc running up the steps again.

Roc knocked at the door.

"Wait a minute, Roc; me and your momma is in here kissing."

"Roc, bring your ass in here. Don't pay attention to your lying-ass daddy."

Roc slowly opened the door.

"Put the letter on the dresser and put your skates on. Me and your momma about to do it in your bed."

Chelsea punched him in the same shoulder. "Stop talking like that around that boy."

Roc placed the letter on the dresser and backed out of the room. "Don't mess my bed up. Y'all can do it on the floor." He closed the door and smiled. He ran down the steps again.

Rico grinned. "So, you think I'm a terrible father?"

Chelsea laughed. "I think you're crazy, but I know you love your son. I just wish you showed him in a different way. All the money in the world can't..." She stared at him. "So, you did steal that money from the casino."

Rico licked his lips and leaned in closer to kiss her.

She held up a hand and gently clutched his face. "Nope. You know I don't fuck around."

Rico pulled back. "Okay. I'm going to jail for the next two hundred years, and you gonna wish you woulda gave me some."

"Whoever wrote you that letter might give you some before you go to jail."

Rico got up to get the letter from the dresser.

"She asked you a silly question at the end of the letter. *Why do WP always get the raw end of the deal in a gray relationship?*"

Rico read the letter. He knew it had been printed from a computer. "I don't know who the hell this is."

"Yeah, right."

He folded the letter and flung it across the room. "I need to check on Trex. He's looking real sad these days."

"Not because you're going to jail. That fool is coming right behind you."

"How dare you talk about my Christian brother like that."

Chelsea burst out laughing.

Rico smiled. He really enjoyed making her laugh. He walked up to her and stopped in front of her. "Stand up, Chelsea."

"For what?"

"Stand your ass up, and quit playing with me." He stared at her, without a smile this time.

Chelsea got up from the bed and was face to face with him.

Rico pulled her closer and hugged her; his head tilted over her shoulder. "Thank you for everything, Chelsea. You was more of a parent than I could ever be to Roc."

She was silent and motionless in his arms. Finally she hugged him. "I'm praying for you, Rico. I hope you don't go to jail."

He was motionless now. They released each other, and he stepped back to look in her face. She avoided eye contact. She couldn't let him see the water in her eyes.

Rico grabbed her chin and looked her in the eyes. "I'm glad to know that you still care about me; that might be better than the pussy."

She smirked and rolled her eyes.

"I could be wrong, though; you still got that fat ass."

Chelsea sat on the bed again. "Get the hell out of here, and go spend some time with your son before you go off on that fed vacation."

"You're right. I'm taking him with me to see Trex. He's fucked up right now because Lynn left him."

"Lynn Gardner? I thought they broke up a couple years after me and you did."

"He had got back with her not too long ago."

"I thought she had better sense than that. She knew he would beat that ass again."

"It ain't like that. She's accusing him of something that happened. She don't have proof; she's just speculating."

"Spec your ass. He did it, and you probably know he did, *whatever* it is."

He leaned in and kissed her on the cheek. "I gotta go. I'll bring Roc back before it gets dark. Then I'm going to the police station; see what the fuck they want."

Chelsea shot him a sad look. "Bye."

"If your man is here when I get back, I'm telling him how you let me tongue you down and hit it from the back."

"He knows I won't jump the fence on him. But he also knows that Big C runs this shit."

Rico laughed and headed for the door. "Tell him I said what up. He seem like a good dude." Rico stopped near the doorway and turned to face her. "Don't you wanna tell me you love me before I go away?"

Chelsea smiled. "See you, saw you, I damn sho ain't gone call you." She laughed again.

Rico waved at her. Damn her laugh made him feel good.

Dan Kapata waited on Perry to return in a taxi. They had placed Carrielli's body in the trunk of a stolen Buick LeSabre, and Perry had driven it to a restaurant parking lot. He was supposed to call a taxi from the nearest gas station. Dan left out of the bedroom and walked to the kitchen. He was thinking about Carrielli. *Perry made a good point.* He stopped in front of the kitchen sink. *Maybe I'm justifying the whole thing.* He took a step toward the refrigerator, and a single bullet entered the kitchen window and pierced the wall.

Dan hit the floor, heart racing a marathon. He scrambled to the living room. *Damn.* Why did he leave the fucking guns in the bedroom? It was strange how he could even think that Carrielli was after him; he'd helped to stuff the dead man in the car. Dan crawled from the living room to the hallway and stopped to listen.

Nothing.

He crawled to the bedroom and felt much safer now. He was in reach of the gun that he had taken from the policeman at the convenience store, and the rifle from the police car.

The Police sniper gritted with disappointment over the miss. He adjusted the mouthpiece on his headset. "Don't ask how, but I missed. Suspect is clearly alert now." The sniper looked through the binoculars again. He could see the hole in the window and the wall.

Dan sat on the floor in the hallway, his back against the wall. He thought he had it figured out. *That goddamn Intrepid.* He would bet anything that those were cops out there. He would bet that the cops had planted tracking devices on all of Perry's vehicles.

Special Agent Johnson pressed the button on the bullhorn. "Dan Kapata, the house is fully surrounded by members from the FBI, ATF, and local police. You and Perry should disarm yourselves and exit the front door with your hands on top of your head."

Dan softly banged his head against the wall. It was time to leave—he knew he couldn't shoot it out with them—but he still wanted to teach the trespassers a damn good lesson. He crawled to the bedroom closet and pulled the carpeted hatch up. He dragged the suitcase of money over.

"Dan, you're running out of time. If you want to talk with me, call 9-1-1 and tell them to patch you through to 658."

Dan lowered himself to the ground. He closed the

hatchway, retrieved the rifle and suitcase, then scrambled under the house.

A gas bomb was thrown through the kitchen window. Another through a bedroom window.

Dan placed the shotgun near a vent. He crawled on the dirt to another area and detached the M-16—the one used in the jailbreak. He could barely smell the gas now. He removed his shirt and tied it around his head, covering his mouth and nose. He crawled with the machine gun to the front vent. He opened a ground hatch and lowered himself beneath the surface with the suitcase. He waited at the top of the underground tube with the hatch closed.

"Dan, you and your son have sixty seconds to surrender." Johnson thought Dan and Perry were inside wearing gas masks. They must be, or perhaps unconscious by now.

After a minute and ten seconds, several policemen attacked the house with more than four hundred rounds of ammunition. The house was hit from all sides, smashing all windows.

The lower part of the house was all brick. Though Dan was protected from the gunfire, he still flinched occasionally.

Finally the shooting settled. Dan opened the ground hatch and waited for the policemen to enter the house.

Ten minutes later he could hear the policemen breaking in using a battering ram. Dan waited a few seconds more, allowing enough policemen to enter the house.

The M-16 swayed in Dan's arms as the bullets ripped through the floor from underneath the house. *Tatter-tat, tat-tat, tat, tatter-tatter.* He swept the area in a wide range, sending more wood chips and splinters in all directions, looking away from the gun flashes and debris. But just that fast the gun cartridge had emptied. Dan had killed three more policeman and had injured four. The four remaining policemen regrouped; it was their turn to return fire through the floor.

Dan submerged and closed the ground hatch again. He crawled backwards for fifteen yards and reached a wide open area of the tube. He had always called this the *Underground Intersection*. He turned himself around and made a left turn. Freedom was only 182 more yards away. A five-minute run in the woods to reach the Dodge Stealth would knock Robert Mayes off the front cover of *Time*.

CHAPTER 27

Rico entered the client-attorney conference room wearing an orange jumpsuit. He was no longer in handcuffs. He walked toward the white lawyer at the table in the center of the room.

The lawyer extended his hand without standing. "I'm Paul Metzer, your court-appointed attorney."

Rico shook his hand. "What's the difference between you and a public defender?" He sat across from Paul.

"Well, the federal government assigns public defenders when they don't think the case will receive any publicity; they assign court apps when they want the public to think they're playing fair." He opened a folder and removed a three-page motion.

"I don't know if you answered the damn question."

Paul lowered his eyebrows and looked away. "Hmm. Let's see...I'm a private attorney that also accepts cases paid for by the government."

Rico held a stoic look. "Does that make sense to you? The same people looking to convict me wanna buy me a lawyer to—"

"There are different departments of government, and there are even different divisions within those departments. Again, one is trying to take you under, while the other division tries to make it look fair."

Rico nodded, impressed with the lawyer's honesty. "Why did they pick you? You must be somebody they can count on for the cross."

"The cross? I don't understand."

"Just tell me why they picked you."

Paul hesitated. "I had a bet with your prosecutor long before you even committed the crime. He lost, and so he would fix it so that I get the next high-profile case—assuming the judge found the defendant indigent like yourself."

Rico leaned back in the chair. "You just said I committed the crime. Why the hell would I want you on my team thinking like that?"

Paul smiled. "When I think a client is guilty, I put up more effort to get him off."

Rico stared at him for a few seconds then began looking around the room.

"The government expects you to have someone hire a private lawyer for you. It seems likely—"

"I'm keeping you as a lawyer." Rico faced Paul again. "But the first time I ask you to do something and you don't do it, I'm sending the world's favorite street villain at that ass."

Paul displayed a look of confusion. "I'm not sure I understand you."

"Good. You don't need to understand everything. Do

what I ask you to do, and you might prosper. But if you ever cross me, you'll have to learn how to beat one your damn self."

Paul cleared his throat. "Okay. Well, let's go over the case."

"You talk and I'll listen."

"I've only seen your indictment and a few other papers. I'll file for discovery materials first thing in the morning. Are there any witnesses you'd like for me to interview?"

"Why would I have witnesses to a crime I didn't commit?"

"I thought you might have witnesses who could vouch for your presence in, say, South Carolina at the time of the casino incident."

"I got a few people who could speak for me, but I'm not tryin to...trying to get them involved."

Paul placed the ink pen behind his ear. "Theft, wire fraud, money laundering, ID fraud, murder, car-jacking, reckless endangerment with a vehicle—"

"Yeah, yeah. Thirty-eight counts, but most of that shit amounts to the same damn charges with different language. And the murder was self-defense."

Paul laughed.

"What's so fuckin funny?" Rico's face held a serious look.

"We can't argue self-defense."

"You heard about it on the news—the guy killed the taxi driver. Then he came after...Robert Mayes with a gun."

"But if we argue self-defense, we'd be telling the jury that you're actually Robert Mayes."

Rico had already gone over the issue with Tank, and they had quickly reached the same conclusion. He smiled.

"I'm just checking. I'll always wanna know whose side you're on. Make sure you keep the right response."

"I don't think that's much of a problem." He pushed his copy of a three-page motion across the table. "I filed this as soon as I knew I would be assigned to the case."

Rico studied the papers.

"The media was displaying your DMV photo, your booking photo, and a photo of the Robert Mayes in the Segron National Bank. They took a viewers poll to see how many people believed that your picture resembled the bank photos."

"And the results?"

"Don't know. The court granted my motion and issued an injunction over the phone against the releasing of any results."

"That's a good sign; you're on the job early."

"I have to be; I bet someone three hundred bucks that I would win this case. Actually, the bet was that I'd win my first high-profile case."

Rico laughed. "So my freedom depends on an extra three hundred dollars?"

"Not really. I plan to give it all I got regardless of the money. This could look good for my career."

Rico poked out his bottom lip and nodded with approval. "Tell you what, you win this case and I'll throw a hundred grand at you."

Paul extended his hand and they shook on it. "Deal."

Tank and Trex sat inside Tank's new midnight blue Suburban. Tank had parked the truck in Janet Orson's driveway on the outskirts of Atlanta, Georgia. He and Trex poured out of the vehicle and headed for the front door. "It seems so...unfair that your fine-ass cousin lives in this two-story house by herself." Tank stopped to admire the interior of Janet's Land Cruiser.

Trex walked by Tank. "Keep on peeping inside of shit; don't be surprised if something blow up in your face. You know she probably got everything she own rigged up."

"I think I'll pull up on her this time with the romance game." Tank walked away from the Land Cruiser.

The front door of the brick home was opened, and Janet stood in the entrance with a look of anger. "Trex, you're a half hour late. You know I don't play that shit." She turned and walked toward the dining room.

Tank entered the house behind Trex and closed the door. He followed Trex to the dining room.

Trex pulled out a chair and sat across from Janet. "There was this...wreck on Peachtree Street and we almost—"

"Don't tell that goddamn lie! I was listening to both the city and county police, and the narcotic and ambulance frequencies for the last two hours. Ain't a damn thing going on over at Peachtree."

Tank laughed.

"I'm sorry, Tank. Have a seat. Do you know what you're getting yourself into by hanging with my lying-ass cousin?"

Tank smiled at Janet and sat to the left of Trex at the table. "I fed him one day, and now I can't get rid of him."

She returned the smile. "Thanks for the compliment you made about me in the driveway."

Trex looked at Tank. "Woman even got her driveway wired up."

"I can't get my hands on any guns or any ammunition

until tomorrow. Y'all can spend the night, and I might have something first thing in the morning."

"We still have most of what you sold us the last time, we don't need guns. My brother is in jail, and we need to set something up with his lawyer."

"I saw Rico's picture on the news. They know damn well Rico didn't pull that big-time shit off in Vegas. I thought they only wanted him for questioning."

"Yeah, they locked him up. He got a nice plan, but we don't trust his lawyer." Tank's eyes shifted toward the sound of a voice coming from the kitchen. It was a scanner, but it was out of view.

"I guess you two wouldn't be down here if I couldn't help you with something. What is it?"

Trex got up from the table. "We need something that we can use to spy on the lawyer." He walked to the kitchen.

Tank leaned forward and rested his forearms on the table. "We need a small monitoring system so we can listen to the lawyer while he's at home. We won't have a problem getting it in his house."

"Damn, it might be a few days before I can get you some hi-tech, good shit."

Trex returned from the kitchen with a popsicle in his hand. "We just came from the Fantasy Spy Shop, but I knew you probably—"

"Fantasy Spy?"

Trex bit the popsicle. "Yeah. That's why we was thirty minutes—"

Janet slammed her hand down on the table. "Damn, Trex! I hope you and Tank didn't talk about nothing important while y'all was in the shop."

Tank leaned back. "Why? What's the deal?"

Janet sighed. "The black salesman is also the manager.

He was selling drugs through the store and got busted with LSD. Word is he's working the charges off by video recording and spying on customers until he can get some useful info."

Tank and Trex looked at one another. They had chatted about the Robert Mayes scheme in the spy shop while waiting on the salesman. Tank got up from the table. "No wonder that muthafucka was watching the Suburban from the window when we drove off."

Trex inhaled deeply and exhaled loudly. "This is a good example. This is why I enjoy meeting muthafuckas at the crossroads."

Janet got up from the table now. "Whatever you're gonna do, you need to hurry. I got personal guns here if you need them, but you can't use them unless I'm invited. We're wasting too much time."

Tank looked at Trex. "Park the Suburban at that pool hall and walk to the spy shop. Me and Janet gonna park in the back of the spy shop. I'll wait on you to open the back door."

Tank and Janet were in the Land Cruiser. Tank's eyes shifted from the side view mirror. He saw that the Suburban was two car lengths away. He glanced at Janet as she drove, and his eyes shifted toward her short shorts and her thighs. "I don't know why female criminals turn me on."

"You ever thought about counseling?" She caught him staring. She quickly yanked at the steering wheel.

Tank looked up, gripping the door handle. "You know how to handle this big ride, don't you?"

She laughed, licked her lips, and shot him the sexiest

look. "What makes you think big rides are hard to handle?"

"Be careful; I might come back to Atlanta and run your man off."

"I never said I had a man, so what makes you think I do?"

"Even anti-social criminals love companionship."

"You like surprises?" Her hands gripped the steering wheel tighter.

"Only from women."

"I'm looking for a good man, but I'm having so much fun with another woman right now."

Tank grinned. "That is a surprise, because I'm looking for a good woman who already has another woman."

She laughed. "You can't handle us; we'll put your ass to sleep in five minutes."

He studied her face and knew she was serious about the lesbian thing. He looked through the passenger window. "Let's talk about something else until this is over. I don't wanna run up in the spy shop with my dick rock-hard."

She laughed again.

Paul Metzer was in the prosecutor's office, twelve floors up from the busy streets of Columbia, South Carolina. Charles Glasser sat behind his desk in a leather swivel chair. "Paul, we'd like to offer you a deal for your client."

Paul smiled. "So soon? I would think that you'd first give us a chance to receive and go over all pretrial discovery materials."

"I'm simply asking you to offer him the deal before he retains new counsel. Surely you don't think he'll keep you as lead counsel."

"Maybe he won't, but I think he understands that deals are made because cases are weak. Discovery materials may give him more leverage with which to negotiate."

Glasser turned in the chair and faced the office window. "Once you receive the discovery materials there will be no offers."

"Let's hear your offer, and I'll take it to him. I think it's a waste of time, but I'll deliver the message."

"If your client is willing to give back all the money he wired from the offshore account, pay restitution on any lost amounts, and plead guilty to the assault on that Vegas policeman and money laundering...we'll drop the other charges."

"So, you want him to plead guilty to the two most serious charges?"

"Hey, we're dropping the Vegas murder charges and the car-jacking; those are the most serious of the charges."

"I'll be sure to relay the message." Paul got up from the contemporary leather chair.

Glasser got up from the swivel chair and walked toward Paul. He stopped two feet in front of him. "Just in case he does decline the offer, what will it cost to learn his defense?"

Paul thought about the question. "A thousand dollars."

"And what will it cost for you to help me get this conviction?"

"Charles, this case really means a lot to you, doesn't it?"

"Look, you wanted a high-profile case, and I got it for you. But I need the conviction, so what will your assistance cost me?"

Paul turned and stared at the doorknob, his mouth twitching during contemplation. "Hmm...is $101,000 asking too much?"

Glasser laughed. "Don't be ridiculous. Seriously, what's it going to cost me?"

Paul thought about it. "Make me your best offer."

"Three thousand."

"Double that and you got a deal."

Glasser extended a hand. "Deal."

CHAPTER 28

Trex had walked a half block from the pool hall to reach the spy shop. He waited at a pay phone across the street, watching two customers inside near the window of the store. After ten minutes, he saw them leaving the store. He jogged across the street when the Cadillac left the parking lot. He needed to get inside before anyone else showed up.

The black manager was about to lock the door. He flipped the *Open for Business* sign around in the window.

Trex watched the hand flip the sign as he approached. *Out to Lunch. Back at 1:00 P.M.* Trex hurried toward the door and turned the doorknob. It opened.

The manager recognized Trex and smiled. "I was just about to take a lunch break. Can I help you—"

Trex pulled out a silenced handgun. "Police, freeze." He whacked the manager on the ear with the side of the gun and watched him fall to the floor. "Don't get it fucked up. *You're* the police; I'm just asking you to freeze." Trex stepped to the large window and closed the blinds. "Get the fuck up and unlock the back door."

The manager got up from the floor, hand pressed against his injured ear. "You can have whatever you want. Please don't—"

"Put some close on your mouth, and open that fuckin back door."

The manager walked to the back door and unlocked it.

Tank entered the back door with a gun of his own. "Did you frisk him?"

"No. I saved that for you."

Tank began frisking the manager. He collected a wallet, a notepad, and an ink pen. He disassembled the pen and found it to be without spy technology.

"Tell me what you recorded us on, and take me to it."

The manager looked at Trex. "I...I don't...*Recorded you?*"

Tank flipped through the small notepad and saw the Suburban's license plate information. *FULL TANK.* Then he showed it to Trex.

Trex looked at the notepad then shifted his evil eyes back to the manager. "Get your hands up." He watched the manager's hands raise. *Pluhnk.* He shot the manager in the hand with Janet's silenced .50 caliber handgun.

The manager let out a compressed yell. He clamped the injured hand between his thighs and bent over. He didn't want to look, but he knew there was a hole clean through his hand.

"Straighten your ass up, and put them damn hands up in the air." Trex touched the man's shoulder with the barrel of the gun.

The manager squealed and moaned. He looked up at Trex. "My hand is killing me."

"Oh, yeah? You just gonna give your hand all the credit? This is the last time I'm tellin you; get your nothin-ass up, hands in the air, and show me what you recorded us on."

The manager slowly straightened up and raised both hands, blood streaming down his left arm. His jaws were filled with air, and his eyes were watery. He walked toward the front of the shop and stopped at the cash register. "The dark glass bubble in back of the cash register is a lens."

Tank looked at the register. He slapped the manager in the face and watched him fall against the counter.

Trex looked down at the speckles of blood on his shirt. "Be careful with that muthafuckin transmission fluid."

Tank looked under the counter and followed the cable from the register to underneath the carpeted floor and up the carpeted wall.

The manager watched Tank follow the contour of the cable. "If I open the register, I can enter a code to stop the recorders."

Tank returned to the manager and slapped him again. "If you open the register, you can probably get the cops here since that cable is connecting up at the telephone jack." Tank aimed a handgun at the manager's chest. The large silencer looked as though it might absorb most of the sound. "Last chance. Where is the recorder?"

"It's...the universal remote control. Over there by the infrared cameras you guys were looking at earlier. The remote is a spy cam and an...audio transmitter; the receiver is in the...in the attic."

Tank squeezed the trigger three times. The silencer on Janet's gun was impressive.

The manager hit the floor.

Trex shot the manager twice more. "You just can't keep them damn hands up, can you?" He looked at Tank. "I'm worried about you, Tank. You act like you like killin people."

"Tell your cousin to come in and help with some of this shit."

Rico sat at the conference table with his lawyer for the second time in two days. "You're late. Why?"

"You asked me to wait on your brother and his friend to show up at my house. They never did."

"I just got off the phone with my brother. He's on his way to your house with the plasma screen."

"You still don't want to tell me what the TV is for?"

"It's for the case. We'll use it in court to show the photos that the media was comparing."

Paul lowered his eyebrows. "You apparently have some strategies that you're not telling me about. Don't you think your lawyer should know your plan?"

"I don't have a plan yet; I have an idea. I'll tell you what it is when it finally turns into a plan."

Paul nodded and began focusing on some documents. "Okay, from everything I've went over so far, it seems as though the entire case depends on you being Robert Mayes. If we can convince the jury that you're not Robert Mayes, then none of the other charges will stand."

"You're looking at me like I'm supposed to cheer. Tell me something that only a good lawyer could figure out."

"To do that I'll need the discovery material. Give it maybe two weeks. I should be on top of things by then. But let's discuss our strategies for jury selection."

"What about it?"

"It'll happen a few days before trial. I want to explain the purpose of certain jury compositions."

Rico nodded with approval, though he hadn't the slightest idea of what *jury composition* meant.

"We're looking to select a jury of mostly men who haven't kept a steady job for too many years."

"Damn. If you wanna cross me, you don't have to let me know."

Paul laughed. "No. I'm not out to cross you—whatever that means. But try to get inside of the prosecutor's head. He is going to want a jury comprised of mostly women."

"Why?"

"Because you're charged with acts of cheating and deceiving. He knows that women aren't usually sympathetic toward cheaters. Most women on a jury would have you face *some* degree of punishment."

Rico thought about Tremaine. He needed to quickly get his mind off of her. "So...yeah, that makes sense. I like that. Now why do you want men who can't keep a job?"

"Because even if they think you're guilty, they can sympathize with a cheater. And they can appreciate a scam which, if they had committed themselves, would allow them to quit their jobs."

"That's good. Who taught you that shit?"

"Law school. Brainstorming with my college buddies. There's other factors like age and the type of jobs but—"

"You keep talking about discovery materials. How much shit is in that package?"

"Everything that they plan to bring up at trial. If it's not included, they can't introduce it at trial. But the courts always allow the government some last minute exception."

"I got a fucked up judge, don't I?"

"No. Uh...actually he's fair."

"Fucked up prosecutor?"

"Sure. Everybody has one of those." Paul smiled.

"He's probably gonna come at you with a deal for me. Let me save you from getting cursed out. Don't bring that dumb shit back to me."

"What makes you think he hasn't already come at me with a deal?"

"Too early. He want me to think he got a tight case."

"So you don't want me to tell you if he does come with an offer?"

"You can tell me when he makes an offer, but don't expect me to go for it. If you act like you got me a good deal, you're getting cursed the fuck out."

"I'll keep that in mind if he tries to make a deal."

"You got a cell phone on you?"

"No. I left it in the car."

"Call my brother's cell phone, and tell him to bring the TV back to your house again. I know he showed up when you came here."

"Give me his cell number and I'll do that for you."

"And if you don't have room for a 71-inch flat screen plasma, try to make room."

"Sounds like a theatre to me. And a benefit. How long do I get to keep it?"

"Until maybe a week before trial. It acts as a computer monitor, and I need for you to get familiar with all the operations and how to use it with a computer."

"No problem. Was that thing expensive?"

Rico leaned forward. "Costs eighty-nine thousand. Shipped from overseas, and won't be sold in the US until 2006."

"Let's say I like the TV, and let's say I win the case.

Instead of the hundred thousand you promised, would you consider the TV and twenty thousand as the reward?"

"I'll *consider* it just for you, but ain't no muthafuckin way you gonna get that deal. How about the TV and five grand?"

Paul stared in Rico's eyes. "The TV and ten grand and you got a deal."

"That's a bet."

"That's only if I like the TV."

"You'll like it. You and your wife. It even comes with one of the most advanced universal remote controls."

Perry Kapata walked out of the Pineville Police Department and got inside the Corvette that was waiting for him at the end of the walkway. He looked at his girlfriend. "Drive."

She put the car in gear, and they left the area. "You don't want to talk about it?"

"Everything's fine. They dropped the aiding and abetting charges."

"You said they would."

"They found my car parked at the place my dad was staying. I knew that wasn't enough to prove I aided him with anything."

"It's a good thing you weren't there." She glanced at him.

"I almost was until I heard all the gunfire and saw a couple of cops ahead detouring traffic. They thought I had escaped through the underground tube with my father. The taxi driver cleared me."

"So now what? I haven't saw you in nine days; shouldn't we get a room before we drive to Tennessee?"

"Yeah. I was thinking the same thing. I need a shower and some sleep." Perry closed his eyes and thought about Rico. The promise he'd made to his father meant even more now. "Make a left at the light. I want to see my mother before I leave town."

She slowed for the traffic light. "How long are they going to keep the Intrepid?"

"They said at least thirty more days."

She kept her eyes on the road.

"On second thought, we're staying at my mother's house for a few days. I want to find out who Rico hangs out with. I'm sure I'll learn more about him at his trial in December."

She drove in silence. She wouldn't dare try to talk him out of whatever he had in mind, though she badly wanted to.

Perry lowered the sun visor. "Just in case he decides to get selfish and serve a lengthy prison sentence."

Trex drove the moving van while Tank studied a Robb Report magazine. They were delivering the plasma screen to Paul Metzer's house for the second time today. Trex wanted to pass the station wagon ahead, but he knew he had to drive careful. "Something is wrong, you know?"

"Like?"

"The fuckin cops still ain't said shit about the Robert Mayes evidence found in the Charlotte apartment."

"I know." Tank looked up from the magazine. "That's the part I don't like. They probably know it's a frame, but they know it'll help my brother's case."

Trex tapped the horn but the driver ahead seemed to ignore him. "I don't know if it helps Rico, but I'm sure it could hurt the prosecutor's case."

Tank looked at Trex. "What the hell is the difference? You just said the same shit—"

"I'm thinking this whole case is set up—lawyer and all. So it's hard to say for sure if something like that can help the case."

Tank leaned against the passenger door with a look of confusion. "You scare me. You're actually makin...sense. Instead of finding ways to help my brother—"

"We should find ways to cross the cops." Trex smiled. "Now you're seeing shit my way."

"Fuck that. I'll come up with the plan. If I leave it up to you, every cop that investigated the Charlotte murders might be dead in the morning."

"So? I don't see no loopholes in that plan."

"Trex, killing people won't hurt the fed's case against Rico. You should know by now that there's only one thing that beats the cross..."

Trex tapped the horn again. "And that's the mutha-fuckin double-cross."

CHAPTER 29

Trex entered the small law firm and stopped at the receptionist's desk. He thought the black woman must be around twenty.

She smiled at Trex then ended the telephone conversation. "How can I help you?"

"I need to talk to Paul Metzer, but I don't want him to know who's here to see him."

"I'm...not really sure I can keep my job that way."

Trex leaned forward, hands on the desk. "You must be new here."

"I started two days ago."

"I can tell. You're doing a good job, though. And I hope you're single." He walked away from the desk, headed toward Paul's office.

She got up and followed Trex. "Sir, excuse me."

Trex ignored her. He opened the office door and

stepped inside. He closed the door in the receptionist's face.

Paul removed his propped feet from the desk. "Trex, what brings you here?"

A knock at the door.

Trex opened the door and saw the receptionist. "Go away, we're having a conference." He puckered his lips and shot her a kissing gesture.

Paul rose from his office chair. "He's cool, Leniqua."

She frowned at Trex and walked off.

Trex closed the door again. "Paul, you know what? You're lucky as hell."

"How is that?"

"Because I like you. You're cool for a white lawyer." Trex sat in a leather chair.

"Well, thanks. But what did I do?"

"You had a discussion with your wife the other day about the prosecutor and how he wanted you to fuck my partner up."

Paul's eyes shifted left to right. He sat in his office chair again, pretending to be recalling such discussion with his wife.

"Your wife asked you what you was gonna do, and you said you was gonna do everything in your power to win the case."

"I don't remember me and my wife having such—"

"Paul, don't even...don't play it off. I got the recording."

Paul stared at Trex.

"It's too complicated to explain. But don't go home and beat your wife down; she had nothing to do with it."

"You want to tell me what this is all about?"

"We can talk, but don't let Rico or his brother know

that I was here."

"That depends on how interesting this gets."

"The whole Robert Mayes scheme in Vegas—that was me. Rico knows it was me, but he's not gonna fold on me."

Paul leaned back in his chair, staring at Trex, trying to see the resemblance. "Is this your way to give your friend an alibi?"

"No, because that information won't leave this room."

"Then why would you tell me?"

"You wanna win the case, don't you?"

"Sure."

"That means you need all the facts you can get. And you're missing the most important fact."

"Rico doesn't seem to trust me. I don't believe I know as much about his defense as I should."

"What do you wanna know?"

"What does he really plan to do with the 70-inch plasma screen that's been sitting in my living room for two months now?"

"I can tell you everything except that. He only told me that he's using it to display the Robert Mayes photos of the casino."

"Okay, he says he'll have an expert witness to rebut the government's expert on digital imagery. The trial is fourteen weeks away; why doesn't he let me meet with our expert to prep him well in advance?"

"Don't know that, either. He didn't talk to me about the expert, but I'll find out."

Paul stared at Trex. "You're his good friend. Why wouldn't he tell you some of these things?"

"That's just the way it is. I know things about the case that he don't know."

"Things like?"

"A couple months ago, some guys was killed in a Charlotte apartment. The cops called it drug related."

"Black guys? Two of them stabbed in the chest?"

"Yeah."

"I heard all about that case."

"No, you didn't."

"Sure I did. It was on the—"

"No, you didn't hear all about it. For some reason the cops didn't mention the packets of braids, bifocals, Robert Mayes's ID, Quadra Casino receipts, Segron National Bank documents, Las Vegas prepaid cellular service receipt, trimmers, and the gun used in the shootout in Vegas."

Paul rested his hands on top of his head. "Jesus Crisis."

"Now how can you prove that the cops is hiding that good shit?"

"That's the easy part. You just have to tell me how you know that...good shit exists."

"Can't tell you that. You just have to take my word."

Paul snickered. "Where should I take your word, to court? Come on, Trex. Sounds like good evidence. How am I supposed to prove to a judge that the government is concealing such exculpatory evidence?"

"You're the muthafuckin lawyer. It's your job to come up with a strategy."

"You're missing the whole point. There's no reasonable explanation—"

"Do what the fuck lawyers are supposed to do. Get an investigator on the job."

Paul thought about it. "Do you know any of the guys who were killed in the apartment?"

"What kinda damn question is that? Don't put me in the investigation."

"I didn't mean it that way. Do you know of anyone

who might have known about one of the guys in the apartment?"

Trex thought about Lynn. "Not really. She won't associate with me."

"Whoever the she is, I'm the one to associate with. If I can get her to tell me that one of the apartment guys might have been connected with the Robert Mayes scheme, then I'd have a darn good reason to interview the crime scene investigators of the Charlotte murders."

"The shit sounds easy, but as long as she's mad at me, she won't admit that."

"You would know her better than I would. You want to help Rico? You and the lady resolve your differences, then you get her to talk to me."

Trex stood in front of Chelsea's apartment door. He could hear someone inside approaching.

Chelsea opened the door. "Rico called here and said you were coming to pick up Roc. Where the hell do you think you're taking him?"

Trex had no idea of what excuse Rico might have given her. "I thought he explained that to you."

She stepped aside. "He didn't explain anything. Come in; Roc will be down in a minute."

Trex entered the apartment and sat on the center cushion of the sofa.

"Where are you taking my son?"

"To the mall. Rico wanted me to get him something."

"You're a damn lie. Whatever it is, Rico wouldn't even tell me over the phone. It has nothing to do with a mall."

"Chelsea, I can't tell you about it. I'm just doing what your man told me to do."

"Rico ain't my damn man. My man is at work."

"I don't mean..." Trex sighed. "What's taking Roc so long?"

"He was getting out of the tub when you pulled up." She headed toward the kitchen. "I caught Roc cursing at some little girl on the phone the other day."

Trex watched Chelsea as she headed for the kitchen. "Maybe she was short with some of his money." Trex laughed.

"Boy, that shit ain't funny. I know you and Rico still curse around my son. I told Rico about that stupid shit more than a hundred times."

"Now you're accusing me of...I know how to fix this. Roc! Bring your little ass downstairs so we can clear some shit up with your mom!"

Chelsea returned from the kitchen with a frying pan. "Trex, you think I'm playing with you. Don't make me slap the shit out of you with this pan."

Roc came out of his room and stopped at the top of the staircase. "Give me five minutes. No, two more minutes."

Trex grinned at her. "I'm just messing with you, Chelsea. But listen at how you sound. You curse at me, you curse at Rico, you curse at Roc when he's bad. What makes you think he gets that cursing shit from me or Rico?"

"Because men are more influential over boys. He's about to be fourteen. He wants to say and do the things his father does. And since you're Rico's best friend—probably only friend—you get your ass cursed out, too."

"I don't mind you dumping your stress off on me. Whether you know it or not, Rico got Roc set for life. Think about the men who don't curse around their kids but ain't doing a damn thing for them."

Chelsea smirked. She and Rico had had a similar discussion. "What happens when his son needs him instead of the damn money?"

Roc rushed down the stairs.

"Sounds like a domestic dispute that you might have to take up with his father."

"Well that's your friend; get his ass out of jail and I'll take it up with him."

Trex stared at Chelsea. "I promise you, I'm working on that." He looked at Roc. "Let's go. Bring your little raggedy-ass on."

"Trex, what kind of car is this?"

"This is a rental car, Roc."

"I didn't ask you that."

"Infinity Q-45. And watch your mouth when you're talking to grown folks."

"I like this car."

"Damn this car. Your daddy told me to pick you up and have a long talk with you."

"About what?"

"Everything. From sex to crime."

Roc glanced at Trex. "For what?"

"He said you could help me get Lynn back, but I would have to run the whole story down to you."

Roc smiled. "Tell me why she dropped your ass; I'll figure out what to charge you."

Trex hesitated. "I can't believe Rico got me confessing to a young-ass runt."

"How the hell I'm a runt, when I can get your girl back but you can't?"

Trex parked the car in front of a convenience store.

"Lynn think I killed somebody, and now she won't talk to me."

"Trex, you killed somebody before?"

Trex laughed. "Roc..." He paused, shaking his head with disbelief. "Man...I done killed...damn near everybody in this book."

Roc lowered his eyebrows and stared at Trex. "With a gun?"

"Gun, knife—it don't make no difference to me." Trex leaned his head against the headrest.

"So you like to kill?"

"Only when somebody threatens me or the people I'm cool with. Like, remember when you was fighting in the park?"

Roc listened with no response.

"I wanted to kill the guy that pushed you off the other little boy." Trex stared through the moonroof.

Roc's eyes shifted from Trex to the moonroof. He wondered what Trex was staring at. "Tell me how everything started with you and Lynn and why you want her back so bad. I usually charge a thousand dollars, but...damn, Trex..."

"What's wrong?"

"Man, you in some deep shit. I got to charge you *two* thousand dollars."

Trex's head tilted forward and turned toward Roc. "You pull this shit off, I'll give you *ten* thousand dollars."

Roc leaned back in his seat and looked through the moonroof again. "Tell me everything. I might even get her to marry your slow ass."

Lynn answered the door at her aunt's house. "Roc!

285

How are you doing?"

"Fine."

"What are you..."

Roc looked back at Tank's Suburban and tried to wave the truck off.

Tank stepped out of the truck and smiled at Lynn. "What's up, Lynn?"

"Hello, Tank. How is your brother?"

"He looks sad, but he's doing good."

"Tell him I'm praying and pulling for him."

"I'll let him know." Tank got back inside the truck and drove away.

"Roc, why did your uncle leave you here?"

"He'll be back in about one hour. I have to talk to you; it's real important."

"I'm sure it is. Come on in."

Roc walked inside. "Is your aunt here?"

"No. She won't get here until 11:45 tonight. You can sit in that big Lazy Boy chair. You want anything cold to drink?"

"No, thanks." Roc sat in the big chair.

Lynn sat in front of the sofa on the carpet. "What do you want to talk about, Roc?"

"You ever watch wildlife stuff on TV?"

"Not lately. Why?"

"What's the king of the jungle?"

She smiled. "A lion. The male lion."

"But I bet you don't know why he's the king."

"Because he can beat up every—"

"Nope. There's other animals that can whip the lion's ass with—"

"Roc!"

"I mean...I meant to say, that can beat the lion."

"Okay."

"A lion won't mess with a mean baboon, a crocodile, a hippo, a rhino..."

"Then why is he called the king of the jungle?"

"Because he lives like a king. Kings don't get their titles for winning every fight; they're called kings because they get served."

"I understand that, but I think you lost me with the animal story."

"The lioness—that's the female lion—she goes—"

Lynn laughed. "I know that, Roc."

"She does all the hunting. But when she kills, she don't eat. She brings it back to the male lion, and he eats what he wants first. The lioness gets the leftovers."

Lynn was impressed. "I didn't know that."

"Yeah. And *that's* why they call him the king—no other animal in the jungle lives that way."

"I guess you got a good reason for telling me all of this."

Roc looked all around the living room. "The lion protects the den for the lioness and the cubs. He gets his kill when something threatens the family."

"I like that role-playing. That's beautiful."

"Good. Now let's talk about Trex. I'll do all the talking; you just remember that he's the lion."

CHAPTER 30

Charles Glasser approached Ted Wells on the witness stand. "So you're swearing under oath before this jury that you never received a tip from the defendant?"

Clockwork glanced at Rico. "I don't...I've never met the defendant before."

"All right. Take a look at the large plasma screen to your right."

Clockwork looked at the screen.

"The four images you see are different angles of the thief in the casino. Do you know who those images represent?"

"A man that presented himself to me as Robert Mayes."

"Now...did that man give you a fifty-thousand-dollar tip in the form of a chip?"

"No, sir. Nobody ever gave me such a tip before."

Rico leaned closer to his lawyer. "Clockwork is trying to cover for me, but instead he's making shit worse."

"You want me to show that he's lying?" Paul Metzer removed his hand from his mouth.

"No. Let him ride."

The prosecutor prepared to display a video of Robert Mayes tossing a dark green chip to Clockwork.

Roc tapped Tank on the shoulder. "Unc, why don't my daddy get up there and say something?"

Tank looked back. "Because your daddy got good sense. Now quit askin all them damn questions, and watch the show."

Chelsea thumped the back of Tank's head. "Stop cursing around Roc."

Tank looked back at her. "We don't curse around him. No bullshit. Am I lying, Roc?"

"Nope." Roc smiled at Chelsea.

Yvonne leaned closer to Chelsea. "Save your energy, girl. Those knuckleheads will stress you until you give in."

The Honorable Judge Moore checked his wristwatch. "The Court would like the leading counsel for both parties to approach the bench."

Paul Metzer and Charles Glasser arrived together.

"Mr. Metzer, I realize that I granted you permission to use the plasma screen throughout the trial, so long as the government is allowed equal usage. But I don't like it. I think it's damaging to your client."

"Your Honor, you've addressed my client, and he's stated in open court that he knowingly consents to the use of the monitor for the purposes set forth in our motion."

"I'm aware of that; I just don't like how the screen is juxtaposed with the defense counsel's table. Your client is sitting only three feet away."

Charles held up an index finger. "Again, Your Honor, the government does not contest the use and position of the monitor."

"Of course you wouldn't; it's in your favor." The judge looked at Paul again. "I was hoping you'd reconsider."

"No way, Your Honor. My client sees it as a defense."

"...After that he became loud and obnoxious. That's when I asked him to cash out and leave the casino area."

Charles glanced at Rico at the defense table. "And had you already introduced yourself as the casino manager?"

"Yes, sir."

"Mr. Allen, if you heard the man on the monitor talk again, do you think you'd recognize his voice?"

Paul sprang from his seat. "Objection, Your Honor! That question was designed to compel my client to testify to prove his innocence."

"Objection is sustained. The jury will disregard the government's last question. Mr. Glasser, be careful."

"Of course, Your Honor."

"You may continue."

Rico leaned closer to his lawyer. "You got good reflexes. But next time don't object to that bullshit unless I nudge you under the table."

Paul covered his mouth. "Do you understand how harmful the prosecutor's question was to our case?"

"Do you understand that the more shit you object to, the more you make the jury think we got something to hide?"

Charles glanced at his assistant prosecutor. "No further questions, Your Honor."

"Moving right along." The judge pointed his ink pen

at Paul. "Mr. Metzer, your witness."

Paul casually walked toward the witness stand. "Mr. Allen, are you sure you've seen the man on that monitor before?"

"Positive."

"Do you know the defendant, and have you ever met him before?"

Orville Allen studied Rico for a few seconds. "I'm...I'm not...I honestly don't know that one for sure."

"And I honestly believe you. No further questions."

After the first day of trial, Paul met with the prosecutor at the United States Attorney's Office. "Charles, I came to make a deal with you."

"A deal? Paul, you turned my deal down almost five months ago. You even lied and said you'd help me get this conviction. You only led me on just to buy yourself some time to get your shit together. We've gone too far now. No deals."

Paul cleared his throat. "The media at the courthouse was wild. I know a win could make you powerful, but a loss could damage your image. Irreparably."

"My case is looking stronger and stronger. Let's face it, Paul—"

"Lynn Gardner."

"Lynn?"

"I interviewed her, Charles."

"Who is she?"

"Ah, come off it, Charles. You know damn well who she is. The Charlotte police interviewed her a few weeks after her ex-boyfriend was killed. They asked her if she knew anything about Thomas Baker's connection to the

Robert Mayes scam—"

"That's not my jurisdiction. I work in South Carolina, remember?"

"Yeah, but you conspired with the North Carolina police when they told your law officers about the evidence they found in the Charlotte apartment."

Charles smirked. "Conspired to do what?"

"Suppress the evidence. They even warned Lynn not to say anything about the Robert Mayes ID and documents found inside the apartment. Said she'd be interfering with an ongoing investigation."

"So you're telling me you have proof that I had something to do with that?"

"I'm saying you at least knew about it. Rico was in the hospital, and you never found anything to connect him with anyone in that apartment."

"I think this is the hardest I've ever seen you fight, Paul. You..." He laughed. "I get it. That son of a bitch offered you more than I did."

"He didn't offer me anything. You were always using other lawyers to help boost your career; your time to return the favor."

"What are you talking about? I landed you this big case. Have you forgotten?"

"But you also wanted me to throw the damn case. That's like...that's...it's like you're selfish with a goddamn twist."

"You want to bring up a Brady violation because—"

"And I don't have to prove that you knew about the apartment evidence; I only have to prove that you should have known."

Charles leaned back in his seat. "What's your offer?"

"Drop all charges. With prejudice."

"I thought you were talking a ten-year, fifteen-year deal."

"Drop all charges or else we end this negotiation."

"Well I guess I'll see you in court tomorrow, Paul."

"Of course you will. With newly discovered witnesses and evidence."

Tank was at home watching the news when the phone rang. He thought it might be his grandmother since she had left the only message on his answering machine. "Hello."

"Hello, Tank. Are you busy?"

"Depends on who's calling."

"Could it be one of your women?"

"Impossible. I'm always single just weeks before Christmas. Besides, you sound sexy, but you don't sound like nobody I ever fucked before."

She laughed. "This is Janet Orson from Atlanta."

"Oh, shit! What's up, Janet? I talk like that when I think somebody is playing on the phone."

She laughed again. "I was thinking about you and sitting here rooting for your brother at the same time."

"I think he might be okay, but I could use some company. You should come spend the night for a few years. You should bring your girlfriend, too. If you want to."

"I broke it off. I don't think I want to see her again."

What the hell did you do that for? "Drive to my place, and I'll take your mind off her. You should get here by eleven tonight. You can go to court with me tomorrow. You might not get much sleep, though."

"I'll think about it while we're on the phone. But speaking of court, do you and Trex want me to bring anything for the courthouse?"

Tank laughed. That had to have been the funniest shit he'd heard all week.

"What? I'm serious."

"That's what makes it so damn funny."

"Is that a yes or a no?"

Tank thought about it. He cleared his throat. "Yeah. Bring me some good shit."

"I'm on my way." She hung the phone up.

Tank locked his hand behind his head. "We already got some good shit for the court. So make sure you drive safe, Janet."

"Now...can you sort of walk us through those events?" Charles stared at Detective Jim Neely.

"Sure." Detective Neely's eyes roamed over the eight whites and four blacks in the jury box. "While investigating Computer 411, I traced one of the last two numbers back to a pager that had service in the defendant's name."

"And did your investigation reveal any other calls?"

"Yes. Cellular phone records prove that a call came from the car phone of a Lexus 400 LS and was answered at Computer 411 within several minutes of the call to the pager."

"Did your investigation confirm the owner of the Lexus or who might have had access to the cellular phone at that time?"

"I was able to confirm that Ernie Adams, the defendant's brother, was the owner. We know that Ernie was at work at the time, and we know that the defendant operates the vehicle on occasion."

"All right. Continue."

"The defendant's name surfaced again on a faxed document inside the Novelty Bread store just before two of its trucks were stolen and the murder of a co-owner."

"The fax—is that Exhibit 31 displayed on the monitor again?"

The detective looked at the plasma screen again. "That is correct."

"Could you tell us how all of this connects to Las Vegas, Nevada and...the Robert Mayes scheme?"

"Sure. Mark Aldridge—"

"The other computer shop guy that you spoke about before we recessed for lunch?"

"Yes. A call was made from the car phone in his Acura Legend to the defendant's residence shortly before the fax was sent to the bread store. The Acura was later found abandoned in Nevada."

Perry Kapata was in the courthouse restroom. He was washing his hands when Roc walked out of the toilet stall.

Roc walked up to the sink after the white man stepped aside to dry his hands.

"Hello there, little man."

Roc studied Perry but ignored him.

"I'm pulling for your daddy out there. I hope he beats that crap."

Roc frowned. "What the hell is you talkin about? My daddy died when I was three."

"Oh, I'm sorry to hear that. Is that your uncle?"

"He ain't shit to me. I came here with my tutor for extra credit."

Perry threw the paper towels into the trash can. He was disappointed. "You can forget about extra credit with that smart fucking mouth of yours."

Roc turned the water off and shook his hands dry. He headed toward the door. "You're lucky I ain't got that muthafuckin lion with me."

Roc entered his mother's Altima and closed the door. He dialed the number using Chelsea's car phone.

"Studio."

"Trex, you remember that man who was...Dan's son who was let out of jail and was on the news and—"

"Yeah. What about him?"

"I think he followed me to the bathroom in the court-house. He said something to me but—"

"Where's Tank?"

"Everbody is still in the courtroom."

"Lynn is supposed to be moving back in with me. That means you got ten grand on the way."

"How the hell...What the fuck that got to do with—"

"Hey, watch your muthafuckin mouth, you little fucka."

"I think that white man is up to something, and I know him or his dad had something to do with Tremaine getting killed."

"Well, look, when court's over today, find out what he's driving or riding in. I might as well get my shit off again before Lynn moves back in."

"Take me with you this time."

"You too young, Roc."

"You didn't say that when you was testing my creeping skills."

Trex smiled. He had nothing to say.

Paul Metzer walked closer to the witness stand. "Detective Neely, isn't it true that the FBI is looking for Mark Aldrige?"

"Of course."

"The prosecutor asked you to walk us through the events. Did you?"

"I believe I did. Yes, sir."

"Wasn't Mark the only person found in the computer shop after Dave Rutherford's murder?"

"Yes."

"Did you find that Mark was responsible for calling 9-1-1?"

"I did."

"Did you find whether or not Mark was responsible for calling the defendant's pager from the computer shop?"

"No."

"Did you find a mobile fax machine in Mark's Acura?"

"Yes, we did."

"Did you find out who was responsible for faxing Exhibit 31—the document currently displayed on the monitor—to the bread store?"

"No, sir."

"Are you still looking for Mark's brother, Norman?"

"Yes."

Paul scratched his head and shot the jurors a look of confusion. "Detective Neely, was that Mark or his brother Norman, who had the credit card fraud charges on his record?"

"I believe that was Mark."

"I believe you're right. Which means it must have been Norman who had the burglary, the bad checks, and the deadbeat dad charges on his record."

"That's correct."

"And the .38 caliber handgun found under the mattress at the Quadra Hotel had only two sets of prints on it. Tell us, to whom do those prints belong?"

"One set belongs to Norman Aldridge; the other was only a partial print. There wasn't enough discernible points to attribute to Mark Aldridge for certain."

"But there must have been enough points for the state and FBI to suspect that the prints were Mark's, right?"

"I didn't handle that aspect of the investigation, so..."

Paul paced the floor as if contemplating his next question. "If Mark and Norman used Thomas Baker," Paul pointed the remote at the plasma screen, making an image of Lynn's ex-boyfriend appear, "or any one of his friends," he pressed the same button on the remote, displaying the two other men from the Charlotte apartment, "to act as Robert Mayes," he pressed the button again, "you wouldn't know, would you?"

"I don't...I didn't find any evidence of that."

"And you didn't find any evidence of Mark and Norman killing Thomas Baker and his boys in that Charlotte apartment after returning from Las Vegas, did you?"

"I sure didn't."

"Is it possible that Mark and Norman tried to frame my client with a weak trail of phone calls and faxes?"

"I don't believe that to be the case."

"I asked you if it was possible."

Detective Jim Neely let out a barely audible sigh. "Anything is possible, but I don't think it's likely."

"You don't think it's likely?" Paul stared at the detective.

No answer.

"Well is it *likely* that you could explain to this jury how such evidence was found in Thomas Baker's Charlotte apartment?" He pointed the remote at the screen again. "Exhibit 38, the bifocals used in the casino scam; Exhibit 39, fraudulent driver's license of Robert Mayes; Exhibit 40, a packet of hair braids..."

Rico's eyes shifted toward Christine. She was sitting three rows away from Tank and Janet. He'd only noticed her two minutes ago. The black, shorter hair made her look different. If he was closer he'd notice the change in her eye color, too.

CHAPTER 31

After the second day of trial Paul met with Rico in the conference room back at the county detention center. "I got to give it to you; you showed your legal ass when you cross-examined that Neely detective."

"If that's a compliment, thanks."

"There's something I don't understand. The government has a Christine Everson on their witness list—"

"The blonde that we talked about, the lady that gave a statement about Robert Mayes trying to bribe her for internal information about the casino...she doesn't really exist right now."

"What the fuck does that mean?"

"Nobody can locate her. The name she'd used for employment at the casino was fake. A subpoena was issued for her, but that means nothing because the address she gave was fake, too."

Rico laughed. "So, nobody can find her?"

"Nobody knows anything about her."

Rico decided to change the subject. "Your wife shoulda been at the trial to watch you perform today. You did your thing."

"We've been separated for the past six weeks now."

"I guess you fucks up like I do."

"Actually we're separated because of this case."

"Yeah? How?"

"I discussed something personal with her about the case. The information went beyond our home, so I asked her if she'd told anyone. She admitted that she'd told her good friend, a woman whom I believe never wanted us together, and that's where the argument started."

"That don't sound too bad. Sounds like your wife's fault."

"That part was. But after I'd accused her friend of spreading the information even farther, all of a sudden my wife found out about an affair that I had been having with someone else she works with."

"You seem like you wanna cry. Start crying and I'll tackle your ass."

Paul smiled. "No, things aren't that bad."

"So, do you like Matt?"

"Matt Christensen? He's great. He really knows his shit with those computers."

"It looks like tomorrow is the last day of the trial. I don't want anyone to come to support me tomorrow."

"Why not?"

"I like to be all alone—as much as possible—on Judgment Day." Rico stared at a corner of the conference table. "I appreciate you helping to get Lynn to testify. I think she helped the case."

"Don't thank me. Your friend Trex should get the credit for that."

"And who should I thank for squeezing those... Charlotte investigators on the stand?"

"I don't want to accept any awards until the end of the show."

"Then go home and get some rest. You got a big day tomorrow."

Paul got up from the table. "Call me at home if you need me."

Alex Harver sipped water from the Styrofoam cup then leaned closer to the microphone on the witness stand. "I worked with Detective Jim Neely and the FBI. For the past six years I've been employed by the FBI as a digital image constructionist."

Charles looked at the plasma screen. "Did you have the occasion to work with Exhibit 17, the defendant's driver's license photo?"

"Yes."

"Tell us about that."

"Sure. We compared the defendant's license to the photos of the suspect in the casino and the Nevada bank. I was asked to reconstruct those photos on a computer to see the resemblance to the South Carolina license photo of the defendant."

"The Court has been kind enough to allow the use of the large monitor for both parties." Charles turned to face the judge. "May it please the Court, I'll ask that the witness now take a seat at the small table in order to access the computer that is now connected to the large screen."

The judge looked at Paul. "No objections from the defense?"

"None, Your Honor." Paul continued jotting down notes.

"You may proceed, Mr. Glasser."

Charles had Alex step down from the stand.

Alex sat at the small table in the center of the courtroom. He placed his hands on the computer keyboard.

The prosecutor aimed the remote at the monitor and pressed a button. An enlarged image of Robert Mayes from the casino appeared on the screen. "This is an enlargement of Exhibit 9. How long would it take for you to edit that image enough to show the resemblance to the defendant's license photo?"

"Less than a minute. It's already programmed and set for a fifty-second automation run."

"Show us your work."

Alex tapped at a few keys, and the automation began.

"Tell us what's happening now."

"As I speak, the computer is augmenting the height of the eyebrows by thirty percent." Alex paused. "Now it is gradually adding facial hair near the mouth, chin, and the side of the face. You can see the Robert Mayes image slowly depreciating."

The prosecutor nodded with approval.

"Now the braids have disappeared. The bifocals are gone. A final image construction is made to establish what the eyes and the area around the eyes must look like without the glasses."

Spectators and jurors mumbled and whispered about the new image on the monitor. It closely resembled Rico's driver's license photo.

Paul Metzer got up from his seat, leaning forward, hands still resting on the table. "Mr. Harver, when your program deleted the bifocals, how were you or the computer able to establish what the eyes and surrounding area must look like?"

"By using what we call a computer hypothesis."

"And does that mean you had the computer guess until you were satisfied with the results?"

"Well, it simply means that the computer made a mathematical guess, revealing what the area ought to look like once the glasses are removed."

"No further questions from the defense."

At 10:30 a.m. Matt Christensen sat at the small table in the center of the courtroom with a different computer.

Paul approached him with a remote control in his hand. "Before you get started with your automated presentation for us, I'd like to know whether you consider Mr. Alex Harver an authority on digital imagery."

"Pretty much. He did okay."

Paul smiled. "In his earlier testimony, he testified that the software that he was using, *Image IS*, was probably the best on the market."

"And I'd have to agree with him."

"But you're using a different software and graphics program, aren't you?"

"That's correct."

Paul pressed the remote control button. "We have four different images of Robert Mayes on the screen. They represent Exhibits 9 through 12. Can you convert those images right before the jury's eyes, just as Mr. Harver did?"

"I can do it forty percent better, requiring less hypothesis."

"How is that possible when you admit that Mr. Harver uses the best software on the market?"

"I have better software that isn't on the market yet."

"Why should this jury give so much weight to some new, unheard of software?"

"Because the software that Mr. Harver used...I created that and sold it to a large corporation."

The jurors and spectators murmured in amazement.

"Mr. Harver spoke highly of your creation. Are you prepared to show us the work of your new product?"

Matt placed his hands on the computer keyboard. "Just say when."

"We're ready."

Matt tapped a few keys and relaxed. "The computer will handle the programmed conversion without having to stop and enter commands."

The upper left image of Robert Mayes slowly converted and finally resembled Thomas Baker of the Charlotte apartment. The upper right image slowly converted and finally resembled Rodney Waters, another murder victim found in the Charlotte apartment. The lower left image slowly converted and finally resembled Stuart Sutton, the third murder victim found in the Charlotte apartment.

The lower right image took much longer to convert. The courtroom was annoyingly silent. Not a cough. Not a sniffle. Finally the digital image was a striking resemblance of Detective Jim Neely. The chatter from the jurors and spectators grew too loud for the courtroom. The judge calmly banged his gavel against the desktop coaster. "Order in the court!"

Rico parted the crowd of cameras and microphones and rushed up to the dark blue Suburban. He opened the door and was surprised to see the caucasian behind the wheel. He jumped inside and slammed the door, watching the media through the tinted window.

The driver stepped on the gas pedal.

Rico looked at the driver. "I'm sure we've met somewhere before."

She glanced at him and smiled. "What makes you so sure?"

"Probably the fact that nobody can find a blonde white girl named Christine Everson."

She laughed. "Never heard of her. Plus I don't even like blondes."

"How did you talk Tank into letting you drive his truck?"

"I didn't. He talked me into it. He says he didn't have time for you; he's talking Janet into moving in with him."

"How did he recognize you? You look completely different now."

"It was the other way around. I talked to him in the parking lot back there after the second day of trial."

He stared at her. "I don't believe I caught your name."

"Vicki Bauer."

"And where the hell are we going, Miss Bauer?"

"To my house."

"In Nevada?"

"That was Christine. Vicki has a house in Rock Hill."

Rico smiled and reclined his seat.

She slowed the Suburban for the traffic light. "Does the loss of Tremaine change my status and position with you?"

He leaned closer, sniffed at her neck, then kissed it.

"I'm always in search of a strong black woman who won't let me get away with whatever I want to do. I need those...features and qualities in a woman."

The light changed and she stepped on the gas. "If I could spend more time with you, I think I could help you to revise your interest in a loyal white woman who has a black grandmother."

Rico stared at her. "I'll spend more time with you; I at least owe you that opportunity. But I'm too old to change my principles."

Silence. She wondered if she could get closer to him with a lesbian act. She needed to be with a man that wasn't afraid of danger; it was probably just a matter of time before the killers could find her.

Rico thought about Tanisha and Vera. He wanted to change his ways but, damn, it was going to be difficult without Tremaine. He knew of only one other woman who wouldn't let him get away with all the bullshit—a woman much stronger than Tremaine. He smiled. He knew Chelsea didn't want him anymore. *Nothing wrong with trying.*

Perry tailed the Suburban from a distance. He made a mental note of the license plate. If only he could get a good look at the driver. He considered stopping his Corvette beside the truck at the next red light.

Roc rode with Trex in a stolen Buick. He sat up front wearing a knit cap.

"When it goes down, if your little ass panic or start crying, I'mma slap the shit out of you."

"When I get about eighteen or nineteen, I'mma bounce my heel off up in your ass just to show you I ain't no kid."

Trex laughed.

"So, how you gonna...going to stop the Corvette?"

"A fender-bender will do it every time. And you can stop trying to talk proper around me. You're now fuckin with the world's favorite street villain."

EPILOGUE

January 2, 2005. Rico's telephone rang in his new home. "Hello."

"Rico, this is Paul Metzer. Did I wake you?"

"Hell yeah."

"Good, because you lied to me."

"About what?"

"About the damn plasma screen. I'm looking at one right now in the Robb Report. You said the TV cost you $89,000."

"I said it costs that much; I didn't say I paid that much."

"Rico, the TV only costs $74,899. On sale right here in the United States."

Rico laughed. "So, you was caught in the cross."

The lawyer was silent for a few seconds, then he began laughing hysterically.

"Slow down, Paul. The shit ain't *that* funny."

"Of course it is. I sold that damn thing to the prosecutor last week for $96,000. He even got it financed." They laughed together.

"Paul, did you ever get things right with your wife?"

"I tried, but I'm just trying to forget about it now."

"Don't do that. Tomorrow I'll introduce you to a good-ass marriage counselor."

"That shit doesn't work."

"Place your bet. But make it light on yourself, because the counselor is gonna tax your nothing-ass for a thousand dollars."

"You're on. I'm betting you five hundred, and I'll pay the other thousand when you're ready."

"We'll jump this shit off tomorrow."

"Wait a second. Is this another cross that I have to beat?"

Rico laughed. "No, but there's another ass I have to beat if you don't have my son's thousand dollars."

Dan Kapata sat on the sand, his shoes only inches away from the waters that surrounded Rey Island, and less than seventy-five miles out of Panama City. He used a satellite phone to make what he considered to be an important call.

Paul Metzer clicked over. "Hello."

"Listen up, I have important shit to do, so I just as soon skip the fucking pleasantries—"

"To whom am I—"

"I used to be known as Dan Kapata; I haven't decided

who I'll become as of yet. But if you would be so kind as to pass this message to a well-known client of yours—"

"Uh...I'm assuming you're talking about Mr. Adams. We were—"

"That's a good assumption. Now, I have a message for you to give him."

"I can do you one better; he's on the other line. Hold on." Paul set up their three-way conference. "Rico, you there?"

"Yeah, but I was about to hang up on that ass."

"Rico, Rico, Rico. The thief who prays to a lot of gods."

Rico was silent.

"Hey, I was thinking...or maybe wondering what your...*enriched* life would be like if you knew an old friend could stop by to visit you anytime in the near future."

"Yeah, well the suspense don't sound too bad. But if you show up unannounced, it's probably gonna...going to be a nasty twist to your story."

"Sounds groovy to me. Oh, and congratulations on your trial victory, but there's still a few charges that I have to press against you."

"That don't sound like no friend of mines—"

"Hey, I gotta go now. But I promise you...I promise you I'll stop by and see you sometime when I get my new life together. And by the way, you wouldn't happen to know who killed my son, would you?"

"Not at all. I heard it was just a traffic accident gone bad. Two in the temple—you know how that road rage is."

Dan pursed his lips and nodded. "When you get the time, could you put some flowers on the grave for me?"

"I'll do that for you—if I get the time. But if you come by like you promised, I think I can get a better deal on two sets of flowers."

Dan laughed. "Now that I know you're a millionaire because of me, I have more incentives to collect on that killer interest."

"And that just gives me more incentive to fuck your momma's son up."

Dan gripped a handful of sand. "You can stop praying to your gods; soon there will be a new devil in town. Until then, stay out of trouble. I wouldn't want anyone to steal my glory." He terminated the call and lay back on the sand. Eight years seemed too long to wait. He'd give it a try, though.

AUTHORS WANTED

at

Infraread Publishing

P.O. Box 223

Bronx, New York 10462

www.infraread.net

Infraread Publishing is presently seeking authors of well-Written fiction, preferably in the suspense/thriller category.

REQUIREMENTS:

First three chapters, query letter/synopsis
Double-spaced text
One side only, 1" margins
Typed manuscript in 10 pt. or 12 pt.
Word count & copyright notice in right corner
Name & permanent address in left corner

Do not send entire manuscript

Due to the volume of submissions, we will respond only we are interested in reading your entire manuscript.No submission will be considered without SASE.

Send to: ATT: Submissions

Infraread Publishing

P.O. Box 223

Bronx, New York 10462

www.infraraead.net

Order Form

InfraRead Publishing
P.O. Box 223
Bronx, New York 10462

Name:_____ID#_____
Address:_____
City:_____State:_____Zip_____
Institution:_____
Email:_____Cell_____

Quantity	Title	Price
	Beat the Cross	$14.95

Shipping and Handling (via Media Mail) $3.05

Total: $_____

*Discount for incarcerated customers: $15.00 flat or two books of new stamps. No personal checks. All money orders must clear before we ship. Credit cards and PayPal accepted online. We ship within 14 days!